INFIDELITY

By the same author

FICTION
A Changed Man
Then We Fall
A Family Affair
The Destroyer
The Dam
Very Personal Problems
The Cure
The Detective
Talk to Me About England
A Distant Country
Children of Dust
The Divining Heart

REPORTING
The City
The Church of England
The Doctors
The Nameless: Abortion in Britain Today
Men and Money: Financial Europe Today
The New Militants: Crisis in the Trade Unions
Gentlemen of Fortune: The World's Investment Bankers
Sex and the British: A Twentieth-Century History

BIOGRAPHY
The House of Northcliffe: The Harmsworths of Fleet Street
Richard Burton
Dylan Thomas: The Collected Letters (ed.)
Sir Huge: The Life of Huw Wheldon
Caitlin: The Life of Caitlin Thomas
Dr Freud: A Life
Dylan Thomas: The Biography

INFIDELITY

Paul Ferris

BASED ON A TRUE STORY

HarperCollins*Publishers*

HarperCollins*Publishers*
77–85 Fulham Palace Road,
Hammersmith, London W6 8JB

Published by HarperCollins*Publishers* 1999
1 3 5 7 9 8 6 4 2

A catalogue record for this book
is available from the British Library

ISBN 0 00 225350 X

Set in Sabon by Palimpsest Book Production Limited,
Polmont, Stirlingshire

Printed and bound in Great Britain by
Caledonian International Book Manufacturing Ltd, Glasgow

For Patricia

1

It was important to know if their man was dead or alive, but the records were incomplete, and some aggravation in the field was inevitable. Inspector Horton, who had got his hands dirty in the basement where the CID stored ancient files, emerged from the washroom to see the traffic sergeant slapping the coffee machine, and remarked, 'It's a hard life,' for the second time that day. The first time he was speaking to his wife, who gave him his suitcase after breakfast and said, 'Shirts and socks for three days, is that sufficient?'

'I can always use a launderette. It's a hard life.'

She looked winter-pale; he kissed her ear; a daughter screeched from upstairs that she couldn't find her school bag, and the door slammed behind him in the wind. There was no telling how long he would be away. He handed over a burglary and an arson to a fellow detective inspector, who added the files to a heap on the windowsill and remarked that if 1961 didn't turn out to be a record year for crime, his name wasn't Parkin.

They chatted about the job that Upstairs had dumped on Horton, weighing the chances of finding someone who hadn't been heard of for years but lacked an entry of death at Somerset House.

'Chance of glory, my boy,' said Parkin, leaning back on the hot-water pipes. 'You wouldn't be having the car if they didn't mean business. I can see it now in the *Post*: "Painstaking investigation by DI Harry Horton led to the arrest," et cetera.'

Horton shouted for DC Jones, who had been waiting in the corridor for ten minutes.

'So this is the lucky chap,' came from Parkin.

'Sir,' answered the constable, a young man buttoned tightly into a suit with rain-damped trouser-legs that appeared to have shrunk.

'Your docks inquiry taken care of?' said Horton, a question not requiring an answer, and ignored the gloomy 'Sort of, sir' he was offered. 'We are waiting on the garage. The Humber needed a new tyre. You'll enjoy driving her.'

'Sir.'

'He was just getting ready to pounce, weren't you, Jonesy?' said Parkin mischievously.

'They'll still be there when he gets back. Pilfering is endemic down the docks. I expect they were at it when the Vikings landed in Wales. "Good morrow, what'll you give me for this helmet with horns?"'

Nobody laughed. Parkin left to go to court; the garage rang to say the car was in the yard. Gulls blown up from the river lined the roof, heavy, cruel birds emitting their mixture of gargle and screech, as they'd been doing on the day Horton first wore uniform, twenty years earlier, and some bastard put chewing gum in his helmet.

'A48,' he said. 'Let's see if we can make Chepstow in two hours.'

The deputy chief constable's car that was, before they gave him a Vanden Plas, lumbered east through starved urban landscapes whose patches of greenery reminded Horton of mould, clinging to the brick and tin. Nothing was said, nor would it be unless the constable was spoken to. Horton smoked a cigarette, read the only file they had been able to trace, broke the silence to review what they knew about their man: his wartime food and identity records, his undoubted existence in the early fifties. 'We may be on a wild-goose chase here, if chase is the word,' he said. 'Buck up. Jump a red light or two.'

At Chepstow – hill, perched streets, castle underneath guarding a bridge and the bluish mud-banks of the River Wye – the inspector said, 'I shall leave you here, Jones.'

'Sir?'

'It's all in the file. He had a relative who moved to Chepstow in the 1920s. Now deceased.' He used to pester her for money, sometimes arrive uninvited and refuse to leave the house. Once he used violence. Only fragments of this past were left in the records. Small communities, however, had bottomless memories for impropriety. 'Bank, tradesman, vicar, neighbour, you don't need my advice,' said Horton, becoming cordial as he instructed Jones to follow by train to Gloucester that evening, and meet him at the nick next day, 9 a.m.

Horton changed seats and watched in the mirror as Jones fished a suitcase and package from the back, where they had fallen off the seat. The constable was trying to reassemble a sandwich; it looked like cheese and pickle. Horton nodded and left him on the pavement. Sandwiches lovingly wrapped in greaseproof paper were a phase of one's marriage.

The superintendent at Gloucester, Tommy Dunn, was an old colleague. He had done better than Horton, but by now had reached his upper limit. All old Tommy wanted to talk about was his garden, its descending water, its little pump, its two trees, its promise of peace at last. 'Your Ellen would like it,' he said, and the conversation died away. Reluctantly he turned to Horton's visit. A file had been cobbled together about the missing man. During the war he was in and out of local factories that made detonators and Spitfires and rubber boots. Horton read employment records, entries from payment ledgers, a carbon copy of a memo approving a pay rise of six shillings a week for his 'diligence and application' as a storekeeper. A rolling stone, beyond Horton's imagination.

There were addresses in Bristol to be visited next day. When Tommy said he must come to supper, Horton excused himself on the grounds of a sore throat. In the Hill Crest Private Hotel at 6.30 he made a call from the pay phone by the stairs and said, 'I happen to be in Gloucester. How are you this long time?'

The woman at the other end said she was surprised he had the cheek. He persevered in a professional way, trying to amuse her with his description of the manager shouting, 'Maggie? Hoover!' every time the wind blew leaves in from the road. 'Definitely not the Ritz,' he said.

'I'm sure.' Lisa's voice had composed itself. Its hostile gentility brought back a memory of her saying, 'Steady now,' narrowing her eyes as he touched her, enjoying a kind of carnal antagonism; a lovely woman to have a fling with. Feeling he could say anything, he told her some nonsense about his home life, just to hear her grunt, 'Bollocks' in a voice like a man's, and asked impudently about her husband, Alec. 'I have just this minute seen his car,' she said. 'He is giving the correct hand-signals for entering the drive. He is getting out. I am waving through the window.'

'Does he still go away on business?'

'He's certainly here at the moment. Your timing was never the greatest, Harry.'

The line went dead. Whether Alec's appearance was real or invented, it had been a promising conversation, worth another try, and he meant to linger in Bristol.

The diligent Jones reported next morning that he had found nothing in Chepstow except a solicitor who provided leads in Tintern and Lydney, places not far away. When he hinted that motor transport would be useful, he was told sharply to pull his socks up and take a train, or failing that a bus.

Horton's car made the day's inquiries more comfortable as he did his best with the scrappy file and winkled out citizens of

Bristol who had been acquainted with the suspect years earlier. A landlady thought the man had passed on, but couldn't say how she knew. He'd suffered with his chest, poor thing, and the winter he was in her back room, which must have been just after the war, she'd had to fetch the doctor; who, when Horton reached him in mid-afternoon, got spiders' webs up to his elbows, poking about in cardboard boxes, and said furiously that his records didn't go back that far. But the landlady remembered him; people did. 'There were stories about him,' she said. 'Just rumours,' said Horton. 'Never proved.'

Soon after seven he was in Lisa's avenue, parking the Humber a hundred yards from her house. A tree spattered the bonnet with rain. 'You'd better come round,' she had said, 'but I warn you, I'm not in the mood for monkey business.'

Her tight black dress and strong perfume suggested otherwise; anyway, he was in no hurry. His inquiries in the district would stretch to another twenty-four hours at least. They sat yards apart in frilly armchairs, leaving the sofa unoccupied except for a nondescript ginger cat. Nothing was said about Alec, nor were Horton's domestic affairs on the agenda. They both had secrets. When she asked what Sherlock Holmes was up to in Bristol, he gave her minimal details, and she took the cigarette out of her mouth and said, 'Murder, eh?'

'Murder perhaps,' and wished he'd kept quiet, not offered her a thread. He didn't want his life unravelled, nor hers; that was the point of being there.

'I didn't know you did murders.'

'I've never had the luck. If we find someone, I shall be just the legman. Roll of drums, enter the chief super to take charge. I've seen it happen.' He shifted in the chair and his cuff got entangled in a loop of fabric. As he said, 'Let's talk about you,' a button came off.

'There'll be a nice chambermaid at your Hill Crest whatsit will sew it on for you,' she said, crossing her legs and smiling.

'Or I could ask you. I'll slip my jacket off.' The perfume, when he stood by her, cut through the stench of her strong cigarettes. 'We had nice times, Lisa.'

'So we did.'

'Remember Norwich?'

'I remember your juvenile acronym.'

'You laughed at it. Knickers Off Ready When I Come Home.'

'It ought to be Korwich. That's why I laughed.'

The cat's ears stiffened and it jumped off the sofa as a car drew up outside. There were footsteps. Horton put his jacket on and said, 'I expect that's Alec. This will be one of your games.'

She looked entrancing – her eyes glittered, her dress was almost above her stockings. 'Why do you think I'm in black? Fine detective you are.'

Friends appeared, a sallow solicitor and a jolly wife, come to take her to the theatre. Horton became an old friend of the family. 'What would I have done without you all?' murmured Lisa. Afterwards he was able to admire her performance. At the time he felt murderous. The button cracked in two between his fingers as a bone might in a cock-teaser's throat; a warning, of a sort. 'We are all poorer for Alec's death,' said the solicitor.

Rebuffs were part of the game. He thought about Ellen and the girls, but couldn't bring himself to telephone and have a conversation about nothing. Another twenty-four hours and he might be able to get Lisa going.

At the Hill Crest, however, he found a message from Parkin, sent round by Tommy Dunn, that said more files had been found and asked to be contacted at home. A new name had come up. On the telephone Parkin quoted from a file going back to the 1920s. At last there was something to bite on. Horton left for the north in the morning, after writing a postcard to Lisa that said, 'I'll be back.'

2

The Empire could lose the war; that was what they said in 1917 as U-boats paved the northern seas with wrecks. People tried not to dwell on it at the ports, where the evidence was too obvious. George Shotton made himself act like an optimist, and found that when he gave out good news that he wasn't sure of, such as the success the new convoy system was having, he was cheered up by the echo of his own dubious reassurances. He knew the frailty of ships' frames; saw them sail confidently over the horizon belching smoke, only to vanish without trace; drank whisky with master mariners who had nervous tics and said it was worse than the fucking trenches.

George's life was spent in places like Tyneside, Glasgow, Cardiff. This week it was Liverpool. Looking up at the hull of the *Marston Moor* from the floor of Canning Dry Dock No. 2, he counted the buckled plates where the rivets had popped out; the steel looked like perforated paper. She ought to have gone to the bottom, and would have if the torpedo hadn't detonated prematurely. The pressure had folded the bronze wings of the propeller in on themselves, and a gang was assembling the tackle to unship it. George felt oppressed, an ant in a pit. Flakes of rust, loosened by other gangs hammering out of sight, drifted down; he felt one land on his hat. How would one live in a defeated England?

The dry dock manager, a smarmy chap he hadn't encountered before, asked him if he would agree a figure of eight pounds notional scrap value for the screw.

'More like eighteen,' said George. 'There's some bronze in it.'

'Exactly. I am thinking of the morale factor, Mr Shotton, sir. Gov'ment wants shipwrights at beck and call. They look for little extras.'

'They get their war bonuses. Who else gets your little extras?'

'You're top dog, Mr Shotton. Marine superintendents, men of clout. Say there's ten pounds to share. Five for you, three for me, two for them poor sods.'

'I mean to tell the owners about this conversation.'

'Won't do any good, Mr Shotton, sir. My word against yours.'

He was right, of course. Ascending the sanded tiers that lined the head of the dock, George lifted his head to invigorate himself with a sniff of salt breeze, and got a speck of rust in his eye, which meant calling at Dr Eggins's surgery on his way to the Compton Hotel, to have the organ bathed and the foreign body shown to him on a piece of cotton wool. One couldn't be too careful about one's health at the age of thirty-seven, middle age just around the corner.

His intention was to have an early night, but he was no sooner in the hotel, making his way to the dining room for an omelette, than he was waylaid. Hotels these days heaved with strangers who became pals for an hour, mixed up with the usual crowd, watering them down to a saucier mood than George had grown up with before the war. His colleague Oscar James did the waylaying, making one of his silly introductions ('George Shotton, gentlemen, diligent to a fault. He and I work out of the same hellhole in Cardiff'), and George nodded politely to the pals he wasn't going to have time for. Among them was a chap with a squint who managed the nearby Alhambra, and was insisting they all come round to see the show, in particular a wench whose songs would rouse the dead, not to mention her figure.

'Tempted, Shotton?' said Oscar. 'See a bit of life?'

'I'm always tempted. But I've got a seven o'clock start in the morning.'

'It's Saturday. I thought we were going back on the express after breakfast. I most certainly am, or the kiddies will want to know why.'

'I mean to fit in a couple of victuallings and a prop-shaft survey. Good night all,' and he went for his omelette, brushing past a couple of overdressed women ('officers' wives', if challenged) who were looking for trade, as they were in all the hotels, and then to the dark bedroom, where the chambermaid had laid his pyjamas diagonally across the pillow, and he was interested to see, when he looked closely, that on the fly was stuck a whisker of what looked like pubic hair. His, presumably; hers, in the madness of a man's imagination that one had to keep tight hold of or else.

So what would life under the jackboot of the enemy consist of? Would they depose the King, pinch the Colonies, extinguish our pride? Night-time was when George's nerves could turn defeatist. A double dose of Globéol, which swore it was the ideal remedy for neurasthenia and brain-fag, left the black shapes of his dreams unaffected, and it wasn't until he was on the overhead railway in the morning, rattling down to Canada Dock, that his faith in England came back.

A light summer mist over the Mersey was dispersing under the sun. Packs of crenellated destroyers came into focus; troopships like buildings; deep-laden steamers full of wheat and ores, queuing up for tugs, and facing them the eight-mile city of the docks, a thousand cranes already bowing over the holds, warehouses with their doors rolled back, locomotives steaming and shrieking. What a sight! What a consolation!

Later he caught the eleven o'clock train from Lime Street, change at Shrewsbury for the 1.57, arrive Cardiff 4.48. George kept timetables in his head. Marine surveyors went where they were needed, and the war had doubled their work. The more he travelled the more he liked it. In a first-class compartment he could read a newspaper, write a report, have a snooze, and even, now and then, chat with one of the ladies travelling alone who were part of the new order. There was a vitality about these journeys. An attractive girl who once gave him a white feather on the Newcastle Corridor Express blushed when he produced his certificate of exemption and ended up flirting with him in the dining car.

Depart Cardiff eight minutes past five, arrive Penarth twenty-four minutes past. Home. George wasn't Welsh, though his wife was. Home, for the time being – he had no loyalty to places – was a well-to-do township across Cardiff Bay with a dock of its own, a yacht club to which he subscribed without ever yachting, and rows of comfortable Victorian villas.

A ten-minute walk took him to his, square and bay-windowed, its domestic pleasures ready for a man after a busy week helping England: lawn at the back nicely scythed by odd-job boy, smell of frying fish from kitchen, sunbeams spattering parquet floors, kiss in drawing room from wife. It was a warm kiss, straight on the lips, but the embrace was fleeting and May's figure under her loose, creamy dress made no contact. After twelve years, what did one expect?

Arthur, a pretty child with curly hair, came banging down the stairs, pursued by Mavis, a servant of sixteen they called a 'nursemaid'. He had jam stains around his mouth and a piece of bread in his hand.

'You should have finished that before you came down-stairs,' said George, 'but since you are here, shake hands and tell me what you've been up to.'

Five minutes were enough. He was not a very interesting

child but might improve with age. When child and girl had gone back to the nursery in the attic, George said, 'Now, what about May?'

'Your telegram came. Olwen is frying you two fillets of plaice that Father sent over, straight from a drifter. I don't expect you've been eating properly in Glasgow.'

'Liverpool.'

'I get these places mixed up.' Her straight black hair and pointed chin made her look severe, concealing the softness and timidity that he married her for. 'Don't be cross, but I have to go out at six. It's the Vigilance Society.'

It often was. Moral vigilance was in its heyday. George said, 'No sudden epidemic of sin, I hope.'

'The patrols persuaded five girls off the streets last week. One hears the most dreadful stories. Mrs Finch was saying that after the war the entire country will need cleansing.'

'As long as you're free by 7.15. I thought we'd go and see *The Advance of the Tanks* at the Palace. It's the official film – artillery duels, horses sinking in mud, the tanks winning the day. I'll pick you up at the town hall.'

'People don't know half what goes on. It's as if some of the girls have lost their reason. Mrs Finch says there are girls from decent families who simply don't care about their reputation. It's my duty to be at the meeting.'

'Marriage is marriage, my dear May. Where I go, my wife goeth too.'

'I don't even like moving pictures,' she said despairingly.

She was being ridiculous. Tanks were fascinating things, even if you were a woman. Hadn't his brother, Everard, written about seeing one of them abandoned by the River Ancre? Poppies had sprung up all around. 'I showed you Everard's letter,' he said. When he saw she wasn't listening, he told her flatly that she was coming, like it or not. Then he washed his hands and ate the fish, alone in the dining room, like the sole resident of a lodging house, waited on by Olwen the dogsbody.

As expected May wept for the poor horses. Walking home from the Palace, arm in arm through the July evening, he tried to comfort her by saying that animals felt no terror in the human sense. She leaned on him a little; he leaned back, and there, perceptible against his forearm, were hipbone and waist, two pieces of the marital jigsaw to be going on with. It seemed a good moment to mention the doctor in Liverpool, to say that Eggins had said never mind the eye, it was the nerves he had to get a grip on. Eggins, in short, had diagnosed wartime nerves. Life today was more difficult for all of us. Any disharmony in one's affairs might thus be the straw that broke the camel's back.

To his surprise, his wife smiled. 'Oh, George!' she said.

'Have I said something funny?'

'I shall buy you a nerve-food at the chemist's on Monday. I know you like taking things.'

'It may cure the symptom. But will it cure the cause? Eggins and I talked man to man.'

He felt her lean the other way. Women were clever devils who always knew when one had physical love in mind. He shouldn't have played the Eggins card, but then, what card should he have played? The layout of the house, the several bedrooms (not counting the room at the back, where Olwen slept, and the attic for the boy and his nursemaid), made it that much easier for May to play dodge the husband.

When it was time for bed he waited downstairs with a dressing gown over his pyjamas, sipping a soda water. After a quarter of an hour he knocked on the bathroom door and called, 'Everything all right?'

She turned on a tap. 'I am cleaning my teeth. Don't wait for me, there's a dear.'

At this point he often gave up. What made him persist

was the quiet rationality of the evening they had spent. He was supposed to be a happily married man. The fact that lapses from fidelity had been known to occur was beside the point. Scores of sensible wives in Penarth and district must be undressing at this moment in the knowledge that husbands with all manner of imperfections awaited them.

George made sure their bedroom door was shut, with a strip of light showing at the bottom, so that she would think he was in there, and went to sit in the big guest bedroom, unlit, concealed in the bay between curtains and glass. Navigation lights passed offshore, points of red and green. He was half asleep when May glided in and began to take her clothes off in the dark.

She jumped as he appeared from behind the curtains and put the light on.

'There, there,' he said, pulling her down to sit on the bed, making two fingers run up and down her underwear, whispering, 'Here comes little mousie to give you a surprise.'

'I have had the colic, that is why I am sleeping here, so as not to disturb you,' she said firmly. 'But I have seen the specialist about the other thing. I was meaning to tell you tomorrow. He says I have made some progress. After the war, if I build myself up with the right foods, I may be strong enough to have another child.'

Children were a red herring. Since pregnancy had made her ill, and Arthur's birth had been difficult, the solution seemed obvious to George, who had no wish for another child anyway. It was merely a matter of taking precautions. 'What a pair we are,' he said, 'always trotting off to doctors,' and without pausing he fished out a paper packet from the dressing gown and suggested she look the other way while he donned a new make of appliance imported from Scandinavia, highly recommended by Dr Eggins.

May sobbed, fists in her eyes, telling him to put the light

out before she died of shame, begging him to leave her alone, gasping that those rubber things made her ill – 'Make me pregnant. Go on, make me die, then you'll be happy' – inconsolable, legs jammed tight together.

It was only a French letter. He was only a husband of average tastes. 'There,' he said, 'that wasn't too bad, was it? I'm only human, you know.'

Because he knew it was what she liked, George said in the morning that he would accompany her to church, although he fancied a lie-in. He felt deliciously lazy. She had sent Olwen up with a tray of bacon and black pudding, and the general wellbeing lasted the walk to St Augustine's, greeting acquaintances, radiating gentility.

The congregation made the air thud with 'Christian Soldiers', which, from the approving looks that a handful of men in uniform attracted, was being sung for their particular benefit. Summer visitors to the coast varied the civilian pattern of dark clothes with a light-coloured suit or two, and even some unsombre dresses on young married women.

The vicar was giving them the popular Psalm 58, which might have been written to describe the Germans, *Their poison is like the poison of a serpent: they are like the deaf adder that stoppeth her ear.* George agreed with the sentiment, but he felt languorous and far away, and his thoughts kept turning to a summer wife in the next pew who wore a slanty hat and pearls in her pink ear lobes. *As a snail which melteth, let every one of them pass away: . . . The righteous shall rejoice when he seeth the vengeance.* George was imagining what she had been up to with her consort the night before, when an usher touched his shoulder and whispered, 'Urgent message, Mr Shotton, if you would kindly step outside.'

George shuddered, expecting the worst, Olwen with a telegram from his family to say that Lieutenant Everard Shotton had been killed in action. May held his arm as they went out. There was no Olwen. His father-in-law, Captain Loader, was sitting on a tombstone studying a book of Admiralty tide tables.

'George,' he said, 'can you get up to Sunderland overnight?'

'Paddington on the 8.10 express, King's Cross sleeper to Newcastle. In Sunderland as early as you like. May doesn't mind, do you, May?'

'It's not my place to mind.'

'Quite,' said Loader.

George got on with his father-in-law, who in any case paid him a useful forty pounds a year to look after each of the five tramps that constituted the Loader Steamship Co., plus proved hotel expenses and first-class rail fare, not the second-class that independent marine surveyors usually received. He also paid for Mavis, the nursemaid, and gave his daughter an allowance.

Mrs Loader was dead. She'd been a woman with a fiery complexion who had a habit of laughing triumphantly when she scored a point, and did it once too often for George, who called her a parrot that ought to have its neck wrung. 'My daughter's marriage will end in tears,' she replied, and after that she never spoke to him.

'Surely he can go in the morning,' said May, perhaps confident that she would not be molested two nights running. 'Let him have one day in the week when he is not careering about Great Britain.'

'These things are beyond my control,' said George – it summed up what he felt about the marriage too – and strolled around the churchyard with Billy Loader to hear about something simpler, the *Cathays Park*, running pit props out of Bergen with a Norwegian crew, whose captain was insisting that eleven trips were enough for anyone in those wicked waters, and he had dreamed about being torpedoed on the twelfth.

'Get another crew?' said George.

'Easier said than done. Solberg as you remember's a good mariner, knows the trade, sailed with the same men for years. They know the Jerries know we haven't got the right timber. There's mines in the Rhondda down to a couple of weeks' supply, so stopping the stuff coming in puts a smile on the Kaiser's face. At the same time I see profits going out the window. I want Solberg appealed to. Threatened, if you've got anything to threaten him with. He's got some yarn about sluggish steering but that's all blather, as you can tell him when you've looked at it. Offer him money, even, as long as it isn't too much.' The face under the woolly white beard was cavernous and tired. 'Not your job, I appreciate.'

'I'll do my utmost, Billy.'

'Give you the opportunity to call on your family.'

'So it will.'

As if one wanted to live in the past.

Walking down Fawcett Street from Sunderland station, George could hear riveters busy at Austin's Pontoon, below the bridge. Even at seven in the morning smoke overhung the Wear from funnels, exhausts, galley vents, braziers, smithies, tar boilers and rubbish heaps, hundreds of gulls diving through it, screaming for floating bacon rind and porridge and dead fish. Downstream the *Cathays Park* was tied up between a collier and an armed trawler.

Captain Solberg was eating breakfast in his cabin. 'Just happened to be in Sunderland,' murmured George. The captain shouted for another plate of salt cod, and George ate the vile stuff till his gums were sore, because he knew that comradeship was the answer. He accepted a glass of schnapps, he discussed the war and the price of everything, he admired the photographs of Mrs Solberg and several Miss Solbergs, he talked about family life, he even invented daughters of his own, a Gwendolen and a Harriet, to improve the intimacy of two men of the world, beginning to warm to one another.

'These are black times,' said the Norwegian. 'You have heard about my decision?'

'Captain Loader is a sympathetic person. No one will blame you.'

George had a look at the steering and found a corroded linkage that enabled a repair to be put in hand. In the meantime, why didn't Solberg be his guest that evening? They could dine at the Palatine and play some billiards, or stroll across to a music hall, or whatever suited.

Over dinner the captain got drunk, and George wasn't sure if he grasped what he was being told about how safe the new convoys were. Solberg left the table saying, 'Billiards is for boys,' and it became apparent that he wanted a woman. Rather than let him wander down to Town Moor and the dockside drabs, whom he seemed to know about, George steered him to Kings Cinema, only a step away, where a middle-aged woman with placid features was 'waiting for a friend' in the tearoom, and took him away, her arm locked into his.

Prostitutes were a desperate measure. Billiards at the Palatine with someone else on his own was the answer as far as George was concerned. On the way out of the cinema he paused to read the posters in glass cases. Coming shortly was a Beautiful Story with tender touches of Pathos. All this week was a Great Problem Picture, the drama of a shop-girl's temptation and a strong man's love.

A woman laughed and he turned to see a pair of young or youngish things, one long-jawed and auburn, the other chestnut-curly, wide-mouthed, toothy, standing behind him. Both had their hair crammed into berets that gave them a fashionable military look.

'Are you going in, ladies?'

'Coming out,' said Auburn. 'Bit of a swizz. Shouldn't bother if I was you.'

'Care for a stroll?' asked George.

'What do we think, Mame?'

'We think strolling is an overrated pastime. We think . . . he's got a dear little moustache. We think we'll miss the train if we don't hurry.'

'Allow me,' said George, mock-polite, and escorted them to the station.

South Shields was their destination. It was only twenty minutes up the coast, and for a lark he bought first-class tickets. They ended up in a jolly hotel called the Golden Lion, where friends were supposed to arrive but didn't, and a certain amount of supper went down, accompanied by champagne. The auburn one was Agnes, the curly one Mamie. Local vowels clung to their speech, as they did to his, softened by living in the south. The talk was all gossip about pals, lurching from name to name: Norah – 'some girl!', broke an artillery captain's heart – Nancy, who said what she thought – a flat in London, W. where they often went – 'Number 43 Elgin Crescent,' said Mamie dreamily, watching ice cream melt on a spoon – a particular friend of Nancy's, one Rupert (howls of laughter) – Albert, a crafty person connected with the stage – 'handsome devil,' said Agnes – Grace, who worked at the Golden Lion, not one of the London crowd – Kitty, who had been unwise enough to marry a man in the shipyards. The interesting ones belonged down south.

If there was to be a choice, thought George, watching his new friends depart for the cloakroom to do their hair, would it be volatile Agnes, pretty enough, or Mamie, who lapsed into dreaminess, who was almost a beauty? The matter was settled by Agnes, who reappeared with a cheap fur draped round her neck, saying they expected her at home, no distance from the Golden Lion, and it was after eleven already. Mamie too was ready to go, talking about the last train. George whispered in her ear but she shook her head.

The station taxi, a battered limousine, was in the yard, the driver dozing. 'Tell you what,' said George, 'let's go back in style.'

Even if one failed, the pleasure that one had been anticipating was left behind as a residue. Not that one anticipated defeat. The trick was to catch girls unawares, lost in a world of their own, from which they could be enticed at the crucial moment, when an arm around the waist or the gift of a rose (or a silver ring, or a supper) was what their dreams had been preparing them for. Drowsy-eyed Mamie was the obvious choice all along.

They rattled down the coast, curtain drawn tight across the glass between them and the driver.

'So what about you, Georgie?'

'I'm a marine surveyor. I find what's wrong with ships. Are you on the stage?'

'Have been. Ran away from home at eighteen. Ran back again at twenty.'

'I like you a lot.'

'Is that why you're breathing in my face? I'm not one of your flappers. Go away, Georgie. Sit quietly, there's a good boy. You come from round here, don't you?'

'Perhaps I do.'

As girls went, he could see this one being trouble.

'And now you live far away from this horrid place, in a pretty house with a pretty wife and pretty kiddies.'

'My wife is dead and I never had much interest in children,' said George. The fact that half the statement was true seemed a point in his favour. He meant no disrespect to May; even thought of her with affection at the same time as entertaining hopes of his new friend. 'Died of pneumonia,' he added, fanning himself with his hat. 'January the twenty-second 1914. The date is engraved on my heart.'

'Perhaps I believe you.'

Scarlet rays from a furnace, reflected by summer clouds, glowed in the river as they crossed the Wearmouth Bridge. Mamie had asked to be dropped in the Chester Road area, saying she had family there. George himself had been born within two hundred yards of the Chester Road.

As they drove down Fawcett Street she touched his hand. 'I like you, George,' she said. But no kiss was allowed, nothing until the taxi was slowing to a halt, when she took the hand again, gripping it tightly by the fingers this time, and brushed them against her breasts. After which the astonishing woman jumped out of the taxi, turned a corner and disappeared. A cat was yowling behind a fence. George tried to smell scent on the tips of his fingers, and thought he succeeded.

Despite his night out, or perhaps because of it, Captain Solberg was unhappier than ever in his cabin at breakfast, and extreme measures were needed if he was to be prised from the berth and added to a convoy that was assembling off the Tyne. Cowardice was in everyone's blood, said George, but so was bravery. He, personally, had always feared death by drowning. But he had been speaking to a Lloyd's agent, who said that a couple of steamers in Bergen were in need of damage surveys, as a result of which he planned to sail with the *Cathays Park* and earn himself a pound or two in Norway, if Captain Solberg agreed. Because who could bear to be seen giving way to a weakness?

'I take you with pleasure,' smiled Solberg, and they drank more schnapps to celebrate.

Mamie was at the back of it somewhere. From the moment sunlight through the curtains woke him at the Palatine, George hadn't been able to put her out of his mind. His nerves were better too. Listening to destroyers whooping in the mist as the convoy stood off to the north-east, he looked forward to being back in Sunderland in seven or eight days; and he would have been, except that the *Cathays Park* was delayed at Bergen because a crane fell into the hold when she was loading timber, and a telegram came from Oscar James wanting to know what he was doing in Norway, with priority work piling up everywhere.

Solberg frowned when George told him he was sailing in another vessel in a few hours, but he had got over his nightmares – could even laugh about them. A collier in ballast took George out of Bergen with a couple of other steamers and a single destroyer. They were bound for the Tees, and he would have to get down to Wales at once (King's Cross via York and then a mad dash to Paddington), which meant no chance of seeing Mamie. London perhaps was a better place to embark on sexual intercourse, if that should be the outcome.

His nerves went wrong again. On the third night clear skies and a moon left the ships in a bowl of shimmering water, painfully visible, made worse by the destroyer's habit of sloping off for hours at a time. George, who had noted where every buoyancy vest and life raft was, remained in the wheelhouse or walking the deck, afraid to be caught in a bunk if a tin fish came their way. He gave her a minute and a half before she went down.

In the early light he was still there, thinking how beautiful the coal staithes looked as the ship tied up at Middlesbrough in a drizzle. A telegram to Channel Buildings in Cardiff said, 'LANDED.'

It wasn't till the next morning that he saw Captain Loader, who came in clutching a telegram and said, 'Bad news about Solberg, I'm afraid.'

'He hasn't funked it again?'

'Torpedoed thirteen hours out of Bergen. No survivors. Thank God you weren't on board.'

'Indeed,' said George, and felt cold for a second before a sense of being alive surged through him. He was sharply aware of several things all at once. Sunlight on the shorthand typist's freckled arms. His father-in-law urging him not to tell May. The framed faces of Solberg's daughters. Sharpest of all, as if they were the essence of reprieve, the girl from Sunderland's breasts.

3

Lieutenant Everard Shotton came home on leave from Belgium with a damaged eardrum and the story of a lucky escape near Langemarck, which George heard about in letters from their sister, Christiana. A shell burst in the air, and soldiers at open-air ablutions behind the lines were blown outwards, several of them in bits. Everard, who was shaving directly under the explosion, wasn't blown anywhere. A drop of blood came out of his ear, that was all. Chrissie, who was a nurse at Gateshead General Hospital, wrote to George, 'He is a great tonic to everyone. Do come and see us all being so happy. I swear some of Dad's grey hairs have gone black again. I think Everard has a sweetheart but he is being very close. I don't suppose he's told you?'

Sadly, he had not. He never told George anything.

Seeing him was out of the question. Priorities sent George up and down the railways lines but not to the north-east. If he had gone to Gateshead (where the Shottons had moved years earlier) he would also have visited Sunderland to look for Mamie; he didn't even know her surname. But in mid-August he found a breathing space between jobs in Dover and Liverpool, which gave him an overnight stay in London. It coincided with Everard's return to his regiment; they arranged to meet and have supper.

King's Cross, where George arrived at dusk with ten minutes to spare, was like a madhouse, waves of khaki going this way and that in the half-light of shaded lamps, which shone permanently because the glass in the roofs had been darkened with black paint. Soldiers and kitbags choked the refreshment rooms.

As a military policeman was pointing out the wood-and-canvas shack behind platform 2 that George had been told to look out for – a board outside said 'Refreshments for Officers Only' – two bangs were heard above the station roar.

'Air-raid maroons, sir,' said the redcap. 'The underground is that way.'

No one rushed for cover. George went into the station yard, where motor taxis and horse-drawn cabs were continuing to arrive. A single searchlight beam was motionless, illuminating a cloudbank in the east.

A few minutes, and Everard would be there. If he was honest, George could have found the time to go to Gateshead. But it would have meant seeing his father and being drawn into family affairs, things he avoided when he could. There was no particular reason, merely a reciprocal lack of sympathy. Young Everard was different. In childhood, even with six years between them, they had been close; afterwards George couldn't penetrate his brother's amiable indifference, but he never ceased to regret that he had lost someone he might have been able to talk to without reserve. The war was a chance to put things right. George had read a newspaper article that said men in the trenches wrote letters home stripped of everything but the need to describe their feelings. So he wrote regularly to Everard and kept hoping, even when all he got back were hurried notes or field postcards. He thought he might bring letter-writing into the conversation over supper that evening.

Then it appeared that Everard's train, a normal main-line service, not a military special, was late. Boys in brass-buttoned uniforms stood on luggage trolleys holding up blackboards with chalked messages about delays. Trains had stopped arriving. Standard procedure, according to the redcap, was to delay them outside the capital during air raids.

'*Is* this an air raid?' asked George.

Well, there was a rumour that Gothas had been bombing south-west London. 'Last time it happened,' added the redcap, 'no trains got through till after midnight.'

A station official said much the same. They had a bad night ahead of them. Main-line trains might have to be diverted to other stations. Which, he couldn't say.

With a likely two hours to spare, George had the mad idea, which almost immediately became a practical plan, of going to see if the girl from Sunderland was at home in Notting Hill, which wasn't far from Paddington. The address, written down as soon as he'd returned to the Palatine on the night they met, had been in his wallet ever since.

It was twenty minutes by taxi to Elgin Crescent, where Number 43 was in a stretch of respectable weather-worn houses. A brass plate said 'Dr Schmelzer'; an arrow pointed down the steps to 'Flat'. Scratchy dance music could be heard. A starved-looking girl came to the door and regretted that Mamie wasn't at home, but perked up at the news that he was George. His fame had preceded him. 'Come through to the sitting room,' she said, and he met girl number two, a plumper piece of work who was dancing barefoot with a young man and kicking his ankles savagely. She took the needle off the gramophone and said, 'Yes, we've heard about George.'

The hospitable friend was Norah, the cruel one Nancy. 'Then this must be Rupert,' said George.

'He can't dance, can you, Roopy?'

'We do like dancing,' said Norah. She cranked the machine, dropped the needle and held out her arms for George to shuffle her around the carpet in a foxtrot, while Nancy went on with the unfortunate Rupert's lesson.

Between records there was stale lemonade in a jug. An unnecessary fire sagged in the grate. All three of them were in their early twenties, guessed George. Nancy was a telephone operator, Norah had well-off parents and didn't bother to work, Rupert (pointed ears, not much chin) was something to do with Madame Tussaud's, the waxworks; bad lungs had saved him from the Military Service Act. 'Lucky boy,' said Nancy, 'because given what an awkward so-and-so he is, he'd have walked into the first bullet that happened to be passing.'

'That's not fair, Nance.'

'Do shut up. Shall I tell George what happened at the military tribunal?'

'I'd rather hear about you hello girls,' said George. 'Why is it you all love to boss us about? *Kaindly clear the laine. Ay am busy with priority calls.*'

'We've got our job to do.'

A loud thud that sounded like a bomb made the electric light swing.

'Raid still in progress then,' said George, and Norah laughed and said it was only old Smellybags upstairs, falling over drunk. 'I expect the whole show was a false alarm,' she added.

Time was getting on. Nancy, working herself into a temper, wanted to know why people had it in for telephone operators.

'Ay'm afraid Ay have to cut you off there,' George said, and, shaking hands with Rupert and smiling into Nancy's venomous eyes, let Norah show him out.

'Made an enemy there,' she said at the foot of the steps. 'Pity you're going, we could have danced a bit more.'

'I have to meet my brother, on his way to the front.'

'But you'd have stayed a while longer for Mamie.'

'I did rather want to see her.'

'Far as I know she's in Sunderland. Supposed to be coming down for a month, but you never know with her.'

'Mamie what is it?'

'Do you really not know? She's Mamie Stuart. Her family are in Hawarden Crescent, Number 3.'

George had no trouble visualising it. The street he was born in was five minutes away.

'She said you were "some girl".'

'She said you were nice.'

Expecting to find a worse crush than ever at King's Cross, George was surprised at how quiet it was. The khaki had thinned out. The Newcastle express, he was told, had arrived more than an hour since. The Officers Only facilities were being used by a couple of subalterns, talking in whispers over their drinks, and a major who was writing a postcard. They couldn't help with his Durham Light Infantry lieutenant, five foot ten, black hair, red cheeks.

A railway official had the nerve to say it was no use finding fault with the company. He was terribly sorry the Gothas hadn't materialised as promised and killed a few people, but perhaps they would do better next time.

George raised his fist. Fortunately he saw the policeman who was coming towards them.

'This gentleman is upset about missing his brother,' said the official.

'I don't expect you meant to do anything, did you, sir? That was not a threatening gesture I saw, was it?'

'Certainly not,' said George.

'Good. We'd best keep our temper for the Germans.'

The Great Northern Hotel found him a room, but knew nothing about a Lieutenant Shotton. He could hardly tour the hotels of King's Cross.

Kneeling by the bed he prayed for Everard, biting his lip to make it bleed so as to prove the intensity of his remorse.

All the 'cottages', as they called them, were much alike: sturdy little single-storey houses opening on to the street, with three or four rooms for living and sleeping in, a scullery and a wash house at the back, and beyond that a tiny yard with a water closet in a cabin.

The ambitious made improvements. Mamie lay in her sister's new bathtub, pinky-white and steaming, watching condensation run down the brick wall, which was all that lay between her and the backyard. By standing up she could reach the tap on the gas geyser and squirt reinforcements into the tub. Scalding water, she had read, transferred the smell of Parma violets from the soap to the pores and thence the inner skin if rubbed in methodically. What the inner skin was exactly, Mamie didn't know, but she could feel the scent seeping into it, flowing under her curves and ridges, getting into her brain, making her drowsy . . .

'That's four lots of hot water you've had in there,' said Edith, outside the door. 'Your tea is on the table. Henry has gone with the van to Roker so we shan't wait for him.'

Fresh linen tablecloth plus shop cakes in three varieties were further hints of social progress. Edith's small daughter politely passed the plate to her aunt.

'Dolly is not having cake today on account of being cheeky,' said Edith, so Mamie naturally whispered, 'Quick!' and slipped her a coconut slice when her mother was out of the room. Unfortunately Dolly was too dull a child to pop it in the leg of her drawers, and was caught munching.

'You are a wicked little girl,' said Edith, 'and if your Auntie Amy hadn't owned up to giving it you –'

'Auntie Mamie,' said Mamie.

'If Auntie Amy hadn't owned up, I'd have had to fetch Mr Slipper. Now go to the bedroom.'

Weeping came through the wall. It was like being in a reformatory.

'If people started doing what they liked with their names,'

said Edith, 'where would we all be? I have said this to you before, you were a nicer person when you were Amy. We hope you'll come round and use our bathroom whenever you want, as long as you don't spend half the afternoon in there – it's not quite nice – but you do have the knack of upsetting things.' She leaned towards her sister and sniffed. 'You've been using one of those fancy soaps.'

'Lovely, isn't it?'

'Silly girl,' said Edith, becoming friendlier. 'Do think about the future.'

'I do, all the time.'

'Daydreaming isn't thinking. You'll be twenty-four soon. I was married at twenty-four. Henry was running his own business not long after.'

Henry had a motorvan inscribed 'H. Silver, Furniture Remover. Distance No Object', and employed two men. Mamie was glad that her sister had some talent for escape; the lean-to bathroom and geyser were already the talk of Robert Street, and one day the Silvers would slam the front door for the last time and fly away. But it would only be to a suburb with North Sea views and a garden. There had to be more to escaping than that.

'You see,' Edith was saying, 'there's two kinds of men, those who know what's right and those,' and Mamie chorused it with her, 'those who are out for what they can get.' Edith brushed crumbs into her palm. 'You can make as much fun as you like but it doesn't alter hard facts.'

'Are you going to buy a gramophone?'

'Henry and I have better things to do than sit around listening to music.'

'You could move the furniture and dance about like mad when Dolly was in bed, you and Henry. It would be good for your marriage.'

'You're being silly, and I don't think you're in a position to make remarks about your sister's extremely happy marriage when you yourself are in danger of being left on the shelf.'

'I only asked about the damned gramophone. I didn't want a lecture.'

'We don't swear in this house.'

Someone knocked on the front door. While Edith was answering it, Mamie examined the china pig on the dresser and saw several coins in him. These days she never had money for the bare necessities, such as silk blouses that they now asked thirty shillings for, or decent stockings where three pairs gave you very little change from a pound. Nancy said she could wangle her a job at the telephone exchange, which might have been bearable ('some of the men are very larky') if it weren't for her memories of the stage, that adventure in the singing and dancing line, the time she was truly free.

Mamie thought to comfort her niece. As she stepped into the passage, Edith was saying, '. . . at least half an hour ago,' and closing the door.

'Who was that?'

'Somebody wanting an address.' She called, 'Dolly, here's your auntie come to give you a hug,' and the tearful face appeared. After cuddles and a secret penny, Dolly was readmitted to the kitchen without a single admonitory word from her mother. This was suspiciously out of character.

'So who was the somebody?'

'Just a person. Would Dolly like her auntie to give her a bath in the new bathroom?'

'That's enough nonsense,' said Mamie, combative now and too sharp for her sister. Somebody was asking after her, wasn't he, and being told she'd left 'at least half an hour ago'.

Edith was stubborn. It was just a boy.

'WHO WANTED ME?'

'How dare you frighten Dolly?'

She kept saying, 'Who? Who? Who?' until Edith gave in.

Their father had sent a neighbour's boy round from Hawarden Crescent to say George had called. 'It's men all the time with you,' babbled Edith. 'I have a duty to protect you from yourself.'

'You have a duty to lend me two quid,' said Mamie, and raided the pig without her sister intervening. She ran until the house was in sight and it was safe to be ladylike and walk. But George, of course, had gone.

Number 3 smelled of boiled cabbage and pipe-smoke. Captain Stuart had just returned from the yard, doing up his braces. He commanded a harbour tug and lived aboard, except for a day a week when he came home and mooched about the house, annoying his wife. 'I liked your Mr George,' he said. 'I introduced myself, and he said, "I'm always pleased to make the acquaintance of a sea captain." '

'What else did he say?'

Her father thought. 'He said the weather wasn't too good. We agreed it was often like that around the time of the equinox.'

It was too bad. She experimented with different paints on her lips, and launched herself on Sunderland in the hope that she would catch sight of him in Fawcett Street or at a picture house. Then she bumped into Agnes and her new officer friend, and a friend of the friend's, and things got better.

When George was in Cardiff he shared an office at the back of Channel Buildings with Oscar James. There they tried to catch up with paperwork and never did, despite an efficient Miss Boulton who could do shorthand at ninety words a minute and smacked the keys of her Underwood with a swaying motion of the body that Oscar teased her about. He liked to flirt with her, a thick-waisted man in his forties shaking a box of marzipan delights under her nose and saying she was so skinny with all that exercise, she needed building up.

It amused him that George never joined in. Women were still a novelty in Channel Buildings. The Lloyd's agent two floors up employed a Madame Maystad, a Belgian refugee who'd arrived in Cardiff in 1914 after she and her husband fled from the invaders. Oscar thought her 'a fine handsome creature', and winked at George behind her back whenever she came down with an incident report. He flirted with her too, explaining to George that it was what Continental women expected.

'Where are we all going, Shotton?' he said, at the end of a day when both Mme Maystad and Miss Boulton had accepted marzipan delights. A woman laughed on the staircase; the last clerks and typists were going home. 'Good night, Miss Boulton,' he called. 'Don't do anything I wouldn't.'

'I personally am going to the Yacht Club,' said George.

Oscar's desk lamp went out. His bulk came and hovered over George. 'I mean, what is our destiny? We are entitled to a little pleasure in our lives, are we not? If I were ten years younger and didn't have three kiddies, I would be tempted to forget myself with Miss Boulton. I envy you your heart of stone.'

His wife and George's had gone to Ventnor on the Isle of Wight. They had both been ill – Bella James with a cough, May with the tiredness that came over her most autumns as the days were shortening. She had taken Arthur with her as a treat. George was happy to be on his own, unlike Oscar, who was restless without a wife. Bella's sister had come to look after the children, and he talked about 'going out on the town' and 'seeing a bit of life'.

As a rule George was rarely at Penarth for more than a day or two at a time. It had been a busy summer for marine surveyors, badgered by the authorities to rush ships through repair yards at short notice. Only a surge in Admiralty work at the South Wales ports was keeping him there for the moment. Soon he would be off again on the endless railway journeys, which his colleague didn't embrace with the same enthusiasm.

On Friday, the day before the wives returned, George decided to accept Oscar's invitation. He had a tentative arrangement of his own, and the two might be complementary. 'A nice roast at seven,' said Oscar, 'and then we can make our plans. I have had reports of a burlesque theatre by the Cardiff docks where the police don't go. You look shocked. Well, as the poet said, even Aristotle broke wind. You and I will go and see a bit of life, Shotton. They have ladies posing under nothing more than a piece of gauze. What do you think of that?'

George agreed they were in for a treat. He arrived a few minutes before seven, and the roast reached the table as promised, though not for another thirty minutes, since the children (no doubt prompted by their father) were demanding that they see Uncle George as soon as he arrived. The sister-in-law seemed to have no more idea of keeping order than Oscar. When finally they ate, the meal meandered along with frequent allusions to cousins and weddings that had to be explained for George's benefit.

Coffee in the drawing room followed, the sister-in-law left them, Oscar peered at his watch; perhaps it was time for the bare ladies. No, it was time to discuss a fascinating article that Oscar had been reading about steel fatigue in steamers. Then a child woke up with a headache and the sister-in-law wanted to call the doctor. Around ten o'clock they agreed with one another that it was getting late for the variety hall where the police didn't go. 'Another time!' winked Oscar.

George strolled down an avenue not far from his home, turned suddenly at a tradesmen's entrance and vanished along the side of the house. Half a minute later Magda Maystad had answered his taps and he was kissing her splendid red mouth in the kitchen. Servant sent away; husband (who owned a rope works) in London overnight for a function. They had been meeting discreetly since 1915; often at long intervals, taking no chances. As long as no one knew, no one was harmed. George was in his own bed at Westbourne Road soon after one o'clock.

A field postcard came from Everard in the morning, a tick against 'I am well'; the minimal statement. The memory of missing him at King's Cross in August was still painful. George's letter of explanation had been long and detailed, involving the incompetence of railway officials and an imaginary meeting with a Lloyd's surveyor. It did cross his mind to tell his brother the simple truth: 'Dear Everard, The reason I missed you was that I thought I had time to visit a young woman first.' But it would have embarrassed them both. So Everard got a respectable explanation, and in return George received a cheery one-page account of whizz-bangs and a gas attack; the King's Cross fiasco wasn't mentioned.

What if he never saw Everard again? *The Times* had its customary calendar alongside the dispatches from the front – 'The War: 4th year: 64th day.' Everard's section of the line wasn't mentioned. Writing to him later in the morning, George spoke of his wife's unwellness, and how he had been fending for himself while she was away recuperating. He also sent two letter cards to the Sunderland girl, one to the north, the other to Notting Hill. Having said yes to some surveys on offer at the London docks, he thought he might take the plunge. The message in both cards was the same: 'Working in South Wales at present. Expect to be in London during the week and will call on you Wednesday about 6 p.m. Warmest personal regards, George.'

May arrived back in the afternoon as pale as when she left. But Olwen had coddled some eggs for her, and she managed to eat them, saying how glad she was to be home. The news that George was going away next day didn't surprise her. She just hoped he wasn't doing too much, and went at once to air woollen vests in case the weather turned cold.

Afterwards he listened to her account of Ventnor. A stranger with binoculars was arrested on suspicion of being a spy. An elderly woman staying in the hotel had known the Shottons in Sunderland before the turn of the century, and remembered George's father. 'Such a pity you don't get on with him,' said May, and he agreed that it was. Chance meetings made him uneasy. Since childhood he had believed that the less people knew about him the better.

Arthur brought back crab shells, a dried starfish and a bag of sea-worn pebbles; he was upset when his father painted them with the letters of the alphabet, and he spent an hour cleaning off the paint with soap and water supplied by Mavis.

In the morning, George was in the spare bedroom doing physical jerks as recommended by Dr Eggins when he became aware that Arthur had come in and was watching him.

'This is to keep me fit,' said George, bending and stretching with extra vigour. 'It's what the soldiers do.' He faced the open window so as to ensure ample supplies of oxygen. 'See how I run on the spot? Knees up, knees up, knees up!'

He stopped, feeling breathless. 'Shall Arthur see if he can do it?'

But when he looked over his shoulder, Arthur had gone.

4

London, the Millwall Docks: 4th year of the War, 68th day. A windless afternoon along the Thames had turned foggy between the time George went into the black hole of the *Lady Karenina*'s boiler room, and the time he came on deck at dusk to talk with Captain Loutsch. The dock had ceased to be part of a landscape of cranes and warehouses. Its length was halved, and unending hoots and whistles came from the river he couldn't see.

In an hour he would be at Elgin Crescent. He told himself she was just another girl, but he was on edge.

'You find very nice mechanicals, yes?' said Loutsch when they were in his cabin.

'Hardly. If you want a classification, the surveyor is going to ask for new furnaces.'

'Of course. That is understood. But you are surveyor too, so your word is against his. You are acting for Russian Steam Navigation Company, and we are friends.'

George didn't want to arrive early at the flat, to seem overeager. Miss Stuart was probably the sort who enjoyed keeping men on toast, and he had met more than one of those in his time. Her unique feature was the indecency in the taxi, and even that might have been a playful gesture that he had misinterpreted. Perhaps the rest was a dirty thought.

The furnaces were deplorable, said George, patched with iron and rivets in half a dozen places above the firebox, as much of a threat as U-boats. He went over the vessel's defects, Loutsch smiling and offering bribes, the chronometer ticking above his head, fog coming under the door.

It was 5.30. One of George's headaches was coming on; keeping company with women was harder work than people supposed. 'Excuse me, something I forgot,' he said, and went to the galley, where earlier he had taken the lid off a twelve-pound tin. He brought it back covered in a cloth.

'Here you are, Captain. What the eye doesn't see, et cetera.'

A rustling came from the tin. George lifted the cloth, and Loutsch gazed without expression at several inches of cockroach, feeding on plum jam.

'All ships have insects.'

'You are infested. The Port Health will have to be told. They'll fumigate you tomorrow.'

'You are unkind fellow.'

He was nervous fellow. At the top of the basement steps he hesitated, afraid that Mamie would be at home, afraid that she wouldn't be. The adventure began. Nancy – he might have guessed – answered the door and said she supposed he could come in. A man in his late twenties with long features, introduced as Albert, presumably the 'handsome devil', who was smoking a black cigarette and reading the *Sporting Life*, said it had been another day for three-legged horses. There was no sign of Mamie.

'Still foggy out there, is it?' said Albert.

'Dense. That's why I'm late.'

'Didn't know you were. What are you late for, don't mind my asking?'

'Miss Stuart is expecting me.'

'Ah. Well, Nance and I are going out somewhere. Are you ready, woman?' She was doing something to a hat in a corner, and said she nearly was. 'And have you got that two quid I lent you?'

'Mamie!' she shouted, and banged the wall. 'Where's my two quid?'

Mamie came down the passage and into the sitting room, blue skirt clinging to her legs, eyes widening at George.

'Why didn't you say he was here? You're hopeless, both of you.'

'Albert says I owe him two pounds, so I suggest you pay him what you owe me.'

'Can't,' said Mamie. 'I put it on one of his dead certs and it lost. Serves you right, Alberto. Unless I borrow it from George.' The eyes widened again. 'Which would be inexcusable. Must be going potty.'

'Not at all,' said George, and the money changed hands, Mamie blushing and handing the notes to Nancy, who scrunched them into a ball and threw it at Albert, who caught it and said, 'Ta.'

'So you got my letter,' said George, when the others had gone.

'Ra-ther! Didn't know if you'd come, though. I bet you've got a fiancée somewhere.'

'Wish I had. When you've been married once, you wonder if you can love someone else again in the same way.' He stared into the fire, amazed at how like the truth untruths could sound, as if lying was simply a complicated way of being honest. 'Let's not go into that. I think we should go out and enjoy ourselves.'

'Let me guess. We are going . . . to the pictures?'

'Wrong. I've got us tickets for the theatre. There's a comedy at the Strand. Followed by supper. Does that appeal?'

'You bet. And then what?'

'Then I bring you back here.'

'Try and kiss me in the taxi. Try again at the door. Try, try and try again. Try and get my drawers off.'

She fluttered her eyes and let the words sink in. George had no immediate strategy to cope with a woman's dirty remark that so closely resembled a man's dirty thought.

'Don't mind what you say, do you? Well then, Miss Mamie Stuart, you won't be surprised if I try.'

'You'll find it pretty difficult. In fact, I'd say impossible.' She was all defiance – voice, eyes, that bosom. 'I'd give up any thought of it if I was you.'

'Are we going to the theatre or not?'

'Ask me why you'd find it difficult. Ask. Just ask.'

'For God's sake.' His overcoat was half on. 'Why would I find it difficult?'

'*Because I am not wearing any.*'

It was nearly midnight before Mamie left the bed and brought them bread and cheese, together with a half-drunk bottle of claret, black-ringed with evidence of recorkings. The theatre tickets were still in his jacket, which was still on the floor, underneath his trousers. The light had been on all the time.

Propped up with one elbow on the pillow, feeding her crumbs of Cheddar, George was amazed he had lived so long without finding such extremes of excitement and peacefulness in one bed, with one woman, in one evening. Mamie's repertoire was not much different from his, though one or two of her tricks had a slow-burning quality that made him shiver with expectation while she kept them going, her eyes fixed on his when they happened to be tricks where their faces were juxtaposed.

Each time he fed her a morsel of cheese she licked his fingers clean with her powerful tongue. 'Now we have a little sleep,' she said, cuddling against him; her nipples softened and he heard her breathing change, feeling protective because this was Mamie the sweet little girl. No doubt the other Mamie would be back later, the one who had used the word that women never did, whispering, 'Oh, I do like to fuck!' as she kneeled with her head in the pillow, a beautiful ostrich.

After that first night, they met as often as they could. Persuading Mamie to remain in Notting Hill wasn't difficult. She had always been drawn to London, she told George, after the troupe she danced with in the north disbanded. They were called the Five Verona Girls, but one of them broke her ankle and another left to have a baby; she could never get started again, and by then the war was on, and audiences were less interested in girls who did nothing but dance in a line and sing out-of-date songs. The cool, wry way she talked about it wasn't what George expected. Her dreams had collapsed; so what, baby?

Nowadays Albert arranged odd jobs for her in theatres as a dresser or an usherette, usually for a week at a time when someone was ill. She didn't ask George for money; even insisted on paying him back his two pounds. Presents were a different matter – a hat or two, pairs of stockings, lace collars and a camisole from a war bargain sale of Parisian lingerie (George said there must be a couple of warehouses in Paris devoted to surplus underwear, if the advertisements were to be believed). Sometimes it was easier to give Mamie money and let her do the buying herself, and when the girls had a rent crisis he would pay her share.

'I am becoming a kept woman,' she said one day. 'Does that mean I must be faithful to you?'

'There's no must about it.'

'I'll tell you a secret. Now I've met you, I don't care for other men.'

That wasn't necessarily a good idea. George had his own life and it was better that she had hers. He didn't ask too many questions, nor answer them. He came and went at Elgin Crescent like a lodger. Mamie and her girl friends formed a little world of their own where men were endlessly discussed and never quite trusted. He knew that Nancy called him 'Charlie Chaplin' behind his back because of his slight stature and moustache and black curly hair.

Norah, the one with the half-starved look, began a diatribe against men one evening when Mamie was in the bath. They were two a penny, they bought you supper, they made you promises.

'I could reel you off a list,' she said. 'We all could.'

'Mamie too?'

'She's had her disappointments. She likes you, you know. She told me what you said about being married once and not knowing if you could ever love anyone again. Nice, that. Wish I had a chap who said things like that. Assuming they were true.'

What else did Mamie remember that he might have forgotten? Leading two lives needed practice. His pattern of work had to be changed to include frequent visits to London. Using his Bradshaw he constructed extravagant journeys. Hull Paragon to Liverpool Central by way of London St Pancras and Euston was expensive but feasible. Successive jobs could be wangled so that the route between them went through the capital. Adultery meant being infinitely resourceful.

Sometimes London was squeezed into apparently nonexistent gaps in his schedule. Instead of two hours fifty minutes from Bristol Temple Meads to Swansea High Street, he shot up to London on a November afternoon and shot down again on the Welsh Mail, reaching the Welsh town at dawn, having left Mamie at midnight with strands of hair stuck to her forehead. It was her birthday. His present, a silver wristwatch inscribed 'From George Nov 24 1917 with love' was on the bare arm that tried to stop him going, soft and compelling around his neck. He could still feel it on his skin as he walked down High Street in the early light.

May accepted the absences without complaint; they were

only a deepening of his old habits. He kept in touch with her, to the extent that he fired off telegrams from distant post offices with sparse information such as 'CLYDE TUESDAY FORTH WEDNESDAY' followed by some domestic admonition, 'REMEMBER TAKE YOUR TONIC NIGHTLY' or 'GET BUILDER TO CHECK LOFT RE CURRENT RAINSTORMS'. Business messages reached him via local Lloyd's agents, or he could use the telephone to communicate with Channel Buildings. He had been careful to avoid having an instrument installed at home. If the time ever came when we all had telephones, he thought, what a curb on a man's freedom *that* would be. The telegram was impersonal; altogether more natural.

If awkward questions were to arise, they were more likely to come from his lover than his wife. She didn't pry into his affairs but he often saw curiosity in her eyes. Since there was once a Mrs George Shotton, there must have been a marital home. He invented a house in Newport that he sold because he couldn't bear to remain there. Since then he had led a nomadic life. The nearest thing to a permanent address was a commercial hotel, the Grosvenor, in Swansea – it seemed a sufficiently far-off place – and Mamie could always write to him there.

The Grosvenor was genuine enough (white globe outside full of dead flies, rat-faced manager who smelled of whisky). George stayed there occasionally. The next time he had a ship at Swansea to deal with, he called in and arranged to have any letters put aside for half a crown a week.

As long as he took reasonable precautions, there was no reason why his two lives should collide. But he had a bad experience in the north-east. For the first time since they became lovers he met Mamie outside London. He had business on Wearside, and she travelled down to meet him in South Shields at the Golden Lion. Agnes was there too, by arrangement, the proud possessor of an Artillery lieutenant at a coastal battery in Scarborough, a thin-throated lad called Donald; she wore a ring with a diamond the size of a pinhead, and she and Mamie spent much of the evening whispering together.

Making love in a strange bed, hearing muffled voices and footsteps, and ships' hooters from the docks, kept them awake half the night. They had to book separately, but it was not the kind of hotel that worried about who slept where, and her friend Grace made sure they had adjoining rooms.

It was morning before they talked. A smell of stale beer came up through the floorboards. 'Hold me tight,' said Mamie. 'I think I'm going to freeze to death. Unless I die of thirst.'

George hopped across the icy linoleum to get her the water bottle from the washstand, one hand shielding his penis in case it swung out of his pyjamas and embarrassed him. She giggled, having seen him do it often.

Two months had taught them small secrets about one another. There was his daily habit of snipping at his moustache with nail scissors, one speck at a time. There was her false tooth, or rather two false teeth that she could swap around in the same socket near the front, one ivory and one gold, each of them fixed by a clip at the back; done by a dentist in 1914 because, she told George, it was 'all the rage' in theatrical circles.

He saw the ivory version as she drank the water, a shade lighter than the rest. In half a minute she would start nibbling her lip and making eyes at him. But she was catching the early express for London and he was due at a dry dock. 'I must get going,' he said. 'So must you, if you want me to put you on the train.'

'I want to talk about Agnes. Will she be happy, do you suppose, getting hitched to a little boy who spends his time firing popguns at seagulls in Scarborough? I bet he has girl-friends there too.'

'Who knows?'

'She thinks I'm envious because she's the first of us to get married, apart from Kitty. I told her, I'm happy with Georgie,' and she began to press against him. 'I don't care if he marries me or not.'

'I'm sure Georgie is duly grateful. Now, one two three, I'm pulling off the bedclothes. Four five six, cold water on your bosom.'

'No! No!' she shrieked, but only to make him chase her into the bathroom along the corridor.

Fortunately the London train was running late or she would have missed it, despite an expensive taxi to take them and her two large suitcases – barely enough for clothes, she insisted – to Newcastle Central. Mamie found it hilarious. 'I told you there was plenty of time, Georgie,' she said, and sat with a piece of toast in a corner of the packed refreshment room, nibbling it at the edges like a child.

He was angry with her. The thought of missing trains upset him; so did hints about marriage. From the beginning he had assumed that Mamie's circle was devoted to having fun, not getting married. That was the whole point.

'Sorry,' she said. 'Mamie is sorry. Her little wristwatch apologises. Her little gold tooth says she'll try harder.'

She was absurd; she made him smile. 'I didn't know it was goldie's turn. Let me see.'

Her lips parted and the tooth gleamed. George blew it a kiss. He gave a defiant glance at anyone who might be watching, and found himself looking at his sister, Christiana, who was staring at him from the queue for the tea urn.

'This'll be your train,' he said, and got Mamie and suitcases on to the platform. He kissed her through the window, made sure she had ticket and money, and waved until all he could see was the red lamp.

Chrissie hadn't followed them out. She was standing by the counter, stirring sugar into her cup.

'How wonderful to see you,' said George. Between the nurse's cap and collar her face looked tired; flesh was drawn tight across bones. 'Where might you be off to?'

'The fever hospital at Boldon, helping out. What about you?'

'Some work in Sunderland. No time to breathe, as usual.' Hoping for the best, he said casually that the woman she had seen him with was the widow of a ship's officer, drowned in the North Atlantic a week ago. The agents had asked him to see her off to London, where she had a married sister. 'I could hardly refuse, could I?'

'I never used to believe you, even when I was small. Do you remember telling me you couldn't take me on the dock pier because girls weren't allowed in case the wind blew their clothes off? I was eight. You were twelve.'

'We were going fishing I expect.'

'You could just have gone without me. But you had to make up that silly story. I never minded you telling me the truth, when you did, which wasn't often.'

'I never did it to harm you. I'd never harm you.'

'Nor I you,' she said. 'But we could have been real friends, you and I. I thought the world of you when I was eight.'

'Odd subject to be discussing in a refreshment room.'

'Odd occasion altogether. How is May? And little Arthur?'

'Blooming. I don't see them as often as I would like.'

'I won't ask if you're coming to the house, since you never do. My train's in two minutes. I won't tell them I saw you, by the way.'

'Tell them what you like, Chrissie. I have nothing to be ashamed of. Nothing.'

When they parted, he could tell that she wasn't a hundred per cent certain. People never were. That was their weakness.

* * *

Mamie's Christmas treat included a visit to Madame Tussaud's Exhibition, which she said they shouldn't miss because Rupert would make special arrangements for them if asked. George hadn't been there for years. They arrived in mid-morning, as an observation balloon was being suspended from the ceiling in the Great Hall. A wax Father Christmas leaned over the basket dangling a parcel on which was written 'Peace in 1918'. Below, generals and admirals caked in medals stood on platforms, faces grim but calm, as if they could glimpse victory in the distance, where a string band was playing.

War maps and displays of weaponry attracted George, but Mamie tugged him downstairs to the Chamber of Horrors. It was her day. They wouldn't meet again until after the holiday. She was going to her family in Sunderland, while he would be 'staying with his sister-in-law' for a week in a part of the country he cautiously described as 'not far from Worcester'.

Peering into the faces of criminals, saying, 'Wouldn't like to meet *him* on a dark night!' Mamie danced about the long shadowy room, urging George on. Most of the horrors concerned murder. Palmer the poisoner smirked, Troppmann the engineer frowned, Dr Crippen looked shifty behind rimless glasses as a detective put a hand on his sleeve.

Mamie was the only woman visitor; a few soldiers on leave and a party of men with Birmingham accents noticed her, and there were grins when she pulled her companion to the curtained booths *Not to be Viewed by Children under 14* to savour The Guillotine (bleeding head in basket) and The English Execution (hangman waiting by the drop as prison chaplain, brandishing Bible and crucifix, walks backwards, concealing scaffold till the last minute). It was too melodramatic for George's taste but Mamie was thrilled.

Brides in the Bath made her giggle. This was a new exhibit, adults only, containing the actual tin bath 'As Used in the First Murder, Committed at Highgate.' It rested on linoleum with a straw mat alongside, while a yellow-faced George Joseph Smith, jacket off and sleeves rolled up, looked wildly at the corpse of a woman half out of the bath he had drowned her in. 'Smith was hanged at Maidstone Gaol on 13 August 1915,' said a sign framed in black. 'It may never be known how many innocent females he sent to their death.'

What delighted Mamie was that the corpse wore a garment, a cross between a bathing costume and a cloak. 'Dead ladies in the nude would never do, would they?' she gasped, squeezing his arm. 'Isn't it priceless?'

'They'd have the police in otherwise.'

'But a bathing suit, I ask you.'

She held up her mouth to be kissed and said that if they were quick, no one would see. He could tell she was up to something. 'Must go and find Roopy,' she said, and they arranged to meet by the Western Front panorama in the hall.

A lecturer with a pointer was tapping Belgium and explaining to a dozen listeners what the Third Battle of Ypres had achieved. 'Passchendaele is somewhat muddy at this time of year,' he said, and George was following intently when Mamie reappeared with Rupert, in black coat and striped trousers, and begged to go back to the basement.

The Birmingham party had left. A handful of visitors moved about in the gloom. 'Wait here,' whispered Mamie. Rupert had gone ahead of them. Now he came from behind the curtain around Brides in the Bath and hung up a placard announcing, 'This Exhibit Closed for Repairs'. He scanned the room and nodded. Mamie stepped over the tasselled rope inside the curtains. 'Come on,' she whispered. 'Don't you want to? Such fun.'

'Must be mad,' said George. 'You too,' he said to Rupert.

'I t-told her.'

'Do you realise what would happen if we were caught in

there? Mamie? The police would have us in the cells. There's such a thing as offences against public morals.'

'No need to give me a lecture. It was just a bit of fun.'

He was shaken. Strolling along Piccadilly an hour later, Mamie clung to his arm, her cheeks freshened by the cold weather, and he saw the way men looked at her. Imitation snow was falling in a shop window. He ordered a hamper for Everard at Fortnum's and bought Mamie a silk handbag, as well as a toy tank and a toy gun for an imaginary nephew, child of the imaginary sister-in-law. Christmas was two days away. They would meet again in London on New Year's Eve.

'Will you be a good girl in Sunderland over the holidays?'

'Depends if you'll be a good boy.'

'You know what I shall be doing. Country walks, log fires, keeping the family's spirits up.' He gave threepence to a woman selling lucky white heather, shrivelled inside silver paper. 'By the way, I'd rather you didn't go to that Golden Lion place in Shields.'

'What, in case I meet a man? It's only a bit of fun.'

'Is everything a bit of fun?'

'Not necessarily.' She snuggled against him by a windowful of glassware, which made their reflections seem set in ice. 'I think I might be falling in love with you.'

'Me too,' he said, because he wanted to keep her from temptation for a bit longer; because it might even be true.

5

Sprigs of holly from Cardiff Market decorated the photographs of Loader Steamship Co.'s fleet, set like plaques on the office walls. A square of unfaded paint showed where the *Cathays Park* had been, reminding George, who had been asked by his father-in-law to look in on Chistmas Eve, that forty pounds per year went down with her.

'I sent Solberg's family a letter of condolence,' he said, adding that while he was on the subject, forty pounds a ship didn't look too healthy now that the war was driving up prices. What about fifty-five in 1918?

His father-in-law frowned. With his beard and shiny cheeks, he would have made a tolerable Santa Claus at a children's party. 'We are all short of money these days.'

'Some of us are shorter than others.' George had been looking at his bank statements, which he kept in a locked drawer at the office. Mamie had cost him a hundred and forty-three pounds since October.

'There was something I wanted to ask you about, George. Delicate matter. Will you give me a straight answer?'

'I'll do my best. About a survey?'

'About a woman.'

Captain Loader was so uncomfortable that George feared the worst. Had some rumour reached the old man? He had a sentence ready: 'No one is perfect but I can say in all honesty that I have never loved anyone but May.'

'Do you know of a lady called Elizabeth Fogg?' said Billy.

Fogg was not a name on the danger list. 'A widow? Husband a sea pilot?'

'That's her. A charming person. She has a little house near Penarth dock with a shop in the front room that sells tobacco. I don't want to upset May, you understand.'

'By doing what?'

'Mrs Fogg and I have been acquainted for some time.'

Ah, thought George as the tale emerged – old friend of the late Mrs Loader, two people drawn together for companionship, singing at the piano, her excellent stews. Marriage had been talked about, and perhaps George could mention it to May; it would come better from him. Perhaps, even, if it wasn't too short notice, he could bring Elizabeth for Christmas lunch tomorrow, a family occasion to make her feel at home?

'Delighted,' said George.

Four would be less oppressive than two. He wished it was otherwise. He wished he didn't have Elgin Crescent on the brain. Mamie would have left there by now; the bed half made, stockings dangling off a chair, a smell of violet soap. Once out of sight she had proved as desirable as ever. But it was no use dwelling on her. A Welsh Christmas enveloped him. Oscar gave Miss Boulton a tin of toffees. Collecting boxes came round for workhouses and the crews of lightships. A colliery band played carols in Mountstuart Square.

George did his shopping on the way home, a fox-fur tippet for May and a standby goose with the giblets in a bag. She had left a note to say she would meet him at the church, where he had promised to take her to a carol service. Meanwhile Mavis had bathed Arthur and was staying with him until they returned.

The boy was tearful, not understanding, or not wanting to understand, why he wouldn't see Nursey until after the holiday. She had her own brothers and sisters, explained George, and they would be expecting her. 'Can I go too?' said Arthur, brightening up at the prospect. A hopeless child.

George made his way to the church at seven. The weather had turned cold; snow was reported from the north. Walking up and down outside St Augustine's, he pictured Hawarden Crescent with snow drifted up against the cottages, and Mamie's face at a window, looking out in disgust at this interference with her right to wear high-heeled shoes.

May appeared with Mrs Finch – the Moral Vigilants must have had another of their meetings – and immediately took George on one side and asked what Dadda was doing, talking to Elizabeth Fogg.

'It's a long story,' said George, who hadn't noticed them in the porch, 'but they are coming to us for Christmas lunch. We are to regard her as one of the family. Now, you're not to upset yourself.'

But he knew the carols were ruined for her. As the church emptied, Mrs Finch pinned him down. His wife was in the next aisle, listening anxiously to her father. Days of May feeling hurt stretched ahead.

'You men could do a grand job, you know,' said Mrs Finch, her stalky frame trembling with energy. 'After all, if there were no men there would be no fallen women.'

'I can see you've given this a lot of thought.'

'Men are reluctant to appear on platforms and be critical of their own sex. Look at the scandal of the *maisons de tolérance* in France. They are certainly tolerated by the British High Command. The War Minister will do nothing about them. An entire generation of young men is being exposed to moral corruption.'

'Not quite entire, I hope. I have a younger brother out there with the Durham Light Infantry.'

'I am sorry. I am too eager.'

'I know from my wife how committed you all are,' said George.

He wondered if he had died on the train from Paddington, and Penarth at Christmas was his induction to eternal torment. Now Mrs Finch was telling his wife, who had joined them, about their interesting conversation. She hoped to get Mr Shotton on a platform. May nodded grimly. Tears were in the offing; he could smell them coming, like rain.

Christmases had to be put up with, had even been enjoyed. Christmas 1917 was unbearable for its own special reason. Expecting nothing, George was surprised by occasional pleasures. Gun and tank went down well. Arthur asked about wars and Germans; there was hope for him yet. The house was servantless – Olwen, the dogsbody, had returned to her family in Carmarthenshire for the holiday – and he roasted the goose himself to an even brownness that was much admired. He didn't object to Mrs Fogg, whose hoarse laugh and slightly vulgar tongue appealed to him as much as they distressed May; not that she was anything but polite. In the evening they played bridge and ate nuts.

'You are often away?' Mrs Fogg said to him. 'My late husband was the same. Ships are the very devil when it comes to knowing where a man has got to,' and her laugh came out like a clearing of the throat.

George was away again sooner than he expected. One of Loader's steamers went aground in the north-west on Boxing Day. The news came like a reprieve. He had the Bradshaw out in a flash to find connections for the Solway Firth. Yes, he could get there quickly. Yes, he had to go, it was his duty not to leave it to a local man. No, he hadn't forgotten they were going to Oscar and Bella's; May would have to go without him.

Her unhappiness was worse for being unspoken. The nearest she came to expressing it was when she said, 'I had hoped to enjoy today more than I did yesterday.' She packed his things with her usual care, and included a turkey leg in greaseproof paper in case the train was stranded in the snow.

'My dear sweet May,' he said, 'what would I do without you?' In a way he meant it.

The vessel was the *Parrot*, the company's rustiest coaster, aground north of Maryport on sand and stones at Point of Kells. Snow flurries against train windows made him think of winters in Sunderland long ago. Childhood was a longing for something already lost. In Carlisle, he slept badly on Boxing Night. Busloads of noisy women crunched through the frozen slush outside the hotel; munition workers, he was told over breakfast. The train to the coast crawled across a wilderness of black and white. Closing his eyes, he dreamed that Everard was speaking to him in a language he couldn't understand; he woke to hear a man calling, 'Silloth, this is Silloth,' and gulls fighting over fish guts.

The *Parrot* was four miles away by the coast road, lying in three feet of water. The insurers had already taken it on themselves to begin concreting the hull so she could be refloated, and George had only to endorse the work.

On board he found that Miller, the captain, was drunk, taking pot shots at seagulls with a revolver, boasting that he hadn't let the Lloyd's surveyor see his log. This was just as well, since it hadn't been written up for days. 'You could lose your ticket,' warned George, and stood over him while they concocted a story about condenser trouble and failed engines, and a cross-tide that put the *Parrot* ashore. Perhaps somebody would believe in the captain's competence. George wouldn't count on it.

Pretending to look for charts, he found more bottles of whisky and poured them over the side. 'I ought to shoot you,' cried Miller, so George confiscated the revolver too.

A dinghy with the mate in it was waiting at the foot of the ladder. As the boat rowed clear Miller leaned over the side, shouting, 'I lost two sons in two years. One in France, the other in a fucking rust bucket like this one. Am I having a fair crack of the whip, Mr Shotton?'

George was afraid he wasn't. But then, who was? Twenty-four hours later the coaster was refloated and towed away. His telegram to Loader Steamships said, 'PARROT TO BARROW FOR SURVEY IN DUE COURSE.' The one to May went, 'SOLWAY FIRTH. SNOW. ENJOYED TURKEY LEG.'

Mamie wasn't returning to London until New Year's Eve. George crossed the neck of England, west to east, on the twenty-eighth, a Friday, and reached Sunderland late in the afternoon. Snow was thawing from roofs in Hawarden Crescent. A furniture remover's van was outside Number 3 – 'H. Silver' and 'Distance No Object'. The house door was half open and a child with a toy bear stood in the gap, telling the toy it was too small to walk in the snow.

'You must be Dolly. I've come to see your Auntie Mamie.'

A thick voice said, 'You'll freeze us all to death, little one,' and Captain Stuart appeared, unshaven and in his braces.

'Tell the man it's Auntie *Amy*, Grandad.'

'Come in, come in. I forget your name.'

'I'm George.'

'This is Mr George. My wife, Eleanor, and this is daughter Edith and Mr Silver, who she's married to, and my sister Edna, and little Dolly you've met.'

'He says Mamie,' persisted the child. 'Mamie Amy Samey.'

'I believe you called to see my sister in the summer, when she was unfortunately absent,' said the sister. 'She is unfortunately absent again.'

Hands, but not Edith's, passed him plates of sweets and biscuits, a cup of tea, a glass of blackcurrant cordial. The amiable Captain Stuart explained how his son-in-law had been caught in the blizzards on Christmas Eve, miles away down the coast, stranded there with the van until today. Henry

Silver cracked nuts in his palms and said that furthermore his new bathroom had frozen solid. It hadn't been much of a Christmas.

So Mamie had never got there. 'Amy Mamie's in London,' squealed Dolly, and was warned to be quiet or else.

'I hope Mr George hasn't been inconvenienced,' said the captain.

'I just happened to be passing.'

The sister spoke again, to ask if Mr George lived in these parts.

'I have business here from time to time.'

'I myself had to work on Christmas Day,' said Captain Stuart.

'He commands a tugboat,' said his wife, a small woman with red ears and a look of Mamie about her lips.

'What business?' asked Edith.

George said they had all been most hospitable, but he must be on his way. He pressed a threepenny bit into the child's palm. 'I'll tell you a secret,' he said in her ear. 'I was helping Santa Claus over Christmas.'

'He hasn't got a beard.'

'I'll see Mr George out,' snapped Edith, and closed the living-room door behind them. 'I wasn't born yesterday.'

'I respect a woman who doesn't try to conceal her age.'

'My sister's happiness is important to me. If a married man were to make overtures to her – I make no accusations – I would be an avenging angel. I merely state facts. My sister has a kindly disposition. A bad person – I am speaking in generalities – might be tempted to take advantage of it. He had better beware.'

'I think you can rely on me to do the right thing,' said George, and let himself into the empty street.

Mamie had intended to go home for Christmas, but one thing

led to another. Someone told her that the queues for tickets at King's Cross stretched on to the Marylebone Road. Snow was reported in the north. And then Norah's new boyfriend, Edgar, came up with invitations to a Christmas Eve ball in Harrow.

A girl was entitled to some fun. George would be enjoying roaring fires and presents under the tree at his sister-in-law's, somewhere near Worcester. That side of him was a mystery. The annual dinner party for neighbours sounded stuffy and no fun at all, but she was curious all the same. Worcester itself was as indistinct to her as China; Mamie's England was confined to the north and London. On Boxing Day George was due to borrow a rifle – or something – and join a shooting party with the sister's husband. The thought of him blasting away at the sky was hilarious. Meanwhile she was supposed to languish in Sunderland.

The ball was fatally short of eligible men. The dancing to a proper orchestra was first-rate but she ended leaving in a bus with Albert. Edgar's tickets being exclusive of supper, she would have liked them all to go up West, not back to Elgin Crescent for tinned sardines and a wizened fowl, washed down with some bottles of muck that Roopy had found in Soho. Admittedly it was fun at the time, until (a) the gramophone broke and (b) Norah caught Edgar in the pantry, kissing Nancy.

The jolly Christmas that should have happened by accident didn't materialise. People faded away, leaving Mamie and Norah to talk about how awful men were, and wake up on Christmas morning in time to go round to Norah's parents for turkey and other festivities. Feeling silly in a paper hat, Mamie thought she might as well have been crammed into a living room with her own relatives as into this one with somebody else's, friendly as they were.

They put her up at Norah's for the next few nights. 'Of

course you must stay,' said the mother, who held liberal views on young women. 'You must feel dreadful, not being with your family.'

Or not being with George.

'I think he's genuine,' said Norah. 'I know Nancy doesn't, but she wants everything for herself. Look at her and Edgar.'

'Will you see him again?'

'Depends how hard he tries.'

They spent hours in Norah's room, where she had slept since she was a child, exploring a wardrobe of abandoned clothes, some of them going back to the start of the century: faded bonnets, beribboned underwear, frocks as heavy as blankets. It was a relief to get away from men. Mamie spent an afternoon soaking in the bath – the family had gone to a matinée – talking to Norah, who sat alongside smoking and sucking in violet-scented steam. 'Wish I had your figure,' sighed Norah. 'Your bosom is beautiful.'

'It's my hips let me down.'

'We all want to be something else.'

'Come and get in the bath. There's room for two.'

'I *couldn't*!'

'Yes you could. End to end. I'll pull my legs up. Bags of room.'

'All right, I will.'

They stayed there for ages, gossiping, talking about the dotty suffragettes who perhaps weren't entirely dotty; about movie stars they admired, Alma Reubens and Edna Purviance and Gladys Cooper; about their childhoods in different worlds. Mamie thought it better than Christmas.

Next day, which was Friday, Edgar was there with roses and humility; a square-faced man of thirty who managed a steel-stamping business (which exempted him from the call-up), not to be discarded lightly. Norah said he could take her out as long as Mamie came as well, a temporary punishment. That night Mamie was back in Elgin Crescent on her own.

George's return to London was still three days away. There were men she could have passed the time with but she wasn't keen. Mr George Shotton had more to offer than the rest; at twenty-four you started thinking about the future. She read bits of her favourite Elinor Glyn, the one where the Russian princess tried in vain to seduce Paul, the honourable young Englishman, at some hotel in Switzerland. Paul wasn't the sort to crumple up at a pretty leg. Imagine if she had met George under other circumstances, not in her fun-loving mood but as the Mamie she felt was somewhere inside her, profound and sensitive, whose dark eyes were windows to her soul. George saw the passionate Mamie, but what about the woman within? Come to that, what about the George within? Did he have depths as well? She hadn't forgotten that remark about never loving anyone again since his wife died. Nancy, of course, said that if she heard Mamie repeat it once more she was going to be sick, but Nancy had no soul to speak of.

On Saturday morning she did housework, a Cinderella: lonely, patient, biding her time. Cleaned the grate, scrabbled for coal, lit the fire, beat the mats in the freezing garden, washed the pans from Christmas Eve, put bleach in the bath, ironed a blouse.

The bell rang. What if the thought transference you read about in the papers had sent a telegram from her brain to George's and he was standing outside, like Elinor Glyn's Paul, shy and quiet, the inner George who couldn't live without her?

'Hello, Albert,' she sighed. 'What brings you? Everyone else has shoved off. I've been cleaning the flat.'

'Thought I'd bring some grub round. Also I have tidings of great joy.'

He wouldn't tell her at first. Albert had been a pal since her song-and-dance days – he did stage-management for variety theatres as well as betting on horses – who made a nice enough lover. They liked each other consistently: no more, no less.

'There's a job touring in pantomime for a month from the second week in January,' he said, sitting by the fire with her at his knees, a hint of frying sausages in the air. 'Queen Elf in *Mother Goose*, costume supplied, bit of kicking and stretching, couple of dozen lines and a poem, no singing, three pound ten a week, third-class rail fare, find your own digs. You're always talking about going back.'

'Is it what I want, though? A career, I mean?'

'Gather ye rosebuds. Girls are in short supply, on account of the wages in munitions. Make a few quid and enjoy yourself.' He toyed with her blouse. 'Gloucester, Bristol, Newport, Cardiff, Swansea. Isn't Swansea where the mysterious George hangs out?'

'He isn't all that mysterious. Yes, it is.'

'There you are then. Say thank you, Albert.'

He pulled her on to his lap. Garments landed on the floor. 'Cheeky devil,' she murmured.

'Ignore it,' he said when someone rang the doorbell. Whoever it was kept ringing. She hobbled to the window. A sideways squint where the curtain left a gap showed trouser-legs and a leather valise. 'George, George!' she mouthed. Albert was into his trousers in a flash, kicked his drawers under the armchair and scurried to the kitchen. When Mamie was decent she scorched her face at the fire for a moment, then went to the door, yawning.

Behind the eager kisses she was thinking that it was hardly a girl's fault if men always suited themselves. Hand up leg? That was what legs were for. Arrive unexpectedly? It was a girl's job to be waiting.

'Little hot-cheeks,' said George.

'Asleep by fire.'

'I smelled cooking or I'd have given up.'

'Sausages. Stay for luncheon. Stay for ever, Georgie darling.'

'I came overnight from the north.' He slumped on the sofa. 'Delayed by snowdrifts. So you never went.'

'What with the weather, and I was poorly. Stayed with Norah till last night. How about you? Did you meet ravishing women?'

'Had to leave on Boxing Day. Ship ran aground. Good excuse, really. Rather wanted to see you.'

'Oh, Georgie.' Oh God. Faced with a crisis of such proportions, what did the inner woman advise? Tell the truth? Confess and start again? Fine thoughts, Elinor Glyn-like, occurred to her. But the inner woman was too terrified to pursue them. 'I've had such a nice surprise,' she said. 'Alberto has been round and my career has got going again. A month in panto, including Swansea.'

She told him about Queen Elf. A dish clattered. 'Is that him?' said George.

'It was he brought the sausages. He's such a dear.'

'Is that little squirt the reason you stayed in London?'

'Don't be silly, Georgie. He's just a pal. I swear to you before God I had no idea he'd call in today. I'll tell him to come and say hello.'

George was evidently unimpressed by the apron tied around the waist, and the blackened sausage impaled on a fork for them to comment on. Albert was too cheery. 'She's been missing you badly, old boy,' he said, squeezing her shoulder. 'Would you like me to make myself scarce?'

'And you can take that burnt offering with you,' said George, standing with his back to the fire, proprietorial. 'Mamie and I are going out to a restaurant.'

'It was kind of you to come, Alberto. I was *so* miserable. May I give him a kiss?'

She put lips to cheek, aware of George's eyes. The crisis would have passed if sausage hadn't fallen off fork and rolled under armchair. Before she could move, George pushed the chair back with his foot, revealing the sausage, together with fluff, a *Sporting Life* and Albert's drawers.

'I wonder whose these could be?' said George, examining them with distaste.

'Roopy and Nance were in here for hours one night.'

'Hours,' said Albert.

There was a simple way of finding out, said George, and instructed Mamie to wait in the kitchen.

'I'll do what I please,' she told him, but he looked so threatening that she went as far as the passage and listened. She heard George say something about trousers, and thought Albert laughed. Then a pause; then a croak from Albert, 'He's got a revolver!'

'I'll count three,' said George. 'One. Two.'

Then silence. Then George calling her name.

Albert, white-faced, was buttoning his trousers. George was standing behind the sofa with the gun in his hand. He said, 'I might have known.'

Mamie tried to think how the princess would have responded. 'Am I not deserving of your trust?' she said.

George rubbed the barrel against his cheek. 'Not half you aren't.'

'I'm going to the police,' said Albert.

'Yes, why don't you? Every male they come in contact with is checked to see he's registered under the Military Service Act. You'll be in the trenches in a fortnight.' He put the gun in the valise, which was open on the floor. 'Farewell, Mamie Stuart.'

'Don't go. Please don't go.'

The front door slammed. She saw his legs go up the steps.

'I thought he was going to kill me,' said Albert.

'I wish he had. Now get out.'

When he had gone too, Mamie sat huddled in the chair, eating burnt sausages, thinking about the unfairness of it all.

'I am a tragic woman,' she said aloud, trying to convince herself that she was. But the unhappiness was real enough.

6

On his interminable train journeys George read survey reports or the *Transactions* of the Institute of Naval Architects, did crossword puzzles and wrote letters to Everard, harmless commentaries on the war and his work, with the odd sentence thrown in about May and home life at Penarth. It wasn't until the Mamie Stuart madness was over that he felt driven to tell his brother about her. He had to tell someone.

'I am twenty minutes out of Liverpool, on my way to Hull,' he wrote. 'As usual there are more people in the corridors than sitting down. Fortunately I have a seat in the first class. My neurasthenia has been bothering me of late. I am lucky, of course, not to be exposed to the perils of war, but one can suffer one's private hells while being safe and warm in England. You have not heard me in this vein before. You are a man of the world now. Who knows what will become of us "after the war", that mythical era? Why should I not confide my present unhappiness in you and say that I have been wretchedly involved with a young woman? Her name is Mamie and I brought our relationship to an end two weeks ago, not out of any moral feelings but because I surprised her *in flagrante delicto*, damn near. It was just as well, since I have no intention of leaving May, and girls have a way of getting their hooks into a man. Why then am I complaining? Simply because I found her a most endearing little monkey, and life is not the same without her. You may be surprised at this account of my weaknesses, but you might agree that there is a certain strength in admitting to the weaknesses in the first place. At any rate, I know that my secrets, such as they are, are safe with you. I have always felt us to be closer than either of us has expressed in so many words. God bless you and return you safely to England.'

Writing it was a load off his mind. He carried it around the country for several days, and still had it in his pocket when he returned to South Wales. For the moment he left it locked in his drawer at the office – where he kept his bank statements, and lately the revolver – in case he wanted to add anything to it.

Now that he had stopped leading two lives, George was at Penarth more often. It should have been a relief to be a normal human being again. He got builders to install a gas fire in the drawing room and replace the soft-coal range in the kitchen with a 'Kooksjoie' anthracite model. A house was like a ship, always in need of attention. The boiler was due for descaling; roof slates had loosened in a gale, despite his telegraphed warning; upstairs window-frames warped in the rain and let in draughts that swayed the curtains. Number 244 Westbourne Road was dry-docked, as it were. Hammers, chisels, blowlamps and soldering irons worked nonstop till she was seaworthy.

May was pleased, so pleased that she came to his bed in her flannelette nightdress. She lay on her back, stretched out motionless like a casualty on a stretcher, and said that if a husband cared so much about the home and his wife's wellbeing, what right did she have to reject his advances? His long absences before Christmas had given her time to reflect. 'I am afraid I have been selfish,' she said, and her hand slid across the cold sheet and took hold of his.

George would have liked to say, 'Too late,' or at least 'Not just now.' It was in the nature of private hells that solace came at the wrong time or from the wrong direction and had the opposite effect to the one intended. He could hardly plead a headache.

During his next absence from South Wales, the first leg of the journey took him into Paddington station. With an hour to spare before he left London from St Pancras, he told the taxi to make a detour through Notting Hill. It was only a mile out of his way. What was a mile? He argued to himself that by going along Elgin Crescent he was testing his willpower to prove that his feelings were on the wane. He sat with his fist bunched under his chin. 'Damn woman!' he said to himself – but his lips must have moved because the cab driver caught his eye in the mirror and said, 'Beg pardon, sir?'

On 22 January he was back in Penarth. According to the tale he had concocted for Mamie Stuart – one of the tales – it was the fourth anniversary of his wife's death. He arrived home, earlier in the evening than he expected, to find a committee of Moral Vigilants in possession of the drawing room. Handshakes and gusts of scent; 'Mr Shotton is one of our silent supporters,' from Mrs Finch; his views solicited on building a refuge hut near the dock, in aid of which a public meeting was planned for the following night.

Because he knew that May would like it, he said he might 'look in for ten minutes' at the meeting. Suddenly the fearful Mrs Finch was begging him to say a few words from the platform, and he was agreeing.

It was a perilous business, going out of one's way to please one's wife. A life of major concessions by them both seemed to be in the making. Hers, ironically, were of the flesh, not the spirit. She was stubborn, anxious, insistent; she kept her eyes shut; there was no ardour. In his absence she had purchased a whirling spray so that he would not have to use his rubber goods. How it worked was a mystery, but she kept it on top of the wardrobe and took it with her to the bathroom.

A hospital ship that was towed into Barry docks, after

striking a mine off Hartland Point, occupied George all day, and he was late for the Vigilants. A heap of bloodstained linen had been left on the quay; a nursing orderly was tying pairs of crutches together with surgical tape. That was the real world, thought George, when he was being hurried on to the platform, not mouthing platitudes about moral decay.

He slipped away before the meeting ended. The town was empty; he walked along roads that spiralled downhill, catching glimpses of riding lights and fairway beacons in Cardiff Bay; through alleys that led to railway sidings, level with the cranes and staithes that lined Penarth dock. Ships were loading coal in the half-tide basin, far off, dust clouding the lights. Shouting came from a pub, the Cuba. This was Moral Vigilance country, but they were all at the meeting.

A girl said, 'Hello, love,' in the nasal East Wales accent. Squarish face, darkish hair. Very likely she had come from Cardiff, paying the penny toll to walk through the subway under the river, to where there was less competition. She pointed to a corrugated iron lean-to, open to cinders and railway buffers. Six shillings, full service.

George was tempted; what else was he doing there? But something about her mouth suggested Mamie, a poor parody in cheap red paint that was enough to make him turn away.

He found a road with a few ramshackle houses. A woman with a dog on a lead had paused under a lamppost. 'Thought it was you,' said a throaty voice, and he recognised Mrs Fogg. 'Saw you across there, behind the Cuba.'

'Sharp eyes you've got.'

'You're like me, you like a stroll at night.'

They walked together as far as her house, one street away up the hill. The roar of coal being tipped came on gusts of wind. She talked about the marriage, which would be in the summer, and how she intended that one day she and Captain Loader would move far away from coal ports and south-west gales.

'I envy you,' said George.

'Surely not. A man in the prime of life doesn't need to envy anybody.'

'It was a figure of speech. You and Billy seem very well suited to each other. I enjoyed our Christmas Day.'

'I had a feeling that Mrs Shotton didn't, altogether.'

'I can assure you she did.'

'You know your own wife, of course.' They shook hands outside her house; blue blinds covered the shop window. 'You remind me of my late husband,' she said. 'He was a deep man too.'

A day or two later, when George was finishing a job at Bristol docks, he was offered a class survey on a pair of oil barges dry-docked in the river at Swansea. He always followed the cab-rank principle: if free, take what was offered. The fact that Mamie Stuart was appearing in pantomime at the Swansea Empire was irrelevant. To refuse the work and *not* go there would have been an admission of defeat. 'PLANS FLUID,' he telegraphed to May. 'ENSURE OLWEN EMPTIES FIREBOX AFTER RIDDLING NOT BEFORE.'

Arriving early from Bristol, he spent a hard day at the riverside, followed by a visit to the Lloyd's agent in Adelaide Chambers. Was the logical next step to catch the first train back to Cardiff? Or was it to test his resolve again? Since the reports were needed urgently, he suggested he stay on and write them. The agent and his clerks went home, leaving George to lock up. As he was writing the last paragraph a clock struck seven. A headache that had stabbed intermittently all afternoon was radiating into his eyeballs, and when he saw a woman approaching down the badly lit street he knew that as she walked under the lamp outside he would see a resemblance to Mamie. Everywhere he went he saw her.

Mother Goose began at 7.15. Bursts of laughter could be

heard; the show had started, and he bought a ticket from a woman who was already counting coins in her booth, and went to sit in the circle.

Queen Elf came on after five minutes. Mamie looked different in the costume: taller, the legs thinner, the face less toothy. When she spoke, he felt the sweat on his palms, down his spine. When the crown fell off – there was some horseplay he hadn't followed – the hair underneath was blonde. A wig? Or wasn't it Mamie at all? George realised that only a blind man could have thought otherwise and marched out, banging the door to the stairs behind him and going round to the stage door, where a woman knitting a khaki sock said that Miss Stuart had left the show before it got to Swansea.

A visit to the Grosvenor Hotel rounded off a difficult day. Edwards, the manager, came out of his cubbyhole, fuddled as usual, and pushed the register towards him.

When George said who he was, Edwards peered at him, like a sentry waiting for the password.

'S-h-o-t-t-o-n. I pay you two shillings and sixpence a week to keep letters for me. Do you have any?'

'Ah. There was three, as I remember.'

'So hand them over.'

'She's got 'em now,' said Edwards, and jerked his head towards the stairs.

'Who's she?'

'Your wife, of course.'

Viewed logically, it was unlikely that May Shotton was in a room upstairs reading letters from Mamie Stuart. But it hadn't been much of a day for logic.

'Describe her.'

'I'd have thought you knew what your own wife looked like, Mr Shotton.'

'I'll break your bloody neck,' said George. He reached over the counter and jerked the man towards him by his tie.

'Pretty woman big eyes lovely smile got a gold tooth sorry.'

'When the mood takes her.' George let him go. 'What room's she in?'

'Number 3, Mr Shotton, but she'll likely be in the bath. Terrible lady for baths, your wife. Permanent hot-water shortage in the place since she came yesterday, no disrespect.'

Upstairs was as grimy as downstairs. George tapped the door. 'Go away,' came from inside. 'I'll be here for ages.'

'It's George.'

They stood embracing in the steam, her wetness all over him, breasts dripping on his shirt, bush imprinting his trousers. His headache had gone.

'Will you ever forgive me?' she said, when she was wrapped in a towel and he was sitting on the edge of the bath. 'I know I was bad but now I'm good. I so wanted you to come. I sent you letters and you didn't answer, and I thought, if I say my prayers he'll come and see me in the panto. But I got the sack in Newport. So I came anyway and lived in hope.'

'How long would you have stayed?'

'All week. Nancy lent me the dough. Said I was mad. Said you were married. She's gone to be a lady soldier, you know, the Waacs – to find someone better than Roopy if you ask me.'

'And Albert?'

'He was an old flame. Hasn't touched me for years, and then that Saturday . . . We were just playing about and then you arrived. Goodness, I was so ashamed. Are we going to bed now?'

'Dear Everard,' George began, the next time he was in letter-writing mood, 'My *affaire de coeur* is less straightforward than I led you to believe.' This letter too joined the bank statements and the gun.

7

We shall all get married sooner or later, said Norah, and you might do worse than George. They agreed that a modern girl who had seen a bit of life should think twice before embracing the kitchen sink and a crowd of babies. Look at Kitty, a best friend from Mamie's elementary school, tall and pretty, whose father was a vet at a colliery, several rungs up from a mate on a coaster, which was as far as Captain Stuart had got in those days. What did Kitty do? Married a riveter at nineteen and lived in South Shields.

George offered something else. They couldn't see him sentencing his wife to the kitchen sink. Hadn't he hired a Mrs Lamb to clean the flat and do the laundry? Nor was he going to give her a baby a year, like Kitty's riveter.

The character of George Shotton was combed through in lazy conversations on Norah's bed or in a conservatory with a vine that caught the winter sun. He could talk about anything, they agreed – Mr Lloyd George, women's clothes, profiteering, motorcars; he even spoke of acquiring a motor himself. Money flowed out of his pockets, though he liked to know where it was going, and Mamie thought he kept lists of his expenditure. A smart, personable man, his worst trait no more than a tendency to fuss – it was almost too good to be true, a chap like that without attachments.

Norah believed he was genuine. Mamie had a nightmare of a fiancée somewhere. 'He *says* he's moved in on a permanent basis. Tells me he gets as many jobs in London as he can.

But he still spends half his time shooting up and down the country.'

'He always brings you back a present.'

'For all I know he always brings *her* back a present. Trouble is, I am fond of him.'

'He's potty about you. Can't leave you alone. Let's say he does have a lady love somewhere else – what you have to do is beat her to it. He's sure to marry again, so when he does, make certain it's you. If marrying him's what you want.'

Mamie liked his presence in the flat. She and George had it to themselves. Norah had tactfully moved back to her parents'; Nancy was in Sussex, training for the Women's Army Auxiliary Corps, and Rupert, if he pined for her, pined somewhere else; Albert was seen no more. George's razor and shaving brush stood next to her 'Mysterieuse' bath salts. Files of his business papers lived in a cardboard box under the bed. A Decca gramophone graced the sitting room, available for dancing to after supper. Sometimes she gave solo performances, minus skirt and stockings, to 'Let's All Go Raving Mad' and 'Gnee-Ah!', kicking so high she nearly hit the ceiling. Five minutes of that and he wanted to have her on the spot, and generally did.

But his sudden disappearances upset her. One Friday afternoon a telegram arrived, sent at Paddington post office: 'DUE BRISTOL CHANNEL. BACK SUNDAY EVE. DON'T OVERWIND GRAMOPHONE.' It was the first week of March; she came back from Norah's in time to pick weakly daffodils from the square and be sitting reading Elinor Glyn, a cold chicken's wing waiting for him in the meat-safe, when he arrived. Her present was sugared almonds; he didn't notice the daffodils. She petted him and let herself be kissed, but in bed she said flatly that it had been a dreadful weekend without him, and she was going straight to sleep. 'Come, come, Mamie,' said George, and talked her out of it. But she had served notice, of a sort; she and Norah had agreed that there came a time with a man when you had to take risks.

In the morning, smiling ironically, he invited her to go with him to Deptford, where they were building a concrete ship. 'Since you are so curious about my work,' he said. They walked arm in arm to the Holland Park underground. Deptford was the end of the world. The thing he had gone to inspect was in a dry basin dug out of the clay, white ribs like a skeleton under the estuary skies. Standing on a wooden platform she waved to the men swarming below, who waved back and shouted up compliments. She was cold and bored; an embarrassed watchkeeper boiled up tea for her in a shed while George got on with his inspecting. What she learned from the visit was that he paid attention to her moods.

Bolder, now, she followed him another evening when he announced abruptly that he had a business appointment and would be back at eleven. Norah would have said it was one risk too many. His trilby bobbed a hundred yards ahead. If he turned, would he recognise the raincoated figure scuttling down the other side of Ladbroke Grove? She was terrified; exhilarated; a woman in love, if asked.

Holland Park station again; eastbound train, two carriages in between them; change at Notting Hill, re-emerge into drizzle and darkened pavements at Earls Court. He was in no hurry or he would have used a taxi. Along Hogarth Road, into Cromwell Road, mount steps overhung by Entente flags; the Hotel de Rouen. She saw him deposit his coat and hat in the foyer and enter the dining room.

A functionary in a tailcoat came towards her at once. 'May I assist, madam?'

'I am meeting someone.'

'Unaccompanied ladies are asked to leave their names and wait in the writing room.'

'Don't be silly,' she said. 'I am, I am Rear Admiral Stuart's daughter.'

He retreated, no doubt to consult the hotel register. Mamie looked through the glass doors to the dining salon, and there was George, chatting to a woman whose face she couldn't see properly. She had an impression of smartness and maturity. Had she ever felt so angry; so empty?

A stout, tweedy man with an excess of white beard said, 'Excuse me, my dear,' as he passed her to enter the dining room. He walked straight to George's table. George was standing up and shaking hands. The bearded one was kissing the woman, whose face, visible now, was plain, pleasant and wrinkled; sixty-five if a day.

She never established exactly who they were. But later in the week George was full of himself because, he told her, a Board of Trade inquiry he attended in Leadenhall Street had accepted his evidence. Some drunk captain; some ship called the *Parrot*. 'It was the owner of the ship I went to meet when I popped out the other night,' he said, as if he knew she needed placating.

At least a scene in the Hotel de Rouen would have brought matters to a head. Mamie kept picturing George as she might have surprised him, caressing the hand of a slim young woman, pale-skinned with dark hair. It was the description he had given her of the wife who died, whose name was May; Miss Skinny would have been May reborn, whereas Mamie was just Mamie.

They went to Brighton for a weekend. She was half in love, half looking for a quarrel. They had been lovers all winter. Marriages were two a penny in wartime, but Mr G. Shotton seemed not to have heard. He bought her a cheap ring for her wedding finger and they registered as husband and wife, a necessity she understood but didn't enjoy.

Their bedroom, under the roof, was furnished with worm-eaten pieces, including a bed that squeaked every time they made love. 'Ha ha, they will think we're a honeymoon couple,' said George, which she found less amusing than he did.

Gulls bawling down the chimney woke them early, but not too early for George. In no time he was pawing and grunting. 'Must be something in the sea air,' she murmured, not properly awake.

Light filled the room slowly. She was warm and contented, cuddling up to him, discussing what they would do. First the Lanes, he thought, where he would buy her a trinket; then a walk to blow the cobwebs away.

'This is the life,' he said. 'I have ordered breakfast in bed. Think if a little chambermaid brought it in when we were having intercourse.' He began whispering what the maid would do.

'Drop the tray and run, I imagine,' said Mamie, who liked the thing itself too much to make it part of a silly game. But George went on about the maid's flushed cheeks; how she would take her clothes off; how they would all be under the sheets together like rabbits in a bag.

'You dirty beast,' said Mamie, without rancour.

'No worse than you at Tussaud's.'

'Perhaps I've grown up since then.'

When she saw him reaching under the bed, where he kept his supply of Dr Eggins's specials, she said, 'Not now, there's a dear. I'm a teeny bit sore. Wait till tonight and we'll do one of those things you say we don't do often enough.'

As if she hadn't spoken, he mounted her and put a knee between her thighs to push them apart. A feeling of annoyance that must have been there already made her jam her legs tighter.

'No!' she said. 'Just for once, the answer is no.'

He was panting with the effort. 'Who – won't – get – her – trinket – then?' he gasped.

'Pig!' she screamed, unable to resist his wrenching any more. So the bed squealed, and George grunted, and breakfast arrived in due course (a boy's voice said it was outside the door). Her resentment ran through it all.

Returning from a long soak in the bath, she found him doing physical jerks in front of the open window, wearing vest and underpants. An empty bottle of his vile Globéol mixture was on the dressing table. 'There was not a proper dose in it,' he grumbled, and while she was still getting her lips and cheeks right in front of the mirror, he hurried out to buy some more, presumably to replace the nervous energy expended during the night.

Downstairs she waited in the lounge, where an army officer with captain's pips put his head round the back of a wing chair and wished her good morning.

For a lark she had a little flirt; accepted a cup of coffee from his pot; agreed that Brighton was fun; said that, mm, yes, scorching down the coast to Eastbourne with a party in a motor sounded sublime, but a girl would need to know it was safe; decided things had gone far enough when he said his name was Johnny and asked what hers was – at which point George appeared in the lounge and asked icily if she was ready.

'Bye-bye, Captain,' she said, and he winked and turned back to his *Daily Mail*.

George was beside himself. What did she think she was doing? In the street he gripped her arm as if she was under arrest. Did he mean nothing to her? He had intended to buy her an 18-carat gold ankle chain, if she wanted to know, but that would have to wait until he had an explanation.

'Stop being ridiculous,' she said. 'Am I supposed to have taken a vow of silence? You don't own me.'

'I have always treated you with respect.'

'Ha ha.' They were by the turnstiles to the West Pier. 'I don't know about you but I am going to walk to the end. Might jump off, just for fun.'

George didn't seem to hear. He was peering at the blackboard that had high-water times and sea conditions chalked on it daily. 'Damn, it's March the sixteenth,' she heard him say.

'Are you coming on the pier or not?'

'I have to go and send a telegram. Wait here for me. I shall not be more than a quarter of an hour.'

Again there was that vanishing trick; here one minute, gone the next. She dawdled – bought a picture postcard for her mother and a stick of rock for Dolly, looked at municipal crocuses, tried to fathom George.

An open motorcar came tooting along the front. 'Hello, hello!' shouted Johnny from the back, where men and girls were jumbled up together. The car stopped. 'Just room for one inside,' he said, and she climbed in. They dashed along the coast, wind ripping their faces.

Upset by Mamie, a double dose of Globéol lying heavy on his stomach, George wrote his telegram at the post office. 'HAPPY BIRTHDAY ARTHUR FROM FATHER. WHAT DOES IT FEEL LIKE TO BE A BIG BOY OF FOUR? DO NOT EAT TOO MUCH TRIFLE. MAY: EN ROUTE TO DOVER.'

He supposed he would have to visit Penarth soon, in order to give the child a present. In February he had been there exactly twice. His absences were taken for granted, the house ran smoothly, May had her Vigilants and her child. She was an exemplary mother, teaching it its alphabet, dressing it in sailor suits and little overcoats. The whirling spray was still on top of the wardrobe, but he had thought of a way of dealing with the moment when May's marble hand reached out for his. He'd cleared his throat and said, 'I can live without that, dear.' On the first occasion she said, 'Are you sure?', but afterwards it became a convention. He would lie in the dark, oppressed by desire for Mamie, feeling the carnal heat inside his pyjamas. 'I can live without that, dear.'

Brighton was as busy as in peacetime – busier, probably, since there were big infantry camps not far away. The officer in the lounge still rankled. Mamie had gone from the front, and George strolled down the pier, presuming that she had done the same. He wasn't a walker by inclination – Dr Eggins said it helped with the neurasthenia – but Mamie liked to stretch her legs. It went back to her childhood, she said once. She thought she had only to walk down the road to find meadows with buttercups and a nice clean cow or two. 'Sweet girl,' he had said, 'I wish I'd known you then.'

'I was hopeless,' she'd replied. 'Mental, Edith used to say.'

Outside their cottage in Mainsforth Terrace one day with Edith, a milkman in a hurry drove his cart down the unpaved street and splashed their frocks with mud. 'To think,' said Edith, 'that milk comes all the way from the country to this nasty place.' That summer Mamie stole some bread and an apple, went out to play after breakfast, and set off along the Chester Road. She must have been about nine. A carrier gave her a lift and left her at a crossroads, miles outside the town. Was this the country? All she could see were fields of cabbages and a few hovels that were worse than Mainsforth Terrace. Eventually she came to a derelict farm, more hovels and a public house. Miners with black faces were lounging on the grass with pots of beer; the pit-wheel and spoil-heap stuck up above the hedges, two fields away. The only animal in sight was a three-legged goat on a chain. A colliery official found her weeping; her mother nearly killed her when a policeman brought her home, just as it was getting dark.

Had she told him the story so he would say, 'Sweet girl' again?

There was no Mamie at the end of the pier, nor in the fortune-tellers' booths, nor along the front, nor back at the hotel. He went to the Lanes and bought the ankle chain. In the afternoon he visited the almost-empty Picturedrome and saw *The Advance of the Tanks* for the second time. A naval rating and a girl were canoodling in the row behind; their kisses drove him out before the picture ended, desperate to see if she was back.

The bedroom was as they left it, except that the bed had been made, and Mamie's littered clothes scooped up by the chambermaid and piled on a chair. Her jars and bottles filled the dressing table. The mirror had a dusting of face powder. George sat on the bed and pressed a handful of underclothes to his face. He couldn't get too much of her physical presence; the coarse-stranded hair that was always coming loose from grips; the grey-green eyes, never still; the short, strong, fleshy body that she dabbed with scents he was expected to have opinions on – Chaminade, Serenade, June Roses, Violette, all of them now mysteriously present in her clothes, together with a hint of Mamie herself that steaming baths could never quite eradicate.

George was eating supper in the hotel dining room when she returned. An elderly waiter intercepted her before she reached the table, so that the first words he heard were, 'The boiled fish, please, I'm ravenous.'

She banged her handbag on a vacant chair; her hair under the scarlet beret had a whiff of cigars. He could be angry again. 'Well?' he said.

'Well what?'

'You have been away all day.'

'Is that a crime?'

'Sh-h-h!' said George. The hotel piano was tinkling away,

but Mamie's voice rose above it. 'Have you gone mad?' he said. 'You are here with me. I happen to be paying.'

'So naturally that gives you the right to treat me like dirt. Do you want to know what I did? Went off with a crowd to Eastbourne. Had a puncture on the way – great hilarity – went to a tea dance, went to a rifle range, and got dropped off here five minutes ago with my reputation intact.'

'Are you making this up?'

'What's the matter, do you think I sat on a seat in the park and cried? Not on your life, baby.'

Most of the dining room was trying to listen. The fish followed by treacle pudding put an end to conversation. Not until they were in the bedroom was he able to get more sense out of her; and by then he had the spectacle of a woman getting ready for bed to deal with.

'I thought I meant something to you.'

'So you do, George.' She scrutinised her face in the mirror, rubbing cream in with slow circular movements. 'Would I be here otherwise?'

'Who were these men?'

'Captain this, Lieutenant that.' Fastenings parted; buttons undid. 'And such nice girls, a Patti and a Harriet. And a May, a dark thin creature. Like Mrs Shotton was, what a coincidence. Safety in numbers, see?'

Bare arms and legs stuck out of a core of underlinen.

'All this fuss about nothing,' he said.

'I'm yours, am I? To have and to hold and do what you like with from this day forward. Till you've had enough of me, that is.'

'What is it you want?'

'I could love you so much if we lived together properly.'

She put on a nightdress, removed her knickers under its cover, and lay in bed staring at the ceiling. George undressed and lay beside her. Their hands touched. 'Sorry,' she said, 'but there it is. Will you just cuddle me? Dare say I'll fancy it again tomorrow.'

'Oh,' he said savagely, 'I can live without that.'

He was on a train, writing to Everard, and had got as far as 'Wednesday, 20 March 1918' when they entered the Severn Tunnel. A whiff of sulphur from the smoke got into the coach, bringing back a memory of the time that Everard, aged six, had whooping cough, and their mother took him through the Darlington Tunnel with the window open, instructing him to take deep breaths so that the smoke would get into his lungs and kill the germs. She swore it saved his life.

'I am returning from seeing my son' was as good a way as any to begin. George weighed the words, tapping a pencil against his teeth, as tunnel became cutting became countryside. 'He has had his birthday and is four. I bought him a castle with lead soldiers. He refers to me as "Daddy Bye-bye", if May is to be believed, in reference to my flying visits. Well, one only has one life. I would never dream of deserting May but I no longer feel I am married to her. Our physical relationship is at an end. We shall rub along, as one does. But I am still a comparatively young man, and I am utterly lost in affection for the "endearing little monkey" of whom you have heard so much (yet so little!). Marrying her would be a consummation of our happiness. And matters have now reached a stage where I fear that *otherwise I shall lose her*. Here is irresistible need encountering immovable object. I wish you were in England so that we could sit by a fireside and talk. My dearest boy, what times we shall have *après la guerre*!'

A voice said, 'Beg pardon, sir. May I punch your ticket?'

George, eyes fixed on the landscape, hadn't heard the guard approach. He held out the ticket and glanced down at his letter. The page was blank except for the date, and a heart inscribed 'George' and 'Mamie'.

He was returning to an empty flat. Mamie had gone to see Kitty in South Shields; when he left on Monday he was alarmed to see her packing enough clothes for a summer holiday. True, she had never heard of 'travelling light'. But everything she did alarmed him now. 'Come up yourself if you can spare the time; you'd like Kitty' was hardly a pressing invitation. So he felt a wave of relief when he heard 'Any Little Things' on the gramophone as he went down the basement steps.

'Mamie darling!' he called from the passage.

A woman said, 'Sorry, wrong number.'

It was Nancy, lounging by the fire in her khaki uniform as if she owned the place. 'I gave Mamie four quid for advance rent,' she said. 'Naughty girl, not telling you.'

He stopped the gramophone and put the record back in its sleeve. 'She and I live here now. Things have changed.'

'Will she be in soon?'

'Why do you ask?'

'She thought of joining me in the Waacs. She didn't say? Naughty girl again. I've got some killingly funny stories about the camp to tell her. They're terrified of anyone laying a finger on us. So there's enough barbed wire for the Somme, and redcaps on the go all night. But the troops will do anything to get in. One chap impersonated a colonel.'

'Killing,' said George.

'Where did you say Mamie was?'

'I didn't.'

'Left you, has she?' Nancy crushed a cigarette in a saucer. 'I've warned her about you.'

'Give me the key and hop it.'

She dangled it in front of his face. 'Four pounds. Come on, Charlie Chaplin, you can afford it.'

'I shall have the lock changed by nine in the morning. Now get out before I kick you out.'

'Still got your gun, have you? I heard about you and Albert.'

'Then you know I'll stop at nothing.' He picked up the poker and stared at her.

'You've got another woman somewhere,' she said, retreating down the passage. He followed her with the poker, telling her softly that she was committing slander, that she would hear from his solicitors. The door slammed behind her.

On Thursday he set out for the north-east, preceded by telegrams. The 10 a.m. luncheon express should have got him to Shields by half-past four in the afternoon, but there were mysterious delays. They stopped in north London among chimney-pots and lines of washing; lost more time at Doncaster; were nowhere near York when lunch was served. 'Troop movements,' said the chief steward through the corner of his mouth; later, held on a branch at a signal box, George saw a trainload of blurred faces and khaki going south.

It was dark when he reached South Shields. His room was ready at the Golden Lion, but there was no Mamie – she had looked in and gone away again – and Grace had to send a message round.

Heads turned when Mamie came in, picturesque in greys and pinks, waving her fingers at people she knew, sidling up to George.

'Can't stay,' she said. 'It's like a madhouse at Kitty's. We've got Agnes there. Her Donald's been drafted to France. They say there's men going from everywhere.'

He hadn't heard? Millions of German soldiers had broken through the front line. There was a national emergency.

'Millions?' said George.

'According to Agnes. His platoon won't be off till the middle of the week, so they mean to get married first, if he can get a special licence for Scarborough on Monday. We're all trimming hats and things.'

George went out of his way to be considerate, telling her she was not to worry about being late; he would be awake whatever time she returned to the Golden Lion.

'Oh, Georgie!' she said. Surely he could see that Agnes needed her friends?

Mamie made a front parlour with three women altering clothes sound romantic; auburn Agnes became a widow already grieving for the husband she hadn't yet married, lying dead on a battlefield. 'I can't possibly run back here to sleep, now, can I?'

It was a good performance; she should have been an actress. 'I think I was a fool to come,' said George.

'I'll make it up to you, I promise.' She paused and prodded him lightly in the chest. 'If I get the chance.'

He knew exactly what she meant. One way and another, these were hard times. In his bedroom, the stale-beer smell from downstairs rising through the floorboards, he lay awake and thought of a merciless enemy overrunning Everard and his trench of men. Someone had to lose the war; was it going to be England?

The War: 4th year: 231st day. *The Times* was not encouraging. Half a million Germans had broken through. The British Army, George read at breakfast, was 'battling today for the safety and liberty of these islands and of Western civilisation.'

Is that how his little monkey would end up, carried off by a man in a grey uniform? Unlikely, no doubt. But another lover would do it just as well. Someone would come along. Nobody waited for ever.

Kitty's riveter left for work at seven. Mamie could have done with another two hours at least, but the twins came to look at her and Agnes, and climbed all over the bed. A poor family with children – Kitty had a new baby at her breast – ran to uncomfortable rhythms of its own. The bits that Mamie liked, three girls larking about with hats and camisoles, were intermittent.

Hopes of George were fading; had faded already. She had pushed too hard. Evidently he didn't want to marry her and that was that. Either she reverted to the former state of affairs, which had a lot to be said for it, or she had one last gamble, kissed and said goodbye, meaning it but leaving the door open for an eleventh-hour conversion.

It was after eleven. He wouldn't come now; probably there had been a fiancée after all. She was in the parlour with Agnes, savaging a hat she wouldn't have been seen dead in herself, when he appeared in the street in a light grey suit. Kitty was with a screaming child in the backyard so Mamie went to the door.

He stood looking at her. 'I have been thinking,' he said. 'How would it be if I went and got a special licence for Monday?'

It was an odd way of proposing. But then George was an odd man.

8

The bride wore an outfit purchased at Binns of Sunderland on Saturday, a wool costume in white and navy blue. George bought her an engagement ring, a split circle with diamonds, as well as a thick gold band. He was waiting on the town hall steps when she arrived in her taxi, looking nervous. They had spent the night in separate rooms at the Golden Lion, Mamie having said it was 'only right', a nicety that pleased him.

All George insisted on was a quiet ceremony. Agnes, in any case, was being married seventy miles away, and Kitty couldn't get away from the house. He had ruled out her family, who would be told afterwards, not before, and Mamie was as obedient about this as she had been about everything since the moment she knew she had caught him. His own family wasn't mentioned; Mamie guessed there was some estrangement.

'I understand you are unaccompanied,' said the registrar, adding that witnesses were obligatory, so two of the staff would stand in.

Only once had George's confidence faltered. That was on Friday, when he'd visited the registrar alone while Mamie went off to look in jewellers' windows, and the man said, 'It is my duty to inform you that under the Marriage Act it is an offence to cause a false entry to be made in the Marriage Register. Before I issue a licence, you are required to answer the following question truthfully. Have you ever entered into a form of marriage, whether in Great Britain or elsewhere in the world?'

'Not that I recall,' said George. He meant the words as a pleasantry, but the registrar frowned.

'You must answer yes or no, Mr Shotton.'

Light from a dirty window was spread about the room, grey and even. George felt a coldness down his back. It was only nerves.

'No,' he said. 'I have not.'

The windows in the marriage room were no cleaner. The town hall clock struck the quarter-hour, and the ceremony that began shortly after eleven drew to a close. George Shotton, thirty-seven years, of the Golden Lion Hotel, South Shields, had married Mamie Stuart, twenty-four years, of 43 Elgin Crescent, Notting Hill, London. It was all there in black and white. George signed the register and gave his fountain pen to his wife for her to do the same. Louie Robson and W. Alan Coats agreed they had witnessed the event.

When they were back at the Golden Lion, George slipped out again to send a telegram to Penarth. 'DISREGARD ALARMIST REPORTS. ENGLAND WILL PULL THROUGH,' he wrote. 'TYNE AND WEAR AT PRESENT. UNCERTAIN THEREAFTER.'

9

In a perfect world, George would have sent the Stuarts a picture postcard to say he was delighted to have married their daughter, and when conditions permitted (meaning after the war) he hoped to visit them in more auspicious circumstances than hitherto. But he had to think of Mamie, who stroked his stomach or his chest – or other bits of him, as convenient – whenever the future came up as a subject during the hours they spent lolling in their honeymoon bed at Droitwich Spa, and who said things like, 'Please, Georgie, please. Pa will be so happy,' or, 'Gosh, I want to see Edith's face, even if you don't.'

Preceded by a telegram, they arrived in Sunderland when they had been married a week. Everyone George had already met was at Hawarden Crescent. So were other relatives curious to see (he guessed) what kind of fellow had swept Mamie off her feet.

As they tucked in to boiled ham and beetroot, Edith kept repeating how glad she was; smiling thinly, not quite at ease. The child Dolly was smacked for some sin involving cake and sent howling into the scullery. After the meal, when washing-up got under way, the women disappeared for a while, evidently for the bride to produce the wedding lines from her handbag. (Mamie told him in bed that night that Edith held the document up to the gaslight to see the watermark and make sure it wasn't a forgery.)

'Women, women,' said Captain Stuart, as the last dishes

were carried out. 'My wife was wondering why you went to Droitwich, George, but doesn't like to ask.'

'The Brine Baths Hotel is one of the finest in England. The baths themselves are a cleansing experience. A prophylactic against the influenza, they say.'

'My second engineer died of it last week,' said Stuart.

'It's the saline does the trick. They have a pool you can't sink in at Droitwich. Three pounds of salt per gallon of water. You should have seen Mamie lying in it. She looked like a princess. I bought her a bright blue bathing suit.'

'Bright blue!' said Henry Silver, staring into space and knotting his fingers.

Although George's idea was that they spend the night at the Palatine before returning to London, he let Mamie have her own way, and they slept at Hawarden Crescent, in the bedroom she still called hers. Naked, she bent over a portmanteau where she was assembling clothes to take to London, wriggling her behind, daring him to take advantage of her. The silent house with her sleeping parents seemed to egg her on as much as it inhibited George.

'Silly boy!' she whispered. 'This is our special love-place. Mamie used to lie in bed and dream about the bobby dazzler she was going to marry one day, and now that she has we can do *anything* here.'

Marriage had enhanced their lovemaking. George felt entirely in her power; but then, she was entirely in his. How had he ever lived without her?

In London he found them a furnished flat at Bayswater in a red-brick Victorian block, Craven Court, and they moved in at once, hiring a taxi to bring Mamie's things from Elgin Crescent half a mile away. Luke-warm radiators fed from a boiler in the basement raised the temperature a few degrees. Was this central heating? she asked. Told that it was, she changed into a light dressing gown, insisting she was as warm as toast, which plainly she wasn't. How could one not love someone like Mamie? The flat needed redecorating. Patches of plaster had come down in a bombing raid; there were green stains in the bath. But Craven Court took her fancy. On their first night they danced to the gramophone. 'Just us,' said George, glad that unwelcome visitors, the Nancys and Ruperts, were a thing of the past.

Next morning he left her in the bath, barely visible for steam, and went to the City, ready to think about work again. Apart from a few spring flowers in window boxes, the streets were drab and wintry. Newspaper placards were still ominous. He hadn't paid attention to the war for over a week. 'Fifth Army Crippled – Official,' said one. Another announced, 'Drastic New Comb-out.' They were scraping the barrel for men.

Messages were waiting at the Lloyd's Register office in Leadenhall Street. Surveys had been offered at Goole, at Barry, on the Clyde. 'PLEASE ADVISE YOUR LOCATION,' Oscar had wired, followed by 'WHERE ARE YOU?' and 'WHERE ARE YOU? URGENT.' There was even a telephone message, two days old. 'Captain Loader asks that you contact home at once. Mrs Shotton dangerously ill.'

George felt a twinge of resentment at the 'Mrs Shotton', as if the title had been stolen from Mamie. But poor May might be dying, might be dead already; most likely a victim of the influenza epidemic. Fate played strange tricks. Feeling the imminence of tragedy, he found an official with a telephone and waited while the operator called the exchange, the minutes ticking away, the instrument sweating in his hand. But the City in wartime was badly placed for nonpriority calls at 10 a.m. George was told his connection would take until the afternoon, so he sent a telegram to Channel Buildings, 'ON WAY', with another to Craven Court, 'URGENT BUSINESS IN WEST. BACK SOON', and caught the next train from Paddington.

The battlefront map in his newspaper showed that the section of front line where he understood Everard to be, north of Ypres and west of Passchendaele, had not been overrun. He watched the familiar countryside go by, toying with sentences for a letter. 'I have some desperately sad news about my wife,' he scribbled on the back of a bank statement. Then: 'Every cloud, I suppose, has a silver lining. I could say that to no one but you. Am I a bad egg? No, I am an ordinary fellow being candid with the one person who will understand and not condemn him as callous. The human heart – what a mystery, eh?'

Memories of May in the old days flooded back. He used to tease her about her shyness; she never minded. On the train, when they were leaving for their honeymoon, he couldn't think why she kept picking at her clothes and the luggage, until she said how awful it would be if the hotel found confetti and discovered their secret.

By the time he arrived at Westbourne Road, George was calm and grave – ready for anything, he would have said, until Elizabeth Fogg, of all people, confronted him in the hall and gave him the news.

'A what?' he said.

'A miscarriage, with complications. But she is much better. When Dadda telephoned to London, we were all fearing the worst. Today she's as right as ninepence. A very brave girl, your wife is, George. She deserves a spot of cherishing.'

'I thought it was the flu,' he said angrily, and went upstairs two at a time.

The nurse was told to make herself scarce. When he kissed May, who was pale but surprisingly fresh-looking, she pushed herself higher on the pillows and said, 'What a nuisance I am, aren't I?'

'I think we can say it was an unfortunate accident.' He sat on the edge of the bed, not too close. 'It's been a great shock to me, you know.'

'It was to me, dear. I had no idea of my condition.'

'I assumed that women did.'

'You mustn't blame yourself. As I told Elizabeth, it wasn't your fault.'

George was doing his best to make allowances for a woman who might have died. 'I'm surprised,' he said, 'that you find it necessary to discuss me with anyone, let alone Mrs Fogg. I thought you couldn't stand her.'

'She and I are going to be real friends.' May smiled mysteriously. 'I misjudged her. One does, you know. I felt I could depend on her, whatever happened.'

She slid her hand across to be held and he gave it a pat. 'Put your head on the pillow beside me,' she said. 'You've been working too hard, I expect. Rushing around England.'

'I am perfectly all right.' He went to the window and did some deep breathing. 'I didn't know till this morning you were ill. My head's in a whirl. I've been up to my eyes in Admiralty work.'

'Will you go back at once?'

'Not till tomorrow. Try and get some sleep.'

Downstairs the Kooksjoie simmered. Olwen was cleaning spoons; Elizabeth Fogg had gone shopping for delicacies to tempt the invalid's palate, leaving a message to say she would be back in the evening to cook supper. The boy Arthur was brought downstairs by Mavis and said, 'Hello, Daddy Bye-bye. Will you take me to the beach?'

The sun was shining fitfully; he supposed he had a duty. They set off, along salty grey avenues that looked less familiar to George than Craven Court, as if he had changed from being a resident to a visitor. He held the boy's hand and told him about seagulls and daffodils, both much in evidence when they reached the public park on the cliff.

At the top of the steps that led down to the promenade, George stopped to point out the island of Flat Holm. 'Can you see it? That's where a man called Mr Marconi sent the first radio signal across the sea. Before you were born.'

'What happened to the baby in Mummy's tummy?' said Arthur.

'Now look here.' George had never heard of such precocity. 'Who has been telling you nonsense?'

'Dunno.' Arthur waved his arms, making a gull swerve and drift seaward. 'I saw oodles of blood,' he said with satisfaction. 'Olwen boiled things in the boiler. Where did the baby go?'

'There was no baby. Mummy had a sort of cut that bled a lot.'

They threw dark pebbles at the sea and George tried to teach him, without success, the flick of the wrist that made a thin one skip the waves. The permanence of the boy, his stubborn awkwardness as he chased seagulls and got his shoes wet, struck George like a revelation of something obvious he had managed to overlook. Arthur would always be there. He would grow up, start school, ask questions to which the answers were increasingly elusive. Somehow he would have to be incorporated into plans of action. One day he would understand for himself how hard it was to do what seemed right without also doing what seemed wrong. All that lay in the future, out of sight.

'What is that there?' said Arthur, when they were back at the top of the steps. 'There. After the flattie place.'

'English coast.'

'What comes after?'

'England, of course.'

'What comes after?'

'English Channel. The Continent. Men fighting.'

'Wish we could see as far as that.'

'Wish we could,' said George.

Channel Buildings was safe enough from family matters.

George pushed his way through the messengers and brokers milling about on the black-and-white tiles of the foyer and made for his office, only to find decorators at work, doing a septennial refurbishment. The furniture was missing, in particular his desk, the one with the locked drawer.

Hurrying to find the temporary quarters, one floor up, he had a sudden conviction that the lock had been smashed and the contents rifled. Miss Boulton, swaying at her machine, gave him an innocent smile, the kind that came with practice, explaining that the contents of the drawers had been boxed and were in the corner. 'All except the drawer that was locked,' she said. 'Mr James said he expected it was where you kept your marzipan delights.'

Oscar had evidently gone to her head. 'Don't try and flirt with me, there's a good girl,' said George. 'Go and find the desk. Then come back and tell me where it is.'

There were tears; a gathering-up of scarf and coat; but the desk was located, in the basement, with the drawer unrifled. George acquired a safe and transferred the contents. His panic had been absurd, a fact that was well known to neurasthenics but provided no consolation. 'The worst hardly ever happens,' Dr Eggins liked to say, failing to see that 'hardly ever' only drew attention to the fatal outside chance.

The lights would be on in Craven Court. Dusk came in London ten minutes earlier than Cardiff. Elizabeth Fogg was roasting a piece of mutton and making a dessert with pears, as well as doing something with calves' livers for May. The house unnerved him, property of that other Shotton. The invalid, propped up in bed, rummaged in her handbag and produced a cheque signed by her father for a hundred pounds, to pay for nurses and doctors and convalescence. It had acquired the camphoric, asexual smell of all her possessions. George folded it into his wallet and said, 'You shall have your supper on a tray.'

'Everyone is so kind to me.'

Mrs Fogg had sent Olwen and Mavis to the pictures, and George heard her singing to herself in the kitchen. He was by the gas fire in the drawing room, sipping a whisky, when she appeared in her apron and said, 'Does the master of the house have any instructions for Cook?'

'I eat what's put in front of me. Will 7.30 be convenient?'

'The minute your father-in-law gets here.'

'Because I need an early night. I must be away first thing tomorrow to have a word with the surgeon. Then back to London.'

She had remained in the doorway. 'Do you mind if I speak out of turn?'

'Speak away. You are going to be one of the family.'

'May is afraid this house gets on your nerves. She would do anything to make you happy.'

The preposterous words sank in. 'This house? Our home? Which I've lavished money on? Thirty-six-gallon hot-water cylinder? Sundry appliances? Electric lighting? Tip-top roof? Roses in profusion?'

'It is merely a feeling she has. That you never feel at home.'

'I don't know which I resent more, my wife having such a silly thought or her telling you about it. Do I seem not to belong here? Is that what's being alleged?' Flustered, he stood up, letting the *Cardiff Echo* slide off his knee. Gas flames sucked at a page, which caught fire. He kicked it clear and stamped on it. The woman remained in the doorway.

'I am very fond of my home, as it happens. Where else would I be at ease with the world? In digs in Hackney? Commercial hotels? Sleeping compartments on railway trains? Please give me credit for some common sense.'

'You have made your point,' said Mrs Fogg, and retreated to the kitchen.

He had overdone things. During supper he admitted that now and then, returning from a long absence, he took a while to adjust. But the rest was May's imagination.

He spent the night in the box-room, shape of things to come. In a strange way, finding a new wife made it easier to feel kindly towards the old one. He hadn't wished May dead. He merely recognised that death was a well-known means of solving the unsolvable. Death must have saved a million marriages. 'Take good care of yourself, dear,' he said as he left.

To round off the visit he sat across the desk from the eminent Barrow-Morgan, FRCS, and asked for an appraisal, man to man, of Mrs Shotton's health.

'The constitution is delicate, as you are aware. We must get the blood back. A strict regime is called for. Her diet will be liver, liver, liver till she hates the sight of it.'

'Tell me frankly,' said George. 'She could have died?'

'Not in capable hands. Having said that, the sudden emergency is never without hazard.' He was a younger man than George had been expecting, clean-shaven; the capable hands were creamy white. He opened a folder and closed it again. 'One needs to take care. You would agree with me there?'

'Whatever money can buy. I am away a great deal on work of national importance, so the whole thing came as a blow.'

'Quite. By the way, I would strongly advise against resuming conjugal relations for three months. Some men find this harder than others.'

'I shall make a note of the date,' said George grimly.

'And consider a French letter, eh, Mr Shotton? I find it better to speak plainly about these things. The method is wisely used. A further pregnancy in the foreseeable future would not be helpful.'

'Oh, you must tell me more. Fer-rench let-ter. How kind of you to give me the benefit of your vast expertise.'

'Please don't be offended.' A white palm was raised. 'It is merely that the whirling spray is famous for its unreliability. As the present case confirms.'

'A man does his best for his wife. He succumbs to . . .' the words almost failed George but he whipped them into line, '. . . a moment of passion, having been assured by her that precautions are in place. He then finds himself being lectured by a doctor as though he were a schoolboy. Offended is hardly the word. Outraged I would say. Kindly let me have your account to date. I shall go elsewhere next time, if there is a next time.'

Perhaps this, too, had been an immoderate response. Penarth had caught him unawares; he was a traveller needing time to adjust.

The transition back to Craven Court, on the other hand, was painless. Voices and a smell of Turkish cigarettes greeted him as he opened the front door, early in the afternoon. His wife had Norah with her, a breath of the old life he supposed he had to put up with.

'What dark horses you are, you two,' she said, watching them kiss.

'Why don't I take you both out to tea at the Ritz? I have an unexpected cheque in my pocket.'

Norah said she knew when to make herself scarce. As the lift gates clashed, Mamie was already in the bedroom. Squares of sunlight lay on the carpet. An Elinor Glyn novel was on the arm of a chair, with a leaflet advertising hats as a bookmark. Her tooth-box was on a windowsill, golden tooth inside in its cotton wool. It caught the sun, like a jewel.

10

We are blissfully happy, Mamie said in her letters home. She had to be happy. It would have been intolerable to marry a chap with money, who gave her a silver handbag engraved 'MS' when they had been married three months plus a dressing-table set in tortoiseshell and more silver costing nineteen pounds at Mappin & Webb, and find fault with him because he was away from home a lot. To her girl friends she wrote about clothes and theatre trips and aspects of George, such as his decision to shave off his moustache ('It was those Charlie Chaplin jokes that did it'), and if she mentioned the business trips, it was only to say that his absences made her feel free.

They were letters of hope and expectation. It was true that their address was now 12 Runcie Road, Bristol, and not Craven Court, W11, but things would soon improve. They were agreeable furnished rooms, as rooms went. A vulgar card to Agnes was on the table waiting to be posted, a plump lady at the seaside with a man leering at her bathing costume and saying, 'This is the place to tickle your fancy!' Mamie had written, 'Gorgeous weather down here. What's it like up there? George is talking about buying a little car. Honk-honk!'

She intended walking to the postbox when it got cooler, but at seven o'clock it was still as hot as ever. Tinned sardines and a loaf were ready in the kitchen for the meal she couldn't be bothered to make. For the umpteenth time she read the irritating label:

Equal to bacon, streaky or lean,
The excellent succulent 'Flapper Sardine',
Equal to butter – equal to beef:
The housekeeper's constant joy and relief.

Through open windows came the sound of a brass band, far off, playing in the stand on the edge of the Clifton Downs. It was six weeks since they moved to Runcie Road, without warning, in typical George-like fashion. He came back to Craven Court from a trip and said, 'I'm taking a few days off. Can you start packing your things?'

'I love surprise holidays.'

'It's Bristol. We're going to live there, you see, out at Clifton. Don't look so upset. I need somewhere convenient for the west coast ports, so I can see more of you. I was there yesterday and found these very pleasant rooms. A Mrs Rogers, widow. The carrier's coming at eight in the morning and we go down in the afternoon. And here –' he pulled something from his pocket – 'is a pair of –' waving them about – 'high-class tailor-made drawers, sold to me in Bristol by a girl who blushed when I asked her if she thought they'd make an appropriate present for wifey. You'll like living there.'

The sardine tin had lost its key. Mamie went downstairs to see if Mrs Rogers had a spare one, and found her with a visitor, a thin straw-haired woman, slightly younger than Mamie. 'This is my Maggie,' said the landlady. 'Her Jack went back to France last night so she's in the dumps.'

A key was found but Mamie couldn't escape. Was hubbie in the forces? asked Maggie. 'Mr Shotton is a reserved occupation,' said her mother smartly, as if it conferred distinction on the house. 'An exceedingly nice gentleman, I may say.'

'When he's here,' said Mamie, and thought it polite to ask what Jack did.

Jack was a sergeant in a rifleman's company, in civilian life a greengrocer. Now one of his sisters ran the shop, and it was she who was looking after the kiddies while Maggie came up to see Mum, who suffered with her legs. Swollen white limbs, networked with blue, rested on a footstool. 'Must be off,' said Mamie. 'Have to catch the post before supper.'

Maggie said she would go with her for company. 'I'll show her the Observatory and then go home. Haven't seen Clifton Observatory? Oh, you must.'

Breaths of wind were cooling the street. Maggie's thick green dress was wet in the armpits and there was a hint of sweat even in the open. They walked in silence until Maggie said, 'You don't have kids, then?'

'Not been married long. Tell you the truth, I don't think either of us is keen.'

'I've got two at present and I shouldn't be surprised if there's a number three, now that Jack's been home. Mum said to me when I got wed, make the most of the first six months because it won't ever be like that again.'

They were at the pillar box. 'Someone as pretty as you are doesn't have to worry,' said Mamie. She flipped the postcard at the slot and missed.

'That's flannel, Mrs Shotton, if you'll pardon the expression.' Maggie stooped and picked the card off the pavement, saying, 'Thanks all the same,' lost her balance, leaned heavily against the box, said, 'Oh hell.'

The paint was wet. One sleeve was smeared with red. A boy giggled and ran off, and they saw the 'Wet Paint' sign in the gutter.

'It may come off with petrol.'

'Better mine than yours' – which was silk in a creamy brown.

'I'll go back, if you don't mind,' said Mamie, but the girl's disappointment made her relent.

The Downs were straight ahead. Desultory cricket was

being played by young men, one of whom, on the boundary, whistled after them. Couples strolled in the lovely evening; a flock of birds streamed overhead like smoke. Sipping lemonade at a stall, Maggie said a man had tried to take her out not long ago, an engineer on the railway. 'I was tempted,' she said. 'He had those deep brown eyes and lovely hands, not a working man's hands at all.' She sipped and dreamed. 'I never told a soul.'

'I knew a man like that when I was on the stage.'

'You weren't an actress!'

'Dancer, mainly. I was with the Verona Girls, you may have heard of them, and he ran a theatre in Leeds. He had fingers like a girl's. Married, I need hardly say. I was only nineteen. Didn't know any better.'

They reached a stone tower, admission twopence. 'My treat,' said Maggie. A winding staircase led to a darkened room within a room at the top. A soldier with his arm around a girl was cranking a handle, and a magnified picture of the Downs, seen through mirrors and lenses, revolved slowly on a circular table. Grass and bushes slid across the concave surface. A horseman cantered down a track in reddening sunlight; a young man in a trilby stood on a mound, as if looking for someone. The picture went on turning and the suspension bridge appeared; a motorcar and a wagonette carrying children could be seen, and below, on the Avon at the bottom of the gorge, a string of barges, already in dusk.

The couple left and Maggie turned the picture back to the Downs. The man was still on the mound. 'That's him,' she whispered.

The penny dropped. 'Go on, then, if you're going,' said Mamie.

'Should I?'

A handbell rang and the ticket-man shouted up the stairs. Watching the girl hurry across the grass, Mamie thought of the thousands of wives in England who must be up to the same tricks. The women-police even thought it worth going round to soldiers' houses where the wife was suspected of having a fancy man (according to Nancy, who knew one of them), so as to have her army pay allowance stopped if wickedness came to light. Think of all those women-who-ought-to-be-ashamed, not setting out to be immoral but finding it happen to them because when it did, it seemed a natural event. Mamie knew the feeling. These days, however, natural events like that were not on her menu. If the thought of little Maggie being drawn down to her engineer in a hollow of the Downs made her envious, it was only for a moment and only because the habits of men and women were so enthralling.

It was getting dark by the time she was back in Runcie Road. Doors and windows were open. A child cried, a pianola jangled 'Ta-ra-ra boom-de-ay'.

Going upstairs, she saw gaslight in the bedroom, and jumped with fright to find George stretched out on the coverlet, collar and jacket off.

'Where might you have been?' he said.

'Grumpy!'

A kiss didn't work. He watched her change into something flowery and start folding the creamy dress into tissue paper. 'You knew I was coming.'

'You said one day this week. I'm not psychic.'

'I've been here over an hour.' He fussed about the bedroom and stood in the doorway in his socks. 'The larder contains a single tin of sardines. One might as well be in Elgin Crescent.'

'Sometimes I wish I was. Excuse me, I want to pass.'

A bad-tempered George wagged his finger. Why had she changed her clothes? He didn't want her going out again. She pushed past him and went downstairs. Mrs Rogers was in the hall, leaning on a stick.

'Nice walk, dear?'

'Will you give this to Maggie when she's here next? The bust needs taking in.'

'Oh, it's lovely. But you shouldn't.'

'Can't stop. Mr Shotton wants to lock me up for the night.'

'My wife has a wonderful sense of humour,' said George from the top of the stairs.

'If I move my leg you can hear the chain rattle.'

She ran back to her husband. They were only having a tiff; it was a hot night; he had been travelling for hours.

'So tell me what the point is of giving away an expensive dress,' he grumbled.

'Her daughter ruined the one she had on when we were out walking.' In a whisper, in case her voice carried through the floorboards, she told him about Maggie's soldier husband and the assignation on the Downs, curious to see how he would respond. He thought it threw an unfortunate light on a nation at war.

'Poppycock!' she shrieked.

'If it was me, and you were misbehaving, I'd bring my rifle back from France, and bang!, that would be that.'

'What if you were the man on the Downs?'

'I wouldn't be. I know better than to go after married women. Why go looking for trouble? Much better to have a wife who never says no.'

'What a cheek,' she murmured, and knew that the bickering was over.

This time he stayed almost a week, working at Bristol docks. Furnished rooms in a suburb on a hill were different when he was with her every night. She tried to make him see what it was like, living in the middle of nowhere. They would find something better, he promised; gave her a few pounds for clothes and a few more for food; attempted intercourse with her in the bath on the morning he left and nearly caused a flood; went off to South Wales in a loving mood, assuring her he would be back in time for the August Bank Holiday.

In Bristol next day she called at the Food Control office for a lark, to see if they would give her a job. A manager with missing fingers and a medal ribbon in his lapel asked her to read a paragraph from a newspaper and spell 'receipt', then offered her a temporary post on the spot, collating ration cards and checking discrepancies, start 9 a.m. tomorrow, because the army was still bleeding Britain dry, and good clerks were worth their weight in gold.

It was just something to do. She eyed his damaged hand, he eyed her rouged lips and jaunty hat, and the encounter ended up as neither one thing nor the other, neither a patriotic act nor a proper flirtation. She liked him; the trouble was that she liked most men as a matter of course. When he looked at his watch and suggested they pop round the corner to the National Restaurant, which offered a sensible bacon hotpot for tenpence, by way of acquainting her with what the job was about, she could have wept for men. Next day she stayed in bed reading an old Marie Corelli and never went near the place. Georgie would soon be home.

A telegram came instead. 'REGRET RETURN DELAYED TILL AFTER HOLIDAY BY CIRCUMSTANCES BEYOND CONTROL. CONSULT LOCAL NEWSPAPER FOR DETAILS OF EVENTS IN PARKS. DEVOTEDLY GEORGE.' Out of affection for his funny message she went as far as glancing at Mrs Rogers' copy of the *Bristol Post*, and found a couple of fêtes and a Pageant of Empire, before the sound of the pianola down the road brought her back to the empty days ahead. As a precaution more than anything, she counted the coins in her purse, pawned her silver wristwatch and borrowed a pound from Mrs Rogers. Having the cash to travel became the excuse for actually doing it. Half a day later she was in

London, at Norah's house, only to be told by a housemaid that the family were in the country.

Instinctively she thought about men, not wickedly but as a practical means of getting on with a holiday weekend. She supposed men were out of the question, even Albert; especially Albert. What she came to London for was nonstop gossip with Norah, drinking iced tea, hearing about Edgar (lately reappeared on the scene), trying on hats, deliciously poised between the old life and the new. Instead of which she was stranded on a pavement with luggage.

Nancy, she thought.

The London she used to know was just under the surface. A passing taxi took her east along streets with memories. A theatre now in use by the army was where she'd met a tenor in a musical comedy who'd taken a fancy to her. A pet shop reduced by lack of imports to rabbits and a jackdaw, by the look of it, was where a warrant officer bought her a parakeet that said, 'Hello, Lord Kitchener!' and died a week later. Baker Street station was where Albert was briefly arrested for indecent behaviour in a public place.

Even Tussaud's, where she tried tempting George in a fit of devilment, belonged to another existence. Today's boy soldiers had drained-white faces; their sweethearts clung tighter. But the same Rupert was there on duty and knew where Nancy could be found. 'Dover,' he grunted, and gave her the telegraphic address at Dover Castle where she worked shifts on the switchboard. 'Will you go to see her?'

'Might do. Any message?'

'Did she get the pineapple I sent her? Somebody brought a box of them back in a hospital ship. They auctioned it for charity and I bought it.' His wing collar looked as if it was going to cut his throat. 'You think I'm an idiot, don't you?'

'I don't think Nancy's your type.'

'How the d-devil do you know what my type is?'

'You're quite right. I'll tell her to buck up and write you a letter.'

They met on Bank Holiday Monday. Two nights at boarding houses, the first near Victoria station, the second in Dover, had eaten into Mamie's funds. 'I came down for a lark,' she said, when they were strolling by the coils of wire and red warning signs below the cliffs. Nancy, firm-figured inside her uniform, saluting officers left and right, said it was like old times. The Lord Warden Hotel had a tea dance at four and all the girls would be there. Furthermore a light cruiser in the basin was having civic dignitaries on board for a buffet lunch, and Nancy understood that Waacs were welcome to liven up the place.

The reception was jolly enough. Officers made a fuss of Mamie, everyone packed together under canvas screens in the stern, and the commander wanted to know how long she planned to stay in the town. 'Not long enough, Captain, *je regrette*,' she said sweetly. Thundery squalls ran across the harbour, and she was surprised to learn that the war had changed course. The last time she noticed, the Allies were losing. Now, apparently, it was the Central Powers who were finished, and it would all be over by Christmas. But wasn't that what they said every year?

Larks at the Lord Warden were much the same, except that the officers wore khaki instead of blue, and Nancy, who had a first lieutenant she called Pudding in tow, was determined to pair Mamie off with Eric, a major, who breathed over her and brushed her bottom with his fingers.

'He's besotted with you,' said Nancy in the ladies.

'He isn't my type. I told Roopy you weren't his type and he was furious. Did you ever get the pineapple?'

'Swapped it for twenty Player's.'

'I don't think you like men all that much. I saw you kick Pudding's ankle. Reminded me of Roopy.'

'You and I could live together after the war, Mamie. What a time we'd have! Wear trouser suits and go to nightclubs.'

'I'm married, do you remember? He's called George. I know you don't like him but he suits me. He's very generous.'

'Well, don't say I didn't warn you.'

Having singled out George's generosity, Mamie could imagine the cutting remarks from Nancy if asked for a loan. So she had to let Eric the major buy her dinner, and borrowed a couple of sovereigns so she could 'pop up to town tomorrow'. Eric was allowed to escort her back to the boarding house and kiss her in the shadow of a hedge. 'Don't spoil it this time,' she whispered when he tried to put his hand up her skirt, implying there would be a next time. Another fool of a man. She left Dover unscathed next day, after giving George one in the eye with a telegram, 'HAVING LOVELY TIME BY SEASIDE. WISH YOU WERE HERE. REPLY C/O PADDINGTON TELEGRAPH OFFICE.' It would remind him what sort of wife she was, the unknown quantity.

The Paddington office had nothing addressed to Mrs Shotton. Restless, she hung about the station for hours, determined not to return to Bristol until George did. Finally she lost patience and went home to Sunderland.

Everything was the same; her bedroom at her parents' cottage smelled of polish and mothballs; George, they assumed, would be joining her shortly. Edith took a harsher view. The price of a soak in the brick bathroom at Robert Street was a lecture on a wife's duty to live where her husband lived and to adapt her domestic schedule to fit the needs of the breadwinner.

'Where would Henry be if he came in tired after a day's work and found I had gone to the pictures? You don't marry a man and then send him a telegram saying you've gone off somewhere.'

'He knows where I am. I did him a nice little telegram this

morning. He loves telegrams, does George. I said, "GOSH I'M HERE."'

'Try and act like a married woman, Amy. Life isn't doing as we please. I may have found fault with George to begin with –'

'That's putting it mildly. You thought he was a really bad man.'

'He has married you and that's enough.'

'He might still be a bad man. I'm not saying he is. He's rather sweet as a rule. But being married to somebody doesn't automatically make them perfect. Does it?'

Edith had no time for what she called 'clever arguments', and was delighted when a stern telegram arrived, warning that George was on his way. 'I wouldn't like to be in your shoes,' she said.

'Bet you he forgives me by supper-time,' said Mamie. She ran her hands down the side of her skirt. 'Or breakfast. Definitely by breakfast.'

11

George had fully intended to be with her for the Bank Holiday at the start of August. Events intervened; when did they not? There was nothing wrong with his plans, as such, which had to accommodate two wives and usually did. One minute he and Mamie were romping in the bath at Mrs Rogers', the next he was at the railway station, vanishing into thin air, enjoying the sensation of keeping one step ahead of his loved ones. Safety lay in schedules; depart Bristol Temple Meads 9.45 a.m., change at Cardiff, change at Whitland, arrive Pembroke dock 3.45 p.m. Admiralty business around Milford Haven took a couple of days, and before returning to his little monkey the schedule allowed him to pop in to Penarth to see his father-in-law and Elizabeth Fogg get married.

Flying visits took care of May and Arthur these days. They rarely lasted more than a night, and he had learned to enjoy them as interludes, as if his passion for Mamie was the routine, and Westbourne Road, where he made polite conversation with May and retired early to the box-room, the idiosyncrasy. He had had the mattress changed for something harder; lying on it brought him closer to Everard and his dugout.

Arriving at the house, he was startled to find the path from pavement to front door covered in newspapers. He moved one with his foot and saw a strip of plum-coloured carpet. Arthur hopped out saying, 'Don't, Daddy, don't!' and put the paper back. 'It's CLEAN. It's for the WEDDING. Daddy, do you like Hercules?'

'I expect so,' said George, not listening. Roses filled the hall; a waitress was laying tables; an elderly man in a short black coat appeared and said, 'Good morning, sir. Is it concerning the cake?'

'I didn't know I had a butler,' said George. He looked in the kitchen, where Olwen was scrubbing a pan and a woman in an apron was whisking mayonnaise. 'Or a cook.'

Upstairs, he called to May, and she came out of her bedroom, closing the door. 'Dressing the bride,' she mouthed. 'She looks lovely.'

'I wasn't told the wedding breakfast was going to be here.'

'Dadda's house is such a gloomy old place. I knew you wouldn't mind.' It wasn't a phrase he connected with May. She always assumed that he minded. 'Now, don't worry,' she said, 'Dadda is paying for everything.'

'As long as the excitement's not too much for you. We have to think about your health.'

'I feel so much better these days.'

'Life goes on pretty well without me, doesn't it? I console myself with that.'

'I wish you were here more often.' She looked up and down the landing and whispered, 'Mr Barrow-Morgan has sent me a letter asking if I would mention his account to you.'

'Impertinent fellows, always after their guineas.'

He just caught, 'I could pay it myself. Dadda has given me a cheque,' the last word only a movement of the lips.

George knew what was going on. Elizabeth had persuaded her husband-to-be to give his daughter some money of her own in case. In case of what? And how much? George would look after it for her, as he always did.

'Leave Barrow-Morgan to me,' he said, and as he spoke, a dog yelped and his son came down the attic stairs with a black hound on a piece of rope, saliva dripping from its jaws.

'Arthur!' said his mother.

'It's all right, Daddy likes Hercules.'

The dog danced about on its rope, jaws crunching. Bits of coal fell out of its mouth.

'It's only while they're on their honeymoon, George. He's a Labrador. They pine in kennels.'

'He eats STICKS, Daddy. And EARTH.'

The creature was smelly. 'He has to go somewhere by tonight,' said George. 'I don't want any tears. Olwen will chain him up in the garden.'

Elizabeth popped her head out of the door. 'I *am* sorry,' she said. 'I thought you wouldn't mind him for a week. On account of you not being here all that often.'

'My concern is hygiene,' said George. The door was pulled shut and he addressed himself to Arthur. 'Do you know how many germs a dog has got on him? Millions.'

'But you said.'

'I didn't know Hercules was a dog.'

'I suppose he could have been one of the guests.' George heard it through the door, and Mrs Fogg laughing in her throat.

He rose above events. He bore no grudge against her. Penarth was the shadow-world that he visited to be alone with his thoughts for a day, where he kept an eye on May and Arthur, then forgot them every time the train pulled out of Cardiff station.

Hercules whined by the rubbish bins. George heard him when they returned from St Augustine's in mid-afternoon, led by Billy and Elizabeth in a carriage and pair, with neighbours out on the pavement, clapping. A cheerful crowd poured into the house, shipowners, sea pilots, relatives. Oscar and Bella James went out to see the dog, which they had promised to look after. 'Has Arthur got a kiss for his Auntie Elizabeth?' said the new Mrs Loader. But Arthur's face was white with grief and hatred.

Although windows were open, the air thickened through the afternoon as food and drink went down. Voices rose, faces sweated. Elizabeth, sitting next to George, was quieter than usual. 'I'm nervous,' she said. 'At my age, fancy! We are going to Somerset. What are your plans for the summer?'

'Plans? Keep going until the autumn, I suppose. Then think about winter. I don't have plans, as such.'

The ladies left them alone for a while. Chatting to men he had known for years, whose common ground was Channel Buildings or the Yacht Club, he was already anticipating the hard mattress, the austere bedroom, the half-written letter to Everard that he would try to finish before he slept: 'I was reading in *The Times* how inventors send hare-brained ideas to the Ministry of Munitions. Put magnets on balloons to pull rifles out of men's hands! Squirt cement over soldiers to petrify them! Fill artillery shells with fleas to spread disease! I found myself thinking about the periscope I made from brass tubes all those years ago. I seem to remember you looking over the wall and seeing the woman next door hanging out the washing. You can't have been more than seven.' Or was his memory playing tricks? Did he merely intend to construct the periscope? Uncertainty had made him break off the letter.

The air was heavy with cigar-smoke. Wives trooped back from upstairs, radiating eau-de-Cologne. Short speeches were made, toasts drunk.

Half a dozen unopened telegrams that the chap in the black coat had forgotten were brought in on a salver, and George was asked if he would read them out. Then it would be over. The hired motorcar that would take the couple to Exmoor was waiting outside with its chauffeur, surrounded by children from the neighbourhood. Only Arthur had ignored it. He was with Hercules, feeding him rubbish from the bins.

George slit the envelopes one at a time. 'Mr and Mrs Harris, Craigcefnparc, send hearty good wishes.' (Applause;

they were known.) 'I am sure that yours will be a long and happy union. Miss Dawson of Oswestry.' ('My aunt aged ninety,' said Elizabeth; prolonged applause.) 'Everard –' He stopped and said, 'I'm sorry, this is about something else. Will you excuse me?'

The valise stencilled 'G. Shotton' was on the spare-room bed, unpacked since he left Pembroke Dock. A hint of perfume suggested that one or more of the women guests had been in there.

'What has happened?' said May, breathless from hurrying after him.

'Missing on August the first. Two days ago. The telegram's from my sister. She wants me to go to Gateshead.'

'Shall I come with you?'

'Better if I go alone. Get it over quickly. If he's been killed I shall go to Belgium after the war and see his grave. Will they have graves, do you suppose? Or just one big grave for them all. Like a plague-pit.'

'Shall we pray together? There is life everlasting, I know there is. I knew it when my mother passed away, when I thought I'd die of grief.'

'No, just a plague-pit,' he said, detaching himself from her hand; from the piety and solicitude. 'I must be off. Don't overexert yourself. Remember you are a semi-invalid.'

'Elizabeth tells me not to think of myself like that.'

'And I am just your husband, aren't I? Well, I can't watch over you all the time. I'll keep in touch.'

'Your telegrams mean a lot to me.' He detected no irony. She had a kind heart. Now she was promising to pray for Everard. One admired a kind heart but did one ever love it?

'Go and say goodbye to your guests,' he said. 'I shall leave through the kitchen.'

Arthur was kneeling beside the dog, trying to teach it to

beg for a bone. It had eaten too much to care and lay with its tongue out, panting.

'You can keep him in the house all week. Tell Mummy I said so. And give him some water or he'll die of thirst.'

'Hercules and I were going to run away,' said the child.

'It wouldn't have worked.'

Holiday trains were crowded, but not in the first class. The horror of thinking Everard might be dead was replaced by the certainty that he was alive. One saw notices in the personal columns every day: 'Lieutenant so-and-so has been missing since 25 April. Can any brother officer give information?' Missing men turned up in hospitals and enemy prison camps; they lost their memories or their names got mixed up.

George's optimism wasn't shared by his parents when he reached Gateshead. The house was practically in mourning, his mother, who suffered from headaches, sedated in a room with the curtains drawn, his father, a quarrelsome draughtsman brought back from retirement to work in a shipyard, determined to 'face facts' and not live in hope. He wouldn't hear of the 'affinity' with Everard that gave George confidence in his brother's survival. 'What affinity?' he said.

Death was presumably more bearable than uncertainty. George would have returned next day to Bristol and Mamie, if Chrissie hadn't begged him to stay. Did he remember bank holidays at Roker beach when they were children? Could they go there on Monday, just the two of them? It would be – she hesitated – in memory of Everard. So Chrissie thought he was dead too. 'Have a bit of faith,' he said. But he agreed to take her.

It was thirty minutes by train to Sunderland, then a tram from Fawcett Street. Thousands of families were already on the sands; queues waited for hot water so they could make tea; gulls screamed over uneaten crusts. They walked on Roker Pier, where Everard had lost sixpence, and took pot shots at the Kaiser in the shooting gallery, where Everard had been allowed to pull the trigger. In the maze, where children still rushed up and down, hammering on the wooden walls, Everard's feat in finding his way in and out, unaccompanied, aged six, was recalled. 'Remember?' said Chrissie, and George nodded. He nodded every time she asked, but the gap between his age and Everard's must have been too great; his mind was a blank. What he did remember but kept quiet about was being at Roker as a child, evidently a child in double figures, trying to squint through a broken plank in a bathing hut at a woman undressing inside, and little Everard running up to ask what he was doing.

'I was practically a man when he was still in short trousers,' said George. They had walked away from the crowds to Seaburn and found a cottage with a cardboard sign hung on the gate saying, 'Limonade. Penny a glass.' It was cooler in the parlour than outside. 'We have kept up a lively correspondence.'

'He may never come back.' She had taken off her hat; the skin beneath the eyes was purple with fatigue. 'You live in a world of your own, don't you?'

'Takes all sorts, you know.' He put his hand over her knuckles on the table; work-reddened, bare of rings. For a second he thought to tell her who the girl was at Newcastle Central, but the words wouldn't come, and the nearest he got to his private life was May's miscarriage. He kept Mamie to himself till the following day, when he was on his way back to Bristol, and he could settle down with writing pad and pencil to tell Everard how three furnished rooms were as good as a palace when you were with the girl you loved.

Mamie's absence when he got there was shocking; her flippant telegram saying, 'GOSH I'M HERE' wounded him with its lack of sympathy for a neurasthenic in love who must naturally assume the worst.

He arrived in Sunderland with a brooch for Dolly and nothing for his wife; her eyes filled with tears that didn't fool George Shotton. Some men would have locked her up for a week with bread and water. The idea of giving her a good slap crossed his mind, and he pinched her arm until she squealed. Never do such a thing again, he said. She had 'only' been to Dover? She had 'only' gone for walks with Nancy and attended a tea dance where they danced together? What would he hear next, that she had 'only' kissed a man or 'only' let him fondle her?

'I'm sorry, Georgie. I was unhappy, not knowing where you were.'

Words were cheap. He went on being stern till they had retired for the night, and she slipped in beside him, naked and smelling of violets. Captain Stuart snored in the distance. 'I didn't mean to be wicked,' she whispered, 'but I was so horribly disappointed you weren't coming.' He folded his arms across his pyjamas and lectured her; told her about a family crisis, featuring the brother she knew of, now reported missing at the battlefront; about the sister-in-law (recently gone from Worcester to live with her parents in Scotland, a prudent resettlement) whom George had rushed to comfort. If not entirely true, it was parallel to the truth. 'My poor Georgie!' she said, and he took off the pyjamas and forgave her.

They never lived in Bristol again. Mamie begged him not to make her go back there, and cut tickets from blue sugar-bags, which she inscribed with promises for George to redeem because he wasn't going to make her, was he? The tickets were numbered 1 to 10. 'No. 1. You may kiss my breasts.' 'No. 2. You may remove my stockings.' The activities were not particularly outlandish, though No. 8 involved a mirror. But it was erotic to present a ticket at random and have Mamie read what it said, tossing her hair and looking angry, as if she was being made to comply. The game was her idea, not his; that was exciting, too.

For several weeks he found ships in the north-east, returning most nights to sleep at Hawarden Crescent. The Stuarts were amiable enough; nervous of their daughter, they were now nervous of him as well. The awkward customer was Edith, two streets away. But Edith, to George's surprise, was on his side.

'Mamie needed somebody like you,' she said. 'Not that she was ever a bad girl. But an older man can work wonders. Especially someone who has been married before, like you.'

They were sitting in her kitchen; Mamie was in the brick bathroom, where the geyser thumped intermittently and made her sister frown.

'I tell her half seriously that what married people have to get used to is not being together all the time,' said George. 'It stands to reason. Mr Silver is off in his van.'

'Two vans now, if you don't mind.'

'Nobody hears you complain. Fact of life, the breadwinner is out and about, the wife stays put. Captain Stuart? Out in the bay, days on end. Your humble servant? Visiting half the graving docks in the kingdom. If the war ends this year as everyone seems to think, I suspect I shall be just as busy. Surplus ships changing hands, all of them needing surveys. Men have things to do. You can't change universal laws.'

Edith nodded. 'I can see you're worried about her.'

'Not in the slightest,' said George, irritated that he had not been cleverer at concealing his thoughts. 'We have been laughing about it.'

'I shall keep an eye on her. But take my advice and don't leave too much ready cash, just enough for tram fares and the pictures. She could open a shop with that wardrobe.'

'Exactly,' said George, and was surprised, when the time came, how meekly Mamie accepted a few coins. He was away for most of September, writing letters from Glasgow and Barrow to 'My darling wifey', then planning to bring her to Liverpool for a week, until a flurry of rail strikes made travelling difficult.

'I know you have been disappointed, my own little darling,' he wrote from Penarth, 'but at last the engine drivers appear to have come to their senses, and the minute I have finished with the *City of Timbuktu* and the *Flying Ostrich* and the *Good Ship Venus* or whatever is in the diary for the next twenty-four hours, I am coming home to the best wife in the world with love and kisses and something I had better not mention. By the way, I found one of your blue tickets in my wallet. Which one do you think it was? You will find out.'

May came into the dining room as he was sealing the envelope, ready for the afternoon collection. 'Poor dear,' she said, 'you don't even stop working when you're at home. You never have time for anything.'

'I took Arthur on board a banana boat yesterday,' he said good-humouredly, putting the envelope in his pocket.

'You're very good with him. I was being selfish. I meant me. I was going to ask – but I mustn't. It's not fair. You're off again tomorrow.'

'Sunderland and thereabouts, so I shall be on home ground. I know a family who keep lodgings there, not far from where I was born.' He wondered how far he could go, letting one life glide towards the other; stopping them just in time. He smiled. 'The husband's a sea captain. I can never get away from them, can I?'

'I'll make sure Olwen has your clean shirts and pyjamas ready in the morning.'

'I could stay another day, I suppose.' He was free to do what he liked. Mamie the little animal, May the good housewife, each had her place. Arthur's voice came from the garden, telling Hercules to stop eating firewood.

'Why do you want me to stay?' asked George.

'Harvest festival at St Augustine's tomorrow evening.'

'All right, if you'd like me to.'

'I'd love it,' and she bent to kiss him, where he sat at the table.

He sent Mamie her letter anyway and followed it with a telegram next day: 'REGRET UNFORESEEN TROUBLE WITH CITY OF TIMBUKTU. LANGUISHING PENARTH DOCK. HOME TOMORROW EVENING.' Dullness and peacefulness did him good in small doses. He gave a Loader steamship that happened to be in port its yearly survey; dictated letters to Miss Boulton; sang 'We plough the fields and scatter' standing between his son and his wife; had Billy and Elizabeth round to supper; finally settled down in his bachelor's bedroom to *A Medical Climatology of England and Wales*, a book recommended by Eggins.

A tap on the door was unexpected. So was May, in her nightie, standing like a ghost and apologising for her failings as a wife, at the same time advancing nervously on the bed.

The two wives glided so close, they could have touched one another. There were times he wondered how he had ever managed with only the one, month after month. Having two seemed perfectly normal. His old stock of French letters was still to hand in a briefcase. If he looked over his shoulder, he would see Mamie in the doorway, watching them with a sceptical eye. Perhaps they were both dangerous women in their way. May wriggled beneath him; it was over.

Travelling north, George thought of his brother sitting on the edge of a hospital bed, head bandaged, trying to remember his name. Did Everard know that Germany and her allies were collapsing? 'Dear boy,' he wrote, 'this is the 70th day of the 5th year of the war, and the last leaves of the calendar are falling inexorably. I have never doubted your survival.' Oscar

James had a relative at the War Office who promised to make inquiries.

The sharpened nerves expected Mamie; her eyes would contain an exact reflection of his longing. Instead he got Mrs Stuart – not even the captain, who was at sea – fidgeting and saying the girl was with Kitty in Shields. Even that wasn't true. At Kitty's George was greeted by mysterious turbulence within, infant voices, fried-fish smells; no Mrs Shotton. 'The bairns have caught a mouse in a shoebox,' the husband explained at the door, smiling crookedly. So he was Mr Shotton, was he? 'Try the tearoom at the Ritz' came from down the passage, where George glimpsed Kitty's breast in the orangey lamplight, suckling a child. It was a lifetime since he proposed to Mamie on the doorstep.

He didn't know what to expect of her; or of himself for that matter. She was eating buns with friends: the auburn Agnes and a sly-faced young woman in a fur coat.

'See, girls!' cried Mamie, 'I said he'd find me. You remember Agnes? This is Charlotte,' and a ripple ran through the fur coat, 'a colleague from my professional days.'

He ordered more coffee – there was nothing much else – and waited for an explanation to emerge. A job at the cinema as an usherette was mentioned. Howls of laughter. Could they see Mamie showing people in with a flashlight? She'd be too busy watching the movie.

'Charlie can talk,' said Mamie. 'She's so short-sighted, she wouldn't know if a seat was empty or not.' Once, dancing to military music, she had marched over the footlights and fallen into the orchestra. More howls. 'Fortunately,' said Charlie, 'I landed on my bum.'

They had been Dancing Veronas. They twittered about the past, glancing around to see if people were listening; Agnes looked bored; George asked after Donald – he was with a battery near the Hindenburg Line, he wrote to her every day there wasn't a battle – and consulted his watch, which said after eight o'clock.

'Is it really?' said Mamie. 'Us girls don't have the time between us.'

'You do now,' said George, and slipped the silver watch on her wrist. He had redeemed it when he was last in Bristol.

'Had to pop it in the summer,' she laughed, turning her wrist in the air. 'I knew the old man would get it back for me.'

'As a matter of fact,' said Agnes, 'I don't think that's very nice.'

'We are a misery, aren't we?'

'Time we went,' said George.

Mamie stroked his sleeve. 'Can we stay in Shields tonight? I told Grace at the Lion and they're half expecting us.'

'No. Your ma will be waiting up.'

'Trains may be a problem, Mr S.,' said Charlotte. 'Unless you came in that motorcar you're always talking about.'

'I don't believe I've ever talked to you about anything.' But it was Mamie he was angry with.

'Please, George,' she said. 'I *do not want* to go to Sunderland tonight.'

'You're going if I have to carry you there.'

Once out of the teashop she went limp and petulant. They had a long wait on the platform. They had caught trains there before; stood under the purring gaslights. Everything was different. 'You think it's amusing,' he said, 'making fun of your husband?'

'Didn't do any such thing. Larking with my friends, that's all.'

'It was your manner.'

'Sorry, baby. Truly sorry.'

She was the old Mamie again on the train, thigh against thigh in the empty first class, adoring him, asking breathily if 'love and kisses and something I'd better not mention' was to do with her birthday in November.

'I'm afraid not. I was merely being indecent.'

'I shall be twenty-five, you know.' She stood up, swaying as they pulled away from Tyne Dock, to peer at herself in the mirror between the photographs of Durham Cathedral and Hexham Abbey. 'Will you love me when I'm old?'

He was touched, against his will. 'If you're a good girl,' he said. 'Good girls get loved for ever.'

'Charlie is twenty-six but pretends she isn't. She got some chap to give her that fur coat for her birthday to cheer her up.'

'Lucky girl. Is that what this is leading up to? "George, can I have a fur coat?"'

'Can I? Really?'

'We shall have to see. They don't grow on trees.'

She nestled close; two men in evening dress who were about to get in at East Boldon tactfully went next door; there was a 'secret' she would tell him when they were in bed. The sweetness of anticipation grew until the moment they walked around the corner into Hawarden Crescent and Mamie announced, 'I can't go in. I'm going to be sick.'

She spoke incoherently about Henry; said the van parked outside was one of his; pleaded with George to take her to the Palatine where she would explain everything. He bundled her into the house, and heard Mrs Stuart say, 'Here they are at last.' The bedroom door banged behind Mamie as he went through to the kitchen, where Henry Silver was sitting with his hat in his lap. Mrs Stuart disappeared into the scullery, leaving them alone together.

'What is going on?' said George. 'Mamie nearly had hysterics when she saw the van.'

'I had to come round. Or there'd be worse trouble.'

A fur coat was at the bottom of it; George might have

guessed. Mamie, needing ready cash to buy one, goes to Henry saying that George will stump up, on the strength of which he lends her the money. It is made of sealskin ('Dear God,' said George), and unwisely she puts it on to show Dolly, making it likely that sooner or later the child will forget her oath of secrecy and tell her ma. Mrs Silver on rampage not being something to take lightly, loan needs repaying promptly in case she looks at the ledger and cat escapes from bag.

'I'd have expected a man in business to show more caution,' said George. 'How much?'

Henry bowed his head. 'Twenty-three guineas.'

'I suppose she rolled her eyes at you.'

Henry thought the remark uncalled for; watched George write a cheque he couldn't afford, twenty-four pounds and three shillings; cranked the handle of the van and departed.

Mamie was invisible under the blankets, pillows protecting her head. Her clothes were on the floor. He kicked a corset under the bed and heard metal ping on the chamber pot.

'So we have come to this,' he said bitterly. 'I ought to drag you out of bed and give you a thrashing but I'm not that kind of man.' He rather thought he might be that kind of man, but it was the wrong time for a demonstration, with Mrs Stuart straining her ears. Instead he opened the wardrobe and there it was, its sleek black brushed-down surface shivering on the hanger. 'This goes back to the shop in the morning,' he said.

Muffled noises came from the bedclothes.

'How many times have you worn it?'

'Once.' Her face came to the surface, red and puffy. 'I didn't get it from a shop. I was going to tell you about it.'

'How very kind of you. Bought it from a fisherman who makes them in his spare time, perhaps.'

'My friend Charlie. She knows a man knows somebody in the trade, gets them cheap.'

'Cheap!'

'Forty-two guineas in the shops, and that's without the fox-fur it's trimmed with. I look marvellous in it, I really do.'

'Stolen goods, I wouldn't be surprised.' He threw the coat on the floor and pretended to wipe his feet. 'You can say goodbye to it.'

'Good night, George and Mamie' came from the passage as Mrs Stuart went to bed.

He stood back for a second, time for Mamie's arms to shoot out. Leaning over the side, she dragged the coat into bed with her and embraced it, rubbing her face against the bushy red collar, cooing at it as if it was a child. George was appalled; transfixed. Her breasts were all over it, startlingly white against the oily blackness. Using her knees she pulled the bottom half below the bedclothes.

'There, there. Oozie-woozie. Go to sleep. Oozie-woozie-woozie . . .'

Her voice trailed away. It was all pretence. But there she lay, breathing heavily, arms and legs wrapped around that bloody sealskin, defying him to prove she wasn't asleep. In the end he concluded that perhaps she was. He slept on the far side, occasionally brushed by the creature; the moment lost.

More journeys, more seaports; May-free nights at Penarth, their last episode never referred to; a dream about Everard, while dozing on a suburban train to Gravesend, in which his brother's body was brought back to England wrapped in Mamie's sealskin. The war was coming to an end. Waves of men moved eastward, Germans fleeing before them, giving George a lump in his throat; a white flag came out of the mist in a motorcar; on the hundredth day of the fifth year, it was over.

He managed to get to Sunderland that evening. As he left the station a roar of voices came from Fawcett Street, accompanied by tin whistles, a bugle, desultory sirens from the river. Ragged lines of girls and soldiers were pretending to dance, hemmed in by a crowd. Flames rose from workmen's braziers that boys were feeding with rags and lumps of tar, their shadows flickering on the walls. Women from the shipyards were grabbing hold of men and kissing them. A mouth smelling of onions left grease on George's cheek, and he raised his hat ironically. A hand snatched it and threw it in the air. They were all mad. He half wished he was mad himself, instead of pushing his way down the street to get clear of the mob and reach the Stuarts'. His telegram, sent at noon, said, 'THERE TONIGHT TO CELEBRATE VICTORY WITH MY DARLING.'

Shop windows were illuminated again, in most cases by electric light bulbs hastily strung up, shining on a chemist's red and green carboys or a tray of watches, overhung with Union flags and messages like 'Lest we forget! (R. Kipling)' and 'Hang the Kaiser'.

Binns department store had excelled itself. The big window had a living tableau that contained, as George saw when he was level with it, four British soldiers armed with Lee-Enfields and a Lewis gun, one British officer, one German officer holding a small white flag, and two Queen Alexandra nurses beside a bed where a wounded man in a bloodstained bandage was sitting up and drinking tea; together with sandbags, a few strands of barbed wire and yards of hessian underfoot to look like earth. Gold paint on the plate glass said, 'A Tribute from Binns'.

Youths in the crowd were shouting encouragement, 'Keep your eye on that Jerry!' and 'Never mind tea, give the lad a beer!' The nurses were encouraged to make a wounded man happy, and when a tin-whistler tried a dance tune in ragtime, there were cries of 'Give us a jig!' and 'Take your partners!' One of the nurses strolled across to the window, almost tripping over a sandbag, and waved to the crowd. It was Charlie, the Dancing Verona. She raised her skirt six inches and waggled her leg.

George used his elbows, and by the time he got to the front, the other nurse was dancing with the wounded man, and he had seen who it was. He banged the glass and shouted, 'Mamie!' but to no effect. The British officer danced with the German, who kept hold of his white flag, while the other ranks took turns with Charlie. The crowd cheered when the wounded man's bandage fell off. He pretended to faint on the bed and pulled Mamie with him. To his disgust George saw they were kissing, her hand on the back of his head, her skirt and his nightshirt rumpled up together.

Then a manager in striped trousers appeared from the shop and could be seen reprimanding them. Mamie and the soldier left the window, and so did Charlie. The bed was wheeled away. The Lewis gunners took up their positions again; the German languished with his flag; the manager bowed to the street and was booed.

Mamie refused to see what the fuss was about. Binns had hired her and Charlie at thirty shillings each to take part in a patriotic tableau. Didn't the audience just love it?

'You made an exhibition of yourself. For what? For a few shillings.'

'If you didn't keep me so short I wouldn't need a few shillings, would I?'

'Were you paid to start kissing him as well?'

'Golly, George, you sound like my sister. I was acting. You're always telling me I'm a proper little actress. That's what I was being in the window. Don't you trust me or something?'

'Do you give me your solemn word that you have never behaved immorally since our marriage?'

She blinked. They were in the kitchen at Hawarden Crescent; her parents were round at Edith's. Dresser, tasselled table-runner, baking oven, all pointed to the propriety of an upbringing that she must have found as irksome as George had found his.

'Like me to swear it, would you?'

Drawers in the dresser were yanked open. Mamie produced a pocket Bible in limp brown leather and read, 'To Amy on her confirmation, November 1907.'

'No need to be theatrical,' said George.

'That's what you're being.' She clasped the book to her chest and said in a silly falsetto voice, 'I, Mamie Shotton, do solemnly swear that the only man who has had relations with me since my wedding day is my hubbie. S'welp me God.'

'No need for vulgarity.'

She pushed the book at George. 'Your turn now. I George Shotton . . . go on, say it.'

'Silly girl. I shall always be faithful to you,' he said. The Bible alarmed him; he didn't let it touch him.

'That isn't what you made me say.'

'I didn't make you say anything. I merely asked for an assurance. You've given it to me. The matter's closed.'

'If you say so.' She looked at the clock on the mantelpiece. 'They'll be another hour. Let's have some fun. I dare you. In here, in the kitchen.'

He wondered if this was her way of extricating them both from the conversation. It served its purpose, two minutes kneeling on the hearth rug, but left something unanswered, as if niggling doubts that might have been in his head for months had come to the surface and refused to go away.

The episode was another nail in Sunderland's coffin. 'I have decided we shall live in South Wales,' he wrote to her from Cardiff a week later. 'I frequently have ships in these parts, and you will find the people quite friendly. We shall be in nice furnished rooms to start with, and later on I may rent a house. Darling wifey, I am determined we shall be happy.'

He chose Swansea, a town where he wasn't known. Edwards at the Grosvenor Hotel found him some addresses on the seafront at Trafalgar Terrace, near Swansea Gaol. A Mrs Hearn, a woman in her thirties, kept a house that looked clean and decent. She understood at once when George said that because he was often away on business, he liked to think that Mrs Shotton would have a sympathetic friend. He paid a month's rent from the first of January.

Penarth was only an hour away, so everyone would benefit, the wives as much as their husband, not to mention little Arthur. George remained one step ahead.

12

The crossing from Dover to Ostend, supposed to be four hours, took nearly six because a gale was blowing and drifting mines had been reported. By the time they went backwards up the harbour and berthed at a shining wet quay, it was nearly dark. Roofless sheds and heaps of rubble could be seen. An official examined George's papers and held a lamp to his face. 'Mind how you go,' he said.

A horse-cab smelling of fish took him to the address where he was expected, in the Rue Sans Nom. The windows were boarded up and the bell didn't work, but they heard him knocking, and Magda Maystad appeared, wearing black and looking more Belgian than she ever had in Cardiff. They had been back only a few weeks. Penny candles in the drawing room showed broken chairs and a skeletal Christmas tree in a bucket. Friends were brought in to meet the visitor, and Yvan, the husband, spoke of the honour Mr Shotton was doing them by allowing them to repay in some small measure their debt to the people of Wales. Magda's smile to George or whoever might be watching was guiltless; what a shame there weren't more like her!

He didn't stay long in the morning. The Maystads knew the nature of his visit, and Yvan was ready with coupons issued by the *préfecture* that guaranteed a place on the light railway to and from Bicksbeke, conditions permitting. Stretches of line were supported on timber and rubble, and nothing moved faster than 18 kilometres an hour. Was he sure of arrangements for his reception? Yes, a telegram had gone to a Captain Crawley. And here were some provisions, said Mme Maystad, producing a hamper, and warned him not to leave it unattended.

They took him through the shattered town, on the way to the railway depot, without comment. From the start the train was bursting with passengers. A woman was thrown off for trying to board with a crate of fowl, but others succeeded. George was sure he heard a pig. All around him was chattering, coughing, arguing, the consumption of grey bread and sausage, pipes ablaze with what smelled like burning hay.

A smashed landscape of earth and water went slowly by. Comment would have been useless, even if his neighbours had expected it. What would be appropriate? 'Christ Almighty!' was hardly more use than 'Oh dear!' Craters and ruins thickened as they chugged south and east. 'I had no idea' might have done, although George had imagined Everard's war too often and too deeply to have expected anything but horror. What struck him was the air of an endless rubbish dump, as if wire and concrete and broken wheels and corrugated iron had come down a chute from the sky.

Whenever the train halted, people jumped out to urinate by the track, women as well as men. George joined them once and came back to find a thin man who trembled taking a piece of cheese from the hamper, which he let him keep on condition he shared it; a sensible move, as it turned out, when they reached Bicksbeke in the late afternoon, and there was no Captain Crawley to be found.

The station was a tin shed with planks, at one end of a village with a few smoking chimneys, signs of life sandwiched between the ruins. Most of the passengers had gone. The trembling man, who alighted at the same time as George, showed him a wooden bungalow smelling of paint, on the edge of the road, that said it was the Imperial War Graves

Commission, Bicksbeke Division. Door locked; no one at home.

The light was going. George was uneasy for the first time since he'd fled his wives. He had sent telegrams from Dover. Penarth got, 'EVERARD ON MIND CAN'T REST. REGIMENT CONFIRMS LAST ACTION TOOK PLACE BICKSBEKE AREA. HAVE NICE CHRISTMAS.' Sunderland's said, 'DUTY TO SISTER-IN-LAW REQUIRES I VISIT BATTLEFIELD RE FRESH INFORMATION. LOVE FROM GEORGE.' The journey resolved the dilemma of where to spend Christmas. But now he was there, the landscape, drained of colour except for a pervasive yellowy light, itself became the dilemma.

It was no use waiting for Captain Crawley. All George had to go on was Oscar James's cousin's husband at the War Office, assuring them that the War Graves people said Crawley was 'a conscientious officer'. As if that meant anything in this wilderness.

'I need a bed for the night,' he said. 'Bed. Sleep.' He closed his eyes and cradled his head.

There was one down the road, away from the village, a hostel in the middle of nowhere. 'Dank u,' said the trembler, and put George's ten-franc note under his hat. It was a YMCA, crowded and noisy, with sausages for supper and a bed in a dormitory. Most of the men were British Army Labour Corps, with a few Belgian soldiers and civilian lorry drivers; nearly a hundred all told. 'They are doing reclamation work hereabouts,' said the manager, and it was only when he became aware of the disinfectant smell underlying the coke fumes and sweaty bodies that George realised what they were reclaiming.

In the morning he saw the rows of plain coffins stacked under tarpaulins. The rain had cleared; pools of blue water reflected the sky. Sun came and went in a chill north-westerly. It was almost a fine day. Working parties set out on lorries that went in both directions, moving cautiously past unfilled craters.

An abrasive conversation with Captain Crawley came as a relief. Crawley had received no telegram, which was of small consequence, he said, since he wouldn't have replied to it if he had. A thickset man wearing steel-rimmed spectacles, he sat in front of a wall map stuck with coloured pins and told George that unofficial visitors from England were the bane of his life. One day there would be cemeteries with all the graves numbered, when the relatives would be welcome.

'I haven't come for a lecture,' said George. 'My brother went missing near here in August. That's the beginning and end of it.'

'I don't mean to be offensive. But the scale of the thing is beyond all reason. We think there are four hundred thousand men in graves – ones, twos, twenties, fifties. The Somme and Flanders are the worst. Some bloody fools in England want to leave them where they are – plant trees, give them nice headstones.'

'Why not?'

'Because come the spring the farmers will be ploughing up the flaming land is why not. You can hardly blame them after four years. Which is why we have a small army on double pay smoking free tobacco for reasons I needn't go into, moving them as fast as we can. What happens when the frost sets in? Are we supposed to blow them out of the ground with TNT? And you come here looking. For what?'

'I explained. I had a brother in this terrible place.'

Crawley sighed and made perfunctory notes. George was evidently being humoured. He was allowed to look through 'S' entries on the index cards that clerks were compiling at trestle tables, but found nothing. Before George left, the officer took him to the back of the building, which looked over the canal, and said he thought there had been a night engagement in

August involving the Durhams 'over there somewhere'. The 'somewhere' was a mishmash of lakes, wire and trenches. George caught the whiff of disinfectant again, and saw buckets of identity discs sprinkled with white powder.

A boy with carroty hair cropped short was dawdling in the road outside. Near him or with him was the trembler, who turned away.

'You are looking for a loved one,' said the boy: a statement, not a question. The accent was strong and Flemish but the English was good. He might have been twelve; thirteen at most. A canvas bag was slung over his shoulder. 'I give help, sir. My family occupy a farmhouse in direction Boesinghe, behind the front lines. I learn English from the officers. They were billeted between fightings.'

'When there was a lull,' said George. He felt distinctly feverish after his night in the dormitory, filled with groans and farts. His neck ached. Was he sickening for the Spanish flu? Sunlight flashed on the windscreen of a lorry beyond the canal and hurt his eyes.

'A lull,' said the boy. 'Thank you very much.' He pulled objects out of the bag. Live rounds of small-arms ammunition. Cap badges. A torn black-and-white photograph of a woman. A rusty whistle. A snapped-off bayonet. Reddish identity discs, lying on his palm like autumn leaves. 'I collect,' he said proudly.

'You took those from the dead.'

The boy shook his head. 'In the earth, after blowing to smithereens. They are knocked about,' and George saw they were all damaged. 'Captain Crawley give me five centimes each.'

'Who were the British officers at your farmhouse?'

'Very many, sir. Lieutenant Smith. Lieutenant Humphrey.' He tumbled the discs into the bag. 'Lieutenant Shot-on.'

George shivered. A pair of geese startled him, honking as

they skimmed the dirty green water. He definitely felt unwell. But the unbreakable bond had brought him to the very place, the very person. 'Was he killed?' he said.

'Sir, I can find out. Many people had kindnesses from the officers.'

'But you remember him?'

'He was in the house of my uncle, come to think. I can find out.'

When they grew up they'd drifted apart. Everard was humorous, even-tempered, without much ambition. He liked to stand at the piano when Chrissie played music from operettas and sing casually in his tenor voice, laughing at himself when he missed a note. Two pound ten a week as a solicitor's clerk in training was 'right down my street'. The boy who hero-worshipped his big brother became the man who ticked 'I am well' on field postcards, as if George's letters were not to be taken seriously. It would all come right after the war. Except that after-the-war was here already.

Figures were active beside the lorry, far off on the plain. George's head felt like glass, letting in the landcape. How had Everard endured all this; how had anyone? What if he had lost his memory and kind Belgians were caring for him? The strong, rosy-cheeked fighting man with his black hair and clear eyes is brought blinking into the light. He says, 'Your face is familiar. I must have known you somewhere. I can trust you.' And George says, 'I am your brother. We were inseparable. You have forgotten.'

The boy said, 'Sir, it is twenty-five francs now and twenty-five when I bring the news.'

This limitless cemetery was a dream, a delusion. So was that bloody boy. The man, a hundred yards away, sat on a wall, looking at them. 'I think his rank may have been captain,' said George. '*Captain* Shotton.'

'Yes, I remember. He was captain.'

The valise, of course, had 'G. Shotton' stencilled on it, and was next to the hamper that the trembler tampered with. 'Got you,' said George, 'conniving little bastard,' and grabbed the boy's collar. He slung the bag in the canal and the brat got his head thumped. When he started screaming, George put his hands around his neck.

'I think you'd have killed him if I hadn't come out,' said Crawley, when the boy had recovered. Through the window George could see the two of them trying to fish the bag out of the canal. 'I shouldn't hang about here if I were you. There's motor transport to Ostend at fourteen hundred hours. We can find room for you.'

It was Christmas Eve. The last boat for England had sailed, even if he had been in a fit state to catch it. The Maystads insisted he go straight to bed, where he lay dying, dosed with triple Globéol, washed down by schnapps in a beer mug.

Magda sat on a chair beside him, nurselike, and said, 'May I speak frankly? You are suffering from nervous exhaustion. I have seen it in Yvan.'

'Quite right,' groaned George. 'But it wasn't in vain.'

'You mean you learned something?'

'Enough to convince me that my brother is alive.'

To say otherwise would be intolerable. The truth was always buried too deep for discovery, and wasn't to be confronted this side of madness. A ship hooted in the Ostend fairway, reminder of the safe and commonplace. There was next year to think about, and the new life with Mamie.

13

Mrs Hearn's establishment in Trafalgar Terrace had sea views, sea winds, and often a coating of sand on the front steps that had blown across the street from the foreshore. Life with George was like a holiday gone wrong; Mamie knew what to expect of the apartment before they arrived. Masts and coal staithes in the South Dock were visible from the front room upstairs where she – or they, when George was in town – sat, ate, talked, read; where home was. The one-sided terrace ran west to east between a cricket ground and Swansea Gaol. Sometimes a bell tolled from the prison; Mamie didn't know why.

The houses were respectable but unsecluded. Steam trains passed almost under the windows, following the bay's curve until the line (the L. and N. W. Railway, which George used for journeys to the north) turned inland and disappeared up a wooded valley. Another line carried the electric Mumbles train, which looked like a tram, to the far end of the bay, where a pleasure pier and a lighthouse ended miles of urban sands, and a lonely coast of cliffs and coves began. Mamie went that way for bracing walks on the sands.

More often she wandered into town, where Mrs Hearn had shown her the places to go for life's necessities, apparently cheap food and weatherproof clothes. A youngish woman with dyed hair, Flo Hearn had an invalid husband, two boys and the house to look after. She was proud of Swansea's facilities, particularly of the covered market with its dismaying mounds of cabbages, bowls of cockles and white enamel trays splattered with what looked like blackish-green cowpats, a local so-called delicacy made of seaweed and misleadingly known as laver bread.

For Mamie real shopping consisted of inspecting skirts and hats at Davis the Bon or Lewis Lewis and, best of all, visiting the thirty-odd departments of Ben's, Swansea's version of Binns. The town also had six cinemas and two theatres, so every week she could see up to a dozen shows, depending how many cinemas changed their programmes on a Thursday. A bag of sweets and stories in the dark suited her. But she was terrified it might go on for ever.

As a way of life it was so laughably unlike anything she could have imagined for herself that at first the absurdity that this was her, Mamie Stuart, buying vegetables and baking powder, seemed to confirm its temporary nature. She had thought the same in Bristol; six months later it began to feel permanent. There were even watery winter days, rain pouring from clouds that came down to street level as she hurried in to the Carlton or the Castle for her daily helping of romantic adventures, when she felt so low in spirits that dissent was out of the question. Stare at Lillian Gish in a five-part Love Triangle Drama, a Pathé Gazette and some Mutt & Jeff; go home to tea; think kind thoughts about George and the undying love he always mentioned at least once every visit. Love wasn't to be laughed at.

A few shillings a week, spent carefully, made domestic life easier to bear. The skivvy who brought the coal up from the cellar could be bribed to stay and dust. Flo would make an extra dish of faggots and peas for sixpence, and Mamie could pretend it was hers, convincing George that she had improved since Bristol. Sometimes he worked in Swansea and the small ports nearby for days on end, so he spent more time at home. 'Much nicer for you,' said Flo, and so it was, except when they quarrelled, or the lovemaking went badly or failed to happen at all.

Marriage left you with less room for manoeuvre. When she was just a woman who liked men, Mamie could offer them, and more importantly herself, endless helpings of whatever seemed opportune: not only dirty acts but mysterious depths and the harmony of naked souls in love as depicted in her library books. She could pick and choose. Whereas marriage was a fixed condition that you didn't invent; it invented you. She had joined the Florence Hearns and Edith Silvers. She even wrote to Edith, poking fun at George and his funny ways, asking how women put up with it all, and got a letter telling her to pull herself together.

Mrs Hearn often invited her down to their sitting room in the basement, where she liked to hear about Mamie's exciting life. As a rule she had no time for theatrical persons, the kind who stayed in certain Trafalgar Terrace boarding houses and misbehaved. Mamie, having been redeemed by marriage, was exempt. Flo wanted to believe that Mr Shotton had saved her in the nick of time. 'He was smitten when he saw you on the stage and was waiting for you after the performance, am I right?'

'Actually he picked me up at a cinema.'

Her life with George came out in bits and pieces on winter evenings, and Mrs Hearn turned it into marital cosiness, tending towards marital bliss. 'Absence makes the heart grow fonder,' she said. 'I hear Mr Shotton going up the stairs two at a time when he gets back.'

'He's afraid I've been spending his money.'

But Flo knew it was love. It was all very well being one of the Verona Girls, dancing in northern cities, pursued by men in flashy waistcoats. Her life before Mr Shotton was simply a means to an end.

'I'd go back like a shot if someone asked me.'

'Never! What would Mr S. say?'

'He'd think it was funny. Wouldn't take it seriously.'

The bronchitic Mr Hearn was told to leave his couch in the kitchen to see Mamie dance a few steps to gramophone music, so he would know what an exotic creature they had under their roof; he smelled of cough mixture and picked his ear. She felt sad, prancing about in the basement. Flo was right; she would never go back.

One of her dreams was that George would buy a motorcar and let her drive it. She saw herself speeding about the town, making new friends – how, exactly, a car would help in this respect she wasn't sure, but the thought of freedom from trams and windy pavements was intoxicating.

They went to a garage and George spent an hour looking under the bonnets of motors, asking technical questions that the salesman, an ex-officer with a scarred cheek who said he was Captain Andrews, couldn't always answer. Mamie was taken with something called a Belsize, which had a dickey seat, and even more by a Humber, blessed with a double dickey. 'Madam has put her finger on it,' said the salesman, and began to praise the interior elegance. A test drive would amaze her. George said sharply, 'Never mind my wife, she wouldn't know a gearbox from a back axle,' and began haggling about prices. In the end he decided the only car he was interested in was a Ford, which they didn't have. Captain Andrews smiled bravely and said he hoped to see them again; Mamie was quite taken with his scar.

This time George was home for only one night. The car-buying trip had been exciting, even though nothing came of it. When he was out of the house – sending telegrams, he said – she made some sugar-bag promises for them to use in bed, and arranged with Mrs Hearn to smuggle in one of her fish pies for supper. But it all went wrong. George was moody and they had a row over the pie when a bone got stuck in his throat and had to be treated with mouthfuls of soft bread and water. Afterwards, grey-faced, he said that having nearly killed her husband, she had better ask Mrs Hearn to give her some lessons in plain cooking.

'Matter of fact, that was Mrs Hearn's pie.'

'You'll say anything if it gets you out of trouble.'

Silence might have been wiser, but Mamie was so cross, she went to find Flo, and said would she come upstairs and settle an argument. George sat reading the local *Daily Post*.

'We've just been eating a delicious fish pie,' said Mamie. 'Tell Mr Shotton who made it.'

'Mrs Shotton did.'

'You sold it me for ninepence. When the Hearns have stew, we have stew. When they have rice pudding, we have rice pudding. I'm tired of having to pretend I can cook.'

'She does try,' said Mrs Hearn, adding innocently that there was some blancmange left over downstairs if they would like some.

Why couldn't George find it funny? Her attempts to laugh him out of his crabbiness failed. In bed, things were active enough, in a red-faced, heavy-breathing sort of way, but the promises were too playful to be used, and Mamie flushed them away in the morning, thinking what a waste.

It was nearly spring, the first sunny day for weeks. George had departed for London after breakfast, leaving her slightly more miserable than before. This couldn't go on, could it? She dressed up and swept into town, aching to feel like Mamie Stuart used to feel. At Ben's she spent one pound seven shillings and sixpence on English Violet Perfume and English Violet Soap. This impressive splurge paved the way to opening an account in George's name. The assistant manager barely looked at the receipted bill she produced, for an emerald velour hat that George bought her in January; he concentrated on the hat itself, which Mamie was wearing, and on the other smart things (purchased up north) that covered her: blue serge costume, blue kid gloves, dark-blue kid shoes. All-powerful in his striped trousers, he authorised a monthly account of up to ten pounds.

'I would prefer fifteen,' said Mamie.

'Fifteen it is, madam.'

Knowing that whenever she felt like it she could stock up with spring lingerie and shoes and a hat or two improved her morale. But the same dusty streets led away from Ben's; she saw herself in a shop window and wondered if she was wasted on George. When a man smelling of beer moved into the seat next to her at the Ritz, a cinema down a lane off High Street where she had gone to see Wallace Reid in *The World Apart*, and she felt fingers on her leg, she made a terrible scene, instead of responding with a quick slap in the normal way.

She enjoyed seeing the miscreant flung out. She enjoyed being mollified by the proprietor in his cubbyhole and offered a month of free seats. He also owned the Elysium, so she could have seats there too. 'Edwin Morgan, madam, at your service,' he said. 'The patron is always right.' His crisp cuffs and slender hands reminded her of the man she fell for when she was nineteen, who ran Cornishe's in Leeds, or was it the Avenue? Reputation was everything at a picture house, said the just slightly oily Edwin. Madam was welcome to bring someone with her, friend or husband; the way he said 'husband' made it sound like a question. He saw her to the foyer, touching her arm. Would she make herself known to him whenever she returned? They would fetch him at once if he wasn't there.

Men like Morgan were two a penny, and she would have to be desperate to take them seriously. Still, there was a degree of satisfaction in knowing that they were there, admiring her, going out of their way to be nice to her on the off chance of scoring a hit.

The man from the garage might or might not have been in that category. He came round to Trafalgar Terrace in a Ford motorcar one afternoon in early April, asking for Mr Shotton, and, finding him not at home, suggested that Mrs Shotton herself might like a spin.

At last, an event to lift her out of herself. The scar and a sporty jacket gave Captain Andrews a worldly look. They raced the Mumbles train, overtook a coal lorry and various motorcars, and arrived at the Mumbles Pier in – he consulted his watch – eight minutes fifteen seconds. He hoped she would tell Mr Shotton about her nifty acceleration and the very low vibration factor.

'Don't build up your hopes,' she said. 'If it was me, I might be persuaded. Do you sell many motorcars?'

Leaning back in the driver's seat, he spoke of postwar economic conditions and the boom that would undoubtedly come. He looked at her sideways. 'Not many.'

Watery sunlight glinted on the bonnet, on the bay. They might have been a couple out for the afternoon, the handsome ex-officer who had been in charge of a motor-transport section in France (he told her about his war; he got the scar when a tyre burst and his vehicle overturned) with the enigmatic young woman who might or might not be his fiancée.

'Is Mr Shotton away a lot?' he asked.

'He comes and goes.' Mamie pulled herself together and said it was time she was getting back. At Mrs Hearn's he gave her a leaflet about the new postwar Ford motors, on which he wrote, 'Mrs Shotton permitted me to take her on a test drive to the Mumbles and back, and expressed herself delighted,' before helping her out of the car and waving as she went in.

She thought no more of him until George was next in Swansea, when he asked her, on his first evening, if it was true that she had been seeing a man.

Was this a prelude to having her bottom pinched and some indecency whispered in her ear? George was hostile, waiting. A few pitiful candidates for the job of seducer passed through her mind. The motorcar man was the obvious one. Apart from him, there was only the oily cinema proprietor and the assistant manager at Ben's.

'What a chump you are sometimes,' she said.

'If you've been sleeping with a man, you'd better make a clean breast of it.'

She slapped his face, so hard that it hurt her hand. He grunted, seized her by the arm, shook her till she was gasping, cuffed the side of her head, stood watching as she fell on her knees and began sobbing.

'I want the truth,' he said.

She refused to answer him, refused his offer of a cold flannel for her bruise, refused to do anything that would help him avoid making an even bigger fool of himself.

'You were seen getting into a motorcar,' he said. Silence. 'A man came to the house for you.' Silence. 'What am I supposed to think?' Silence. 'The skivvy saw you.' Silence. 'The last thing I want to do is think ill of you.' Silence.

When it suited her she found the Ford motors leaflet and threw it in his face.

'You'd have been wiser to show me this at the start,' he said.

'*You'd* have been wiser not to go sneaking about, paying the skivvy to spy on me. Go and see Captain Andrews. I'll come with you. "My husband wants to know if you have been behaving immorally with his wife." He'll take you to court for slander.'

George made no defence. He was bitterly sorry; it was only because he loved her; it was only his jealous nature. For the first time since their marriage, Mamie felt she had the upper hand. His advances in bed were repelled and he was told either to leave her alone or go and sleep on the sofa. She forgave him next day; the crowning revenge. 'Darling wifey,' said the penitent, 'we'll do whatever you like today.'

That was easy. A fine April morning hung across the bay. 'See a bit of scenery this morning. Have lunch somewhere nice. Take me shopping afterwards.'

They caught the Mumbles train to a busy village called Oystermouth and hired bicycles so they could ride down the rocky coast and ride back again to the Pier Hotel. It was another version of her childhood adventure, walking off after breakfast along the Chester Road. George hadn't been on a bicycle for years. He wobbled and hit the kerb. 'Come along,' she ordered, making circles in the roadway, her tweed skirt riding up for errand boys to goggle at.

The lovely morning, her victory over George, the thought of being able to do as she pleased, made her fond of Swansea for the first time. The hedges were greener here. They rode and pushed their way to a pub and a chapel on a hill. The great bay and the town across the arc, muddying the air, were left behind. A steep track ran down the far side between fields and gorse, passing occasional set-back houses with shutters and lawns, ending in a hollow that opened on to a beach between cliffs. Mamie's front wheel was trapped in a rut. She descended the last hundred yards like an arrow, shrieking with pleasure, and fell off in the grass. Behind her George came slowly, brakes squealing, trilby straight on his head. Poor George.

The sea was far out. No one had walked on the sand except birds.

'Could we buy this and have it for ourselves?' she said.

'What would we do with it?'

'I'd bathe here naked every day and nobody'd see except you.'

A kiss and a fondle in the middle of nowhere would have been in order, except that at this particular moment she didn't feel inclined for wifely acquiescence. She removed the hand that was caressing her through the tweed and tucked his arm through hers as they walked back up the beach. A boy with a sheepdog was looking at their bicycles. George asked him what the place was called, and he said, 'Caswell Bay, sir.' He whistled to the dog and went along the road towards Swansea.

George, evidently forgetting it was her day out, not his, said they should leave the cycles and walk up the next headland. When they came out on the cliff, she saw what had attracted him, a primitive windmill built of wood, enclosed by a low stone wall, attached to a pump and some earthenware pipes. 'Pumps water for the houses on this side, I dare say,' said George, bending and poking, as if a machine with blades going round in the breeze had anything to do with Mamie's treat.

'Look at the lambs!' she said, advancing along the clifftop, which offered a narrow belt of grazing high above the sea. Ewes baaed and gathered their offspring to safety. No George came with her. She marched on, scattering endearments at lambkins, telling their mothers not to make such a fuss. The next headland and the next cove came in sight. Gulls rose and fell on invisible threads above the sea. It was the pure countryside that should have been a mile down the Chester Road of her childhood, but wasn't.

'Noisy creature,' she told a sheep standing alone by a bank and some alders. It was reluctant to move. Mamie saw the reason, a hole in the ground with bleats coming from it – more of a cleft than a hole, four or five feet across, cut at a steep angle through the rocky ground. Shading her eyes, she made out earth and stones, tilting into gloom and then blackness. The lamb was bleating nonstop;

the ewe stared, challenging her not to care about dumb animals.

'Georgie!' she shouted. 'Help! Come quick!'

He was strolling along the cliff. Now he ran, taking off his hat.

'There's a lamb down there,' she said. 'Will you be a sweet boy and rescue it?'

He told her not to be ridiculous. The lad with the dog would find it eventually. Lambs were always getting stuck in places. Think of his clothes. One would need a torch and a rope, for a start. Furthermore there was a most peculiar smell. They had to get back to the pier for lunch. Also one could drown if there was water at the bottom.

'The lamb hasn't,' she said.

Its heart-rending bleats – she defied George to say they were anything less – made her adamant; so, secretly, did the prospect of getting him to do as she wanted. After all, this was his day of penance. It was deeds she wanted, the proof of married love. But all she said was, 'Oh, Georgie. Oh, please.'

'You really want me to go down there, don't you?'

'Ain't nothing you can't do, baby.'

'What happens if I can't get up again, eh?' He was removing his jacket and looking at a tree.

Seeing it begin to happen, she panicked and said, 'I've changed my mind.'

He broke off a branch and started trimming it with a penknife. 'Go for the police is what you do. Take your stockings off.'

'What, now?'

'I need a sling to bring it up with. If I get that far.'

He knotted the stocking feet together and tied them loosely around his neck. The branch had been trimmed to a short stick. Minus collar and tie, and with his sleeves rolled up, he looked younger and rougher. He scrambled sideways and backwards down the cleft, and she saw his waistcoat disappear, then his head. Stones rattled, far down. The lamb had stopped bleating.

Mamie consoled herself with the thought that any moment someone would walk along the cliffs, and she could tell them, 'My husband's down there, rescuing a lamb. I may need to get help.' But no one came. Minutes passed. Ships moved across the sea; a thrush sang in the alder.

'Geor-gie!' she called. No reply. She lay on the grass looking over the edge, hand shading her eyes, and called again. Solid dark; total silence. She stood up and began calling for help. A fishing boat was coming close in along the coast. Would they see her on the cliff? She had her red blouse off, waving it and shouting, when she heard George say, 'You'll frighten him,' and he came out with the lamb trussed and dangling upside down from his neck.

He had done exactly what she wanted, but somehow he had made a fool of her in the process, or she had made a fool of herself.

'Didn't you hear me shouting?'

'I heard something. I was too busy.'

The lamb had been caught in a length of wire; George hadn't reached the bottom. He thought it was very likely an old ventilation shaft, since lead mining was once common along the coast. Farmers probably used it to dump rubbish and the occasional dead animal. The smell was probably a carcass.

'You've torn that blouse,' he said, cleaning his scratches with spit and saying he must buy antiseptic in Oystermouth. His trousers were muddy and one leg was holed at the knee. He replaced his collar and tie, and Mamie threw her stockings away in a temper.

The lamb rejoined the ewe, butting her fiercely for milk. Mamie had been ready to allow a bit of canoodling behind a bush, if George asked her nicely and was prepared to put up with some teasing about men who couldn't wait. Instead he was absorbed in himself, hurrying them back to their bicycles. Men had to want her more than she wanted them. If they didn't, they must take the consequences.

14

'My dear brother "Somewhere in Europe", You will laugh, one day in the future, when I tell you that you have now achieved the enviable distinction (or otherwise!) of being mentioned on three occasions in *The Times*, the first when they posted you missing, the others in the advertisements I have decided to place at intervals in the Personal column, asking for news of your whereabouts. Only last week I read of a wounded soldier who arrived unannounced in South Wales, safe and well, having been given up by his family a year ago. He received a bad knock on the head, a hospital lost his records, etc., etc.

'Life goes on here with the usual ups and downs. I remain deeply attached to Mamie while keeping up friendly relations with Arthur's mother. Since her brush with death last year she has perked up considerably. Have I been able in all my descriptions to convey what it is about Mamie that puts me under a spell? Beautiful, sensual, fun-loving, capricious in a womanly way that angers me one minute and stirs me into loving her more the next. Will that do? She is emancipated (as are so many girls in England today) and I have to admit that the thought of her entering an immoral relationship makes me very angry.

'Sometimes I feel trapped between my two women and allow myself to think of desperate answers to a situation that doesn't get any easier. (Why did I think it would? I am not an optimist by nature. But I have a strange capacity for *not thinking about things.*) Last month when we were out walking, Mamie asked me to rescue a lamb that had fallen into a lonely cave. The affair was not without danger. When I got down there in the dark, I found myself thinking that my death would solve everything. You will tell me not to be morbid. I came out with her lamb, and small thanks I got for it too. But you must not think me bitter. I have made my bed, etc., etc.

'I keep her tucked away in a house in Swansea, where I have recently rented business premises, and now find it simpler to visit Penarth and see Arthur. I have no wish to be divorced from May, even if that were practicable, which in present-day England it is not, without jeopardising one's name. Technically one "lives in sin", I suppose, though I confess that that strikes me as an exaggeration. Naturally I fear discovery. One is bound by laws that make no allowance for one's deepest feelings.

'You and I will smile when we discuss the niceties of adultery, man to man. As you can see, I write the word without flinching. There is an even harder word to write. All I can say is that when I committed bigamy – your intuition will have told you my secret! – it seemed to me to be a golden solution, inevitable under the circumstances. You will tell me frankly what you think, and I believe I know what it will be. "In matters of the heart, George, nothing is simple. It doesn't do for onlookers to rush into harsh judgements." *Even if* you conclude that I am a scoundrel, I shall take it on the chin. All that matters is the unbreakable bond. Nothing will ever part us, my dearest boy.'

George had been on the Clyde and by late afternoon he would be on the Ouse. England was a place seen through train windows; they passed Sheffield Main signal box as he finished the letter. The Ouse was an afterthought, slipped in between Clydeside and South Wales, where Mamie was expecting him on Wednesday. Now it would be Thursday at the earliest.

He had been in Scotland, surveying decommissioned minesweepers that the Admiralty hoped to sell. The evening he finished, he read in *Lloyd's List* that one of the Loader ships had been in collision outside the east-coast port of Goole. It was George's old friend the *Parrot*, and in the morning he decided to go there without asking. He liked Billy Loader, who never interfered in his daughter's marriage. It would be a gesture if he could nudge underwriters into accepting that the ancient coaster was beyond repair.

The ship was tied up at Skinner's Wharf, downriver from the dock. Her stem was crumpled and the anchor had been thrown backwards into the ship, where it was wedged in the decking. Unfortunately she wasn't holed below the line.

'Captain on board?' he shouted from the quay.

'He'm buggered off,' said a seaman in a jersey who came out of the wheelhouse.

'I'm from the owners.'

'Help yourself. Mind that plank. He wobbles.'

The visit ended in farce. Another surveyor appeared from below, also from the owners, and showed his authority, a letter from Harris Navigation of Middlesbrough. Loader had sold out to Harris a week earlier. Hadn't Mr Shotton's owners told him? Well, that was owners for you.

What was her history, the other man wanted to know.

'Chequered. I wish you well of her.'

Back in Cardiff, at Channel Buildings he found the Loader Steamship offices stripped bare. He looked in on his own office, where Oscar greeted him with ironical remarks about the man with the double-barrelled letter-heading, 'Channel Buildings, Cardiff' on one side and 'Adelaide Chambers, Swansea' on the other, and asked about his father-in-law – 'the cunning beggar!'

George said he had stopped being surprised at the things people did.

'That was a dig at me,' grinned Oscar, and glanced at Miss Boulton, tapping sternly at her machine, to see if she was following the wit.

'More a dig at myself,' said George.

He found Billy at home in Penarth, supervising a carpenter who was making a summerhouse, and a boy with a roller who was trying to even out the lumpy turf that no one had bothered with for a decade.

'I know,' said Billy, 'I forgot. It was unpardonable. It all happened suddenly. Those Harris chaps had been after me before. But I had plans, you know. With all the war surplus coming on the market, I thought to double the fleet and concentrate on coal for France.'

'Might have worked. Element of risk, I suppose.'

'That's what Elizabeth said. As if running ships was ever anything else. She worked on me, night and day. You know how women do? It was time to reap the rewards of a lifetime and all that.' He nodded towards the summerhouse. 'Here I am, reaping.'

'Didn't she want to go and live somewhere else?'

'Now she wants to stay. But we are going to America for a holiday in the summer. America! She has a cousin in Boston.'

He had aged since his wedding, less than a year earlier. His linen jacket and panama hat made him look like a man on a bowling green. 'You'll find your wife blooming,' he said. 'I expect Elizabeth is round there. She usually is.'

They were on deckchairs in the garden. The boy sat on a rug with his back against the one decent tree, reading a comic, the dog Hercules by his feet.

'What a lovely surprise,' said May. 'We haven't had a telegram for ages.'

Arthur waved his hand languidly. 'Hello, Daddy.'

George frowned. 'I believe we get up when we say hello to people.'

'I've been ill. Do look at my spots.' He opened his shirt and pointed at pale scars across his chest. 'Auntie Elizabeth said that if it had been the smallpox I would have been DEAD.'

'It was chickenpox,' said May. 'He was quite poorly.'

'Brave little soldier,' said Elizabeth.

'I should have been here. Oscar James can always contact me through Lloyd's agents.'

'We had the doctor, and Elizabeth is such a good nurse.'

'My temperature was one hundred and two.'

The woman ruffled his hair. 'Arthur Shotton, you are a proper little health fanatic. Come with me and we'll give Hercules his supper.'

George sat in her deckchair and said, 'Health fanatic? One might take offence at that.'

'He does get morbid at times. He is highly strung.' May's pale features were sharp in the sun; the pointed chin more pointed than ever. 'You must remember, dear, I am here on my own, and having a stepmother as reliable as Elizabeth is a comfort.'

'She interferes. Has an influence.'

'Nonsense, George.'

'Precisely. You used not to say things like "Nonsense, George."'

'I do think you want to have it all ways. I wish you had more time for us, and Arthur and I are always delighted when you come, but meanwhile life must go on.'

'I am merely suggesting that if Arthur's wellbeing is involved, I would like an effort made to send me a message. Have you thought of taking him to the seaside this year?'

'As a matter of fact I have. Will you come as well?'

'I can't make promises but I might look in for a day or two. They say Ilfracombe is pleasant. Or Tenby. I leave it to you to make the arrangements. You and Elizabeth.'

He ought to be grateful to be so painlessly freed of responsibility. The clockwork house ran without him, hot water circulated, the Kooksjoie burned like an eternal flame, his son ceased to be an infant. His presence made no practical difference. But he liked to know that wherever he was, there was always somewhere else. Two lives were better than one.

If he left within the next hour he would be with Mamie before dark. Instead he hung on in Penarth until it was too late, content to spend another night in his spartan bed. Supper at the Yacht Club; men talking about strikes and Bolshevism; back later to visit Arthur, asleep at the top of the house. The boy's face was as soft as putty, innocent of awkward questions for a few more years.

15

The car didn't materialise, and it was still trams and shoe leather when Mamie went shopping. Anyway George had made it plain that he didn't approve of women drivers. God knows what George did approve of; certainly not the account at Ben's, which he grumbled at and then closed. And he wouldn't have approved of the man who gave a cheeky whistle from an upstairs window further along Trafalgar Terrace, when she was on her way to buy life's necessities at the market; or of the friendly wave she gave in return; or of the way she stopped dead and said, 'Albert? What a lark!'

He was downstairs in a flash; had been sitting there for an hour, hoping she'd appear; was helping with the show at the Empire that week, and got her address from Norah. 'I thought it was time I forgave you for booting me out that day,' he said.

'Sorry, baby. Let's go on the sands.' They walked through an arched passageway in the railway embankment. 'There's a skivvy at my lodgings who spies on me. Now you can give me a kiss.'

Only dogs and a couple of old men shared the vast foreshore. 'We all miss you,' he said. 'What do you do with yourself down here?'

'This and that. Went to the show at the Empire yesterday.'

'Did you like it?'

'Zelleski the burlesque juggler? Don't make me laugh. Dolly Elsworthy in her latest successes? She's forgotten how to sing, if she ever knew, which I doubt.'

'Got a sweet figure, though.'

'Been seeing it at close quarters, have you?'

'Rather be seeing yours.' Albert was trying it on, raising his black eyebrows. 'How about coming for oysters and a pint of Guinness?'

'Then what? I'm a happily married woman. Mr Shotton isn't far away.'

'How far?'

'Never you mind. I expect he's still got his revolver somewhere. I don't give him any cause to use it.'

'So why does he have you spied on?'

'Because he's that sort of man. Needs to think he owns a woman. But that gives her a weakness to work on.'

Albert put his arm around her waist. Gulls rose and retreated as they walked, dropping back on the hard brown sand beyond an invisible arc of danger. 'So have you got him where you want him?'

'We fight sometimes and he doesn't always win. He's a funny mixture. I have plans for him he doesn't know about yet. Buying me a little car. Moving to London. He has some peculiar reason I can't get to the bottom of for wanting to live in South Wales, but I shall get us to Kensington before I've finished. Might even come round to having a baby, as long as there was a nurse and a nanny.'

It wasn't disloyalty to her husband. Albert, incongruous on Swansea sands in sharp-toed shoes and a wide-brimmed hat like an assassin's, was a visitor from the other side of the world, too far away for it to matter. She might as well have been talking to the gulls for all the relevance an old pal from the theatre had to her life in this town, this hole. His propositions were friendly, not passionate, and all she needed to say was, 'Now then, Alberto!', making him hoot with laughter and run his hand down the rump of her skirt before taking it away and slapping his own wrist.

No Guinness and oysters at the Mackworth, then. What she was tempted to say yes to was a little gathering of artistes at the Empire after the second house that evening – just a drink and a sandwich to celebrate the birthday of Herbert de Vere, England's Premier Pianist.

'He wasn't bad,' conceded Mamie. 'Nice-looking boy.'

'Not your sort. More a man's sort, if you see what I mean. Stage door about ten? Come on, you'll enjoy it.'

Watery sand, mirroring watery skies. Echoes from far away; the Verona Girls, rehearsing on chilly mornings, thighs goose-pimpled; scenes as remote as China.

Because ten o'clock was too late to be seen going out by Mrs Hearn, she sat through the show again. It was much as before, except in the second half, when Zelleski came on. First came the juggling that went wrong, the mistakes made with dexterity and overlaid with patter about what the missus would do to him when he got the sack; then the build-up to the climactic spinning of twenty-four plates on pointed sticks, accompanied by Zelleski's cries of despair, with the manager appearing in a dinner jacket and standing with arms folded, shaking his head.

The routine was ancient: apparent disaster, ultimate triumph. Mamie wasn't bothering to look. Then a plate crashed. Racing down the line, Zelleski panicked and gave a clumsy spin that lost another. Suddenly he screamed, 'Sod it!' and swept them all away. The manager vanished. A few people laughed and a mock-posh voice from the gallery shouted, 'I say, cheps, was that meant to heppen?' Zelleski kicked a broken plate into the stalls, where fortunately it landed in the aisle, and slouched off the stage. The orchestra gave a triumphant fanfare. The curtain came down.

The party was held in the biggest dressing room, which Dolly Elsworthy shared with Margot and Marje, comediennes. Zelleski sat in a corner, looking pale, gulping champagne every time the pianist brought him a glass; they were evidently close, and Herbert kept giving the juggler's shoulder affectionate squeezes.

'Come and meet the poor devil, real name Alf,' said Albert, and took Mamie over. The theatre manager was conspicuously absent. 'Mamie used to have an act herself,' said Albert. 'They were the Dancing Glens to start with, then the Five Verona Girls.'

'Then the Four Verona Girls. We just faded away.'

'With dignity, I hope,' said Zelleski. 'More than some people manage.'

Herbert de Vere was hovering, this time without champagne. Mamie heard him say, 'Do stop moaning, Alf. No point ruining the party.'

'Your party, you mean. That's all you care about. You, you, you.'

'If we're going to quarrel, let's do it in private.'

'Right. I'm ready to go.'

'Well I'm not.'

Mamie told flattering untruths to Dolly Elsworthy. She found kind words for Hector & Lolletta, Song and Dance on the Unsupported Ladder. The room was crammed with people laughing, gesturing, drinking, fog banks of cigarette smoke across the bulbed mirrors. Herbert claimed to have heard of the Five Verona Girls. It obviously wasn't true but Mamie swayed happily, sipping her drink, ears roaring with the noise, savouring the glittery, empty moments. Talk, talk, talk; echoes of another life.

Dolly thought someone should go and see where Alf had got to, and asked Mamie to hold her glass while she went herself. A minute or two later she was heard screaming. The men rushed out. 'There's been an accident,' said Lolletta. 'Oh my God.'

'Brace yourselves,' said Albert. He had returned on his own. 'Alf has had an accident.'

'There, I told you.'

'He's dead. Hanged himself with a fly rope.' Lolletta fainted, crumpling expertly into a chair. 'They've cut him down and somebody's gone for the police. Mamie, you'd better not be here. They'll question everyone,' and he explained that Mamie was a married woman with a difficult husband.

They were out and walking down Oxford Street by the time the bell of the police car was heard. Her legs were like cardboard. A late tram took them to the western terminus and they walked the rest. Afraid to be on her own, she went with him to his lodgings, one of the no-questions-asked houses that upset Mrs Hearn.

There they slid from coffee boiled on a gas ring to talking about the dead man to comforting themselves in bed. Mamie hadn't meant it to happen. Once it did, she relished the experience as much as she used to in the past with a brand-new lover. Albert told her silly stories and licked her ears and made her feel unmarried. Just for once she didn't have to put up with George. 'You – are – delicious,' Albert mouthed at her, and fell asleep as soon as they finished. She found herself waking him up after half an hour and asking for more; from now on, she thought, George had better look out.

Mamie crept in to Mrs Hearn's without being seen, although next day she made a point of explaining about the old friends from theatre days, female friends naturally, who made her join them for supper. Flo had to promise to say nothing to Mr Shotton, who wouldn't understand. 'Our secret!' she agreed. Mamie could only hope.

It was a week or more before George was there next. The inquest had come and gone, reported in the *Post* under a poetical three-decker headline, 'Juggler's Tragic End after Lapse at Empire. Dies By Own Hand. Broken Plates.' Albert was back in the Smoke, and Mamie had looked in on Captain Andrews for a chat. Her browbeaten days were over.

As if he smelled rebelliousness, and wanted to show her who was boss, George waited till she was having a soak in Mrs Hearn's bath and found a letter from Norah, written weeks earlier, in her handbag.

He tried to say it was on the kitchen windowsill ('Windowsill my eye,' said Mamie) and began to quote from it.

'"Everyone thinks your idea is splendid, Nancy is out of the Waacs now and would love to see Charlie again." That's the one who deals in stolen goods. "Masses of people would love to see you again . . . Ma can find beds . . . six at a push . . . Get old George to cough up the rail fare." That's what I am now, is it? Old George. "You sound very fed up. Try telling him to his face he's a pig." A pig? How can you let Norah write you letters like this?'

She sniffled and went into the bedroom for a clean handkerchief, pushed the door behind her and got George's valise from under the bed. Tit for tat. All she could find was a letter in his own handwriting, but it would serve to make the point.

She returned to the living room, reading it aloud. '"Dear Everard, These are testing times for both of us. My life has not been easy of late." I thought Everard was your brother. I thought he was dead.'

'Give it to me, please. It's private.'

'So's mine.'

'Just give it to me.'

'Swap you for it.'

She eluded him as he tried to grab the letter; saw a yellowish look in his eyes; was knocked sideways by a blow to the side of her head, and fell on the carpet.

He drew the curtains and stood with the letter in his hand,

watching her. 'You are putting on an act,' he said. 'I only gave you a push.'

'A pig is what you are. I shall leave you.'

'You upset me. Everard and I were very close.'

'If he's dead, why are you writing him letters?' She had a singing in her ears. 'I don't believe he's dead at all.'

'You may be surprised to know that I don't either. But officially . . .' He showed her a cutting from his wallet: 'Lieutenant Everard Shotton, Durham Light Infantry, *missing, presumed killed*.'

'Sorry, baby,' she said, ready to be friends, but only if he tried. 'I really am sorry. You never talk about him. You never talk about your family.'

'Shall we change the subject? The matter's closed.' He was unapproachable; wrapped in himself. He started peeling an apple, humming a wartime tune, the one about packing up your troubles in your old kitbag.

'You shouldn't have gone to my handbag. You shouldn't have hit me either. I shall write to Pa and tell him.'

'Tell him what you like. I didn't touch you. You're making it up.'

There was no sense to be got out of him. He left her a pound for groceries when he went off to Llanelly docks in the morning.

After the boys had gone to school she went downstairs to see Mrs Hearn. 'Flo,' she said, 'is this nearly a black eye?' She lifted up her hair. 'Is this a bruise? Have I imagined it?'

'Mr Shotton said you'd had a fall. He looked in on his way to the station.'

'He punched me,' said Mamie.

The point was difficult to get across. Mrs Hearn suggested a cold compress; Mamie's account of a quarrel about a letter had to contend with wet bandages and the reassurance that 'least said, soonest mended' had served the Hearn household well. Safety-pinned, she looked like one of the war-wounded whose photos were in the *Post* as more heroes came home.

'There,' said Flo. 'I expect worse things happened when you were one of the Veronas.'

'Unwanted sexual advances, yes,' said Mamie tartly. 'Biffs on the head, no.'

Flo drew up her chair. 'Must have been risky, having champagne suppers in a private room. Did you slap 'em in the face or threaten 'em with the cheese knife, ha ha?'

Presently Mamie asked to borrow a pound till Mr Shotton came back; removed the bandage and put on make-up; packed a suitcase and left the house while Flo was out shopping; pawned the watch again, sent Norah a telegram, and caught a London train at High Street.

Twenty minutes later smoking chimneys had given way to the meadowy Vale of Glamorgan, and a stranger had already invited her to take tea with him after Cardiff, where they put the buffet car on.

16

The Compton Hotel had moved with the times. Gone were the sticky leather chairs in the lobby and the snug where tarts in hats with feathers lay in wait for naval officers. In peacetime the officers were fewer, the women less tolerated. The boss-eyed manager of the Alhambra still drank there with his cronies and boasted about that week's female attractions. George still avoided the circle; Oscar James, whenever their visits to Liverpool coincided, still tried to draw him in.

'You're not looking yourself, old man,' he said, catching up with George in the Smoking Room where he had gone to read *Lloyd's List* in peace. 'Try and get out more in the evenings. I have been hearing about Samuel's in Horse Street where they do select shows for gents and the police turn a blind eye. Just harmless fun. After all, we are bachelors when we're up here.'

'So we are. I am seeing a doctor shortly. I'll ask him if the excitement would kill me.'

A youngish tart in a green hat caught his eye when he took a turn down Church Street before going to bed. A man didn't stroll there by himself late on a summer's evening without expecting female attention. Most of us came to a tart or two in our time. George raised his hat to show there was no ill feeling and kept going, back to the Compton, to his striped pyjamas that a chambermaid had touched and a mattress that naked women must have lain on.

A man without the right woman was at the mercy of his

warped imagination, if that was what God had given him. Mamie, who was as salacious in real life as anything he was able to invent, had saved him from all that. When he went into a register office and perjured himself, it wasn't only that he was afraid of not being able to sleep with her any more, of having to hand her over to men who would. Marrying her wasn't lust pure and simple. It was so he could be freed from something in his nature, which only Mamie could achieve.

What he had failed to recognise was that life with Mamie would be a more violent business than life with May. What happened when a passionate marriage got out of hand? What happened if you had the same need of her as before?

All he could do was hope for the best. Lack of money had already driven her to write. Mrs Hearn, who knew where he was staying, forwarded a letter after a week. It said she had decided to leave England and go to South America, where English dancers were in huge demand. He might hear of her one day in Cuba (her geography was shaky), another chorus girl gone to the bad. Or she might remain in London after all, where going to the bad was just as easy. What did it matter where she went? 'PS, I am staying with Norah. We are going to Kew Gardens tomorrow. I have no money and am living on charity.'

What was he supposed to do, send her a wire saying, 'HERE'S A FIVER. ALL FORGIVEN'? Loving a girl didn't mean letting her do as she liked. Furthermore his health was suffering. Eggins found the nerves as frayed as ever; detected a faint systolic murmur of the heart that might or might not be of consequence. 'Working too hard?' he said. 'Pace of modern living? The wife in good health?'

'I have dreams about my brother who was posted missing in France. I am convinced he's alive. But in the dreams he's dead.'

'Deep waters,' said Eggins offhandedly, and wrote a prescription for a sleeping draught, adding that all in all, George wasn't doing badly for a man of thirty-eight.

'Thirty-nine.'

Eggins's voice rumbled after him as he left: take decent holidays, smoke a good cigar, give the heart a chance.

But one knew oneself better than anyone else did. It was Mamie he ached for, Mamie who was giving him a systolic murmur, whatever that might be.

Oscar's music hall was as ghastly as he expected. It was 3 July, two years to the day since George walked into Kings Cinema and saw Mamie. Too restless to sleep, he went out again after saying good night to Oscar and found the girl in the green hat. Under it were curls with a faint resemblance to Mamie's. Name: Katie. Price: half a guinea. She kept a room in a backstreet hotel; was clean enough; had grey eyes; bucked and kicked under him as if she was enjoying it, fabricating love as Mamie might have done the night they met.

What if Mamie had been willing to sleep with him straightaway at the Golden Lion and take a pound for her services? Would he ever have seen her again; ever have gone mad and married her? Instead there had been that business of drawing his fingers across her breasts and starting up a different process altogether.

Katie, even followed by strong pills and Globéol, didn't result in much of a night's sleep. In the Smoking Room before breakfast he wrote, 'Darling mine, let us start afresh,' and ended the nightmare. 'It is two years yesterday since we met. Two years to the day! Can you imagine how unhappy I was all night? I know you're unhappy too. I won't get cross when we are together because I know I'm so much uglier then. I dare say we have both been stubborn and selfish. Little darling wife, you must return to your husband George. *Come at once, wifey.*'

In honour of her return they stayed at the Adelphi, where there was also less chance of prying eyes. Bowls of carnations and a half-bottle of champagne were waiting for her when she arrived in the evening, unbearably pretty in a green silk dress he had not seen before. 'Mm!' she said, flushed with excitement, and was enthralled by the private bathroom – smelling the jars of bath salts, running water over her hand to see how hot it was.

They sat drinking the champagne, traffic rumbling below in Ranelagh Street, dust rising in the golden air. London had been uneventful. No Charlie, no Nancy, nobody but Norah and her family. Only the visit to Kew, and a picnic in Richmond Park, and a boat down the river to Greenwich; innocent outings that he wanted to believe in and had no good reason to doubt. As for 'old George' and other epithets, Norah had been told firmly not to use them.

He kneeled by the chair to undo her blouse.

'Speed merchant,' she said. 'I bet you've been naughty with somebody since I went.' She used her dreamy voice; her eyes were closed, teasing him. 'Was she pretty?'

'Ravishing. Her name was Mamie. I must have dreamed it. Such dreams! How about you?'

'I don't go in for men. Only my husband.'

'Truth?'

The eyes opened. 'As I live.'

'So we're happy again.'

'Bliss, isn't it?' She watched his fingers on her breasts. 'I had an idea in London –'

She was interrupted by a knock on the door and a voice saying, 'Room Service,' and went to run a bath while George admitted a waiter with a trolley. Supper was unloaded. The waiter hung the 'Do Not Disturb' sign as he left. George replaced his clothes with a dressing gown and waited. Mamie sang, splashed, scrubbed, crooned with pleasure as if she had a baby in the bathroom, or as if she was the baby herself; came out swathed in towel; took in the basket of bread, the trio of cheeses (one of them French and smelly), slab of butter, salad bowl, fruit bowl, bottle of dark red wine; remembered, he was relieved to see.

'The first night we slept together,' she said. 'You were going to take me somewhere and we didn't go. All there was in the larder was bread and cheese.' She let the towel slip and seized a knife. 'I'm ravenous.'

Food before love hadn't been part of the plan, but he was in an accommodating mood. He stroked her spine and watched crumbs lodge in her pubic hair as they lay propped up against pillows. 'This idea I had in London,' she said. 'Shall I tell you about it?'

He held a glass for her to drink. A few drops spilt between her breasts but she wiped them off with a corner of sheet before he had time to use his tongue.

'I thought,' she said, 'why don't we go and live in Kensington?'

Was she mad? He drew circles on her thighs and gave a string of reasons – cost of property, inconvenience *re* west-coast ports, the medical climatologists' view that neurasthenics were at risk in damp and chilly areas like those near the parks.

'Couldn't you say, "one day"?'

'If it's all that important. One day we might.'

'I like London, you see. Can't help it. Went there first in 1912. Charlie had a cousin, lived in Hampstead. It was when the Dancing Glens had fallen through and we were trying to organise the Veronas. We stayed there for a week. It was heaven. I floated. I was nearly nineteen. Do you wish you'd met me then? I didn't know a thing. I was like a child.'

She seemed to dangle her innocence in front of him. Pulling up the sheet to cover her breasts, she told him why she turned 'Amy' into 'Mamie'. When they were in Hampstead, Charlie had shown her a newspaper article about an artiste called Mamie Stuart. This other Mamie had gone to an engagement in a city called Buenos Aires in South America. When she got there, the manager wanted her to sing a rude song about a 'Little Pink Pettie from Peter'. It meant taking off her skirt and performing in her petticoat.

'I've heard of worse things.'

'She caught the next boat back to England and had the law on them. She got hundreds of pounds.'

'So when you called yourself "Mamie", there were two of you with the same name. What was the point?'

'I didn't think of it like that. It sounded glamorous, and I had more right to it than she did. Her real name was Annie Danks. All I had to do was change the "Amy". Go on, laugh at me.'

'I'm touched.'

'Thought I was going to be famous. Spent ten pounds I didn't have on my teeth. Who was going to see when I was up on the stage? I ask you, George, I was so green. Dare say I still am. Need looking after.'

Traces of innocence were soon competing with noise of bedsprings; Amy the sweet child versus Mamie the little whore. They were two nights at the Adelphi before George was due at King's Dock, Swansea, after which he would be off again. He let her spend money on clothes in Liverpool; even let her talk him into having their photograph taken, something he had been cautious about in the past. They collected the prints before leaving and looked at them on the South Wales train. George had kept his hat on, a trilby that hid his hair and came down almost to the eyebrows. Mamie's latest hat, with rose motif, shadowed her face, an oval brooch clipped to the deep vee of her blouse. 'I shall have it framed,' she said. George wondered if he could burn it when she wasn't looking.

Flags were out in the town when they arrived on Friday

afternoon. Mrs Hearn, warned by telegram, had their apartment clean and aired. She had stuck a magazine picture in a downstairs window, showing the King and Queen entwined with laurel leaves. No one had told Mamie that Saturday was Peace Day, a treaty having been signed at last. 'Hasn't it been peace since last year?' she asked George.

'That was an armistice. The treaty makes it official. If you read a newspaper you'd know these things.'

'I've got a hubby who can do all that.'

He smiled at such helplessness, knowing he was supposed to smile at it. Sweet little monkey; cunning little monkey.

After consulting papers at his lock-up in Swansea – he kept his secrets there now – he decided he must spend some more of May's money, and wrote to the bank. He also added a letter to the thick Everard file that was beginning to smell of old paper. Survey reports that had been there for weeks, left for signature by the typist he borrowed from a shipping agent, had to be dealt with. That was all, apart from circulars that had been pushed under the door; one of which wasn't a circular but a letter in May's handwriting.

He tapped his fingers on the table; shadows went to and fro in the corridor, past the frosted glass; he read the letter a second time. The hotel in Tenby where she was taking Arthur had been damaged in a fire, but they had kindly found her somewhere else by the sea. It was called the George and was at the Mumbles. May and Arthur were arriving on Peace Day, and hoped he would spend a little time with them. She had no idea where he was, and Oscar was away, but Miss Boulton in his office said she could try Adelaide Chambers. At the end was a row of Xs, with 'These are from Arthur.'

His initial feeling of alarm didn't last. They would be tucked away there on Saturday, settling in, and on Sunday he left Swansea for Scotland. He might even drop in on them as a surprise before he left. The neatness of the plan appealed to him. If he rearranged his schedule he could spend the morning with the boy and still have time to be on the Clyde by midday on Monday. He liked the idea of going from one Mrs Shotton to the other, four miles at most along the bay; one step ahead, as always. His telegram said simply, 'WILL LOOK IN SUNDAY ABOUT TEN.'

Saturday was overcast and cool. Mamie planned to spend the day reorganising her wardrobe, 'so I won't spend too much money', as she put it. George went along the road to the cricket field, where bands and speeches could be heard, echoing over the sands. Flags at half-mast and laurel wreaths; march past of ex-soldiers in suits; rounds of applause as the Mayor presented medals for bravery in what was now history, that limbo where Everard was; sporting events, including a blindfold race for disabled men and a 100-yards race for men with one leg. George saw no bitterness in the faces, but he wondered what Everard would have made of it.

'I shed a tear,' he told Mamie.

'I've been reading the *Post*, like you said. There's a bonfire and dancing on Mumbles Hill tonight. Could we go to that?'

'Kilvey Hill sounds better. The one above the docks.'

It was unlikely that May would take the boy out after dark. But she was inclined to spoil him, and George couldn't take the risk. He and Mamie joined the crowd on Kilvey, a bleak hillside where a choir sang hymns in the gloom, before rockets and maroons shot up from ships below them in the docks, and the bonfire began roaring like a blowtorch in the damp southwesterly wind, sending trains of sparks to ignite fires higher up the hill. The fire brigade arrived, skidding on the grass; it was too windy for dancing; the two of them gave up and went back to Trafalgar Terrace, Mamie begging him to stop and buy fish and chips on the way, which he let her have as a treat.

The house was silent, Mrs Hearn and the boys still out at

one of the many bonfires. Mamie asked solicitously if there was any medicine he ought to be taking – something she had not done before – and insisted on making him a cup of a concoction called Vi-Cocoa before they went to bed. She read him what it said on the tin: '"Pick-me-up for brain and body . . . nourishing effects on nerve centres . . . direct aids to digestion . . ."'

'I believe you really are fond of me,' he said.

He slept in her arms, and in the morning she packed his valise as neatly as it was done every time he left Penarth. 'You remind me of my first wife,' he said, 'the way you tuck things in with the tips of your fingers.'

'Why notice it now?' said Mamie, and shut the clasp. 'I've packed for you before.'

'She and I came to Swansea once.' He let the two women drift together, halves of a single secret. 'I keep these things to myself.'

'So you should. Tell me how long you'll be away.'

'A week? You'll be a good girl?'

'Always am. Going down to Flo in an hour to learn how to cook a Sunday roast. Think of me making mint sauce.'

'Think of me on the train. It's from Victoria, so you'll hear me going past at nine fifty-eight.'

'I'll wave.' She looked at her watch, retrieved yet again from the pawnshop. 'You'd better hurry.'

He saw her at the window, flapping her handkerchief, and she might have seen his face against the glass of the compartment. At 10.03 the train stopped at Mumbles Road, a shed-and-platform halt halfway along Swansea Bay, where the main line left the coast to go north, out of the town. George got off, and waited for the next Mumbles train to arrive from Swansea on the electric track. The air was warmer; when the train came, children with bathing costumes rolled up in towels were sitting at the front.

Another five-minute journey, this time to Southend, last-but-one stop before the terminus at the pier. The tide was out, but the usually desolate sands were enlivened with families on holiday. Deckchairs had been lined up under the sea wall, and the frame of a Punch and Judy show was propped against a kiosk.

A few steps and George reached the George, set back behind a yard that sloped down to the road. He saw Arthur at once, playing with a toy lorry. May appeared and handed him a canvas bag containing two spades, a child's cricket bat and a hard rubber ball. In return he gave her his hat to look after. 'Luncheon is at half-past twelve,' she said. 'I shall have a lazy morning. Try not to let him fall in the water.'

Father and son crossed to the beach. George took off shoes and socks and rolled up his trouser-legs. There was no danger. He helped Arthur dam a stream and bowled to him on a whaleback of hard sand, out towards the sea, which was creeping in, pressing walkers and dam-builders back towards the promenade. At the far end of the bay, part of the smudge along the foreshore must be Trafalgar Terrace. Was that the secret life or was this? 'My long-suffering May!' he wrote to Everard, preparing phrases in his head, as he often did. 'There were tears when I took my leave.'

A man in a check cap was setting up the Punch and Judy on a strip of grass by the sea wall when they returned. George hurried them through the meal, which included a bony fish that tasted of soap (he thought fondly of Mamie, studying the mysteries of gravy four miles away), and began to say his goodbyes over the biscuits and cheese.

'You promised to stay for the Punch and Judy,' piped Arthur.

'I hope the boy isn't turning into a liar.'

'I promised on your behalf. Half-past two, across the road. Do stay. I made inquiries about a taxi in case you were in a hurry. There's a place along the road.'

'You sound like your stepmother,' he said. 'Very well, as long as a car is available.'

The usual crowd had come from nowhere, and George hoisted Arthur on to his shoulder so he could see better, while May held his leg to steady him. Ten minutes later the fighting was over and Judy's corpse had been thrown out. Jack Ketch was about to hang Mr Punch – a child shouted, 'Oh no you don't!' – when George heard a man call, 'Come on, Mamie, you've seen enough.'

When he turned, Mamie was a few yards behind him, standing on tiptoe to see the puppets. She was in the green silk dress. Her eyes shifted to his, and her hand went up to her mouth as she took in Arthur – who had twisted around so as not to miss Mr Punch turning the tables on Jack Ketch – and May, who was holding the boy steady.

The voice called, 'Ma-mie!' again. It came from a newish motor that might have been a Ford, parked a short way along the main road. The driver's seat was on the far side, so George couldn't see his face, and Mamie was gone in a second. The door slammed and the car drove towards the Mumbles. Jack Ketch dangled from his rope. May said, 'You have gone as white as a sheet. Come along, Arthur, off Daddy's shoulder at once.'

'It was the fish we ate,' said George, and hurried back to the hotel so he could pretend to be sick in the lavatory. He was proud of his resourcefulness when he came to look back. Within a quarter of an hour he had taken May and Arthur out of the hotel, in the taxi with their luggage; he had to consider what Mamie would do, what inquiries she would make. 'That fish you gave us was off,' he told the proprietor, banging money on the counter. 'You don't want a scene? Nor do I. But I have the health of my sister-in-law and her son to consider.'

They went to the first place he could think of, the Langland Bay Hotel, at a safe distance along the Gower coast. The only room available was expensive. May kept saying there was no need, she was sure the kitchen at the George was spotless, but he insisted that his wife and son deserved something better, told Arthur he would post him a shrimping net and a pair of water wings, and was driven off to High Street station across the other side of the town.

The London train that was part of his rearranged timetable left in half an hour. Hot, stale air in the carriage was choking him. How could she have done it? At least he knew the truth about her now. The fact that she might think she knew the truth about him was unimportant. One had to believe in oneself. He could wriggle out of anything.

17

Sunderland was a safe distance from Swansea. London would have been safer still, but without money it wasn't a practical place to be. Mamie didn't leave for twenty-four hours, during which she tried without success to solve the mystery of George, the child and the woman; sleeping with the door locked and furniture piled against it in case he came back. Mrs Hearn, dying of curiosity, saw her off from the station. Mamie went home.

Her arrival alerted Edith to a crisis. So did the clothes that Mamie brought with her to Hawarden Crescent. Visiting the house, Edith was angry at the garments that overflowed into the front parlour. What could a girl do with so many skirts? She hoped it wasn't extravagance that was at the root of whatever the trouble was that they were being kept in total ignorance of. 'When girls leave their husbands,' she said, 'they live to rue the day.'

'Who said anything about leaving him? He needs teaching a lesson.'

'If George has done something wrong, the sooner we know about it the better.'

'George is just George.' Mamie had no idea how it was going to end, but confiding in her sister was hardly going to help. Either she stayed married to him or she took her chances as the wife without means, living on . . . what? Family charity? Disreputable men? Jobs for women had evaporated after the war. Before the end of the year she would be twenty-six. Her friends were married or moving in that direction. Norah was engaged to Edgar at last. Charlie claimed to be working on a rich American, aged sixty, with a weak heart. Nancy still wanted to share a flat, but Mamie had gone off the idea. Taking all that into account, she didn't mean to let George go if she could help it. When Edith warned about ruing the day, Mamie knew she was right, although she refrained from saying so. But hanging on to your husband was one thing. What if the husband you hung on to was as unpredictable as George?

Edith was even rattier than usual. The weather was hot and she was pregnant, an event that everyone had tried and failed to keep from Dolly. Mamie found it ridiculous that the child knew her mother was having a baby, without having the slightest idea what having a baby meant, and tried to enlighten her. The brother she was hoping for before the end of the year was at this very moment inside her mama (though it might turn out be a sister), and was the reason why mamas in general sometimes had large tummies. No, it was not put there ready-made by the angels; it grew from a tiny seed.

Edith called her a wicked woman after Dolly went home bursting with questions about seeds and tummies, and said they didn't want small children exposed to that sort of talk in Sunderland. Wicked Mamie-Amy. She bought sweets for Dolly and told her to keep her eyes open when the baby came, and if she saw any storks or angels, Auntie Mame would pay her a pound.

'Why not give the kid straight answers?' Mamie asked her sister, foolishly inviting the response that if they were talking about straight answers, what about Mamie giving some for a change? For instance, Edith knew that she was in touch with her husband. A letter had been seen arriving at Hawarden Crescent.

'Pity you weren't there or you could have steamed it open.'

'I will ignore that. Does George intend coming to Sunderland?'

'You never know when he'll appear. Or disappear. Whoosh-bang! If you really want to know, I'm frightened of him. He's always up to something. He's like a man who's leading another life.'

Her sister pounced on the words, but Mamie refused to say more. Nothing was clear to her either. George's letter was mainly about her misbehaviour – always suspected it – weakness for anything in trousers – solemn promises reneged upon – travesty of oaths on Bibles – Captain Andrews presumed to be in motorcar – wronged husbands could claim damages – what a scandal for *News of the World* – clean breast the only answer. As for his side of things, explanation was simple – had his dear brother not disappeared in Flanders? – was there not a wife and child? – did George not have obligations? – was grief to be besmirched by unwarranted suspicions? Mamie seemed to hear a comedian cackling, 'I say, I say, I say. That was no lady you saw me with, that was my sister-in-law.' But she knew it wasn't a laughing matter.

The anguish made George ill. He couldn't stop imagining her with men. The glimpse he had of Albert's private parts, that time he pointed the gun at his head and made him reveal his lack of underpants, kept coming back to him with abominable clarity. He dwelled on her copulations, imagining pubic hairs matted into hers, her legs jerking in time with someone's spotty loins. Once he locked himself in his room at Adelaide Chambers and put the revolver in his mouth. The barrel had a bitter taste; he took it out again.

By now she would have received his furious letter of rebuke, together with a list of addresses where she could send her abject apologies as he travelled about the country. There was nothing in Liverpool. In South Wales he attended a Royal Mail steamer stranded off the Gower coast; at the Grosvenor Hotel,

Edwards handed him a picture postcard from Sunderland on which was written 'Liar'.

At Penarth he arrived in a rage, to be told that his father-in-law was ill.

'He strained his heart in America,' said May. 'I think Elizabeth tried to make him do too much.'

The doctors were keeping him in bed. George, visiting him, thought how gaunt he looked, his beard too big for his face, listening despondently to Elizabeth's throaty voice describing American cities, American food, an American wilderness called the Adirondacks that her friends insisted on taking them to.

'I'm not surprised about your father's heart,' George said later. 'I felt tired just listening to her.'

'I wish they hadn't gone there in the first place. But there's no talking to Elizabeth. She likes to get her own way.' She looked across at him, one armchair signalling to another in the pause before the curtains were drawn. 'I mustn't be unkind, because she was very good to me when you and I were going through a bad patch.'

Was this supposed to be a good patch? They lived in a deepening shadow of contradictions. For the first time in two years there was no one else to go to. Arthur had started school, a house, with iron fire escapes, called Penarth College that would drain more pounds away. Mavis the nursemaid had gone. What had been the 'Nursery' was now 'Arthur's room'; his school cap and satchel hung on pegs, and May began referring to him as 'our little man', signs of a future that George wished he wasn't there to notice. He was at Penarth more often now, a normal man in a normal marriage, except that he had to discourage his wife from visiting him in the spare room. May waggling her limbs in the air, making herself more amenable just as Mamie was making herself less so, was too much to bear. He took the Eggins's specials from their hiding place and flushed them away like poison.

Her girl friends were easier to talk to than her family. Mamie gave them speculative versions of the story. George had written another angry letter after she called him a liar, so there was more to speculate about. 'Old George has a fancy woman in South Wales,' she wrote to Norah. 'Isn't it priceless?' To Charlie she said, 'Do you know what I suspect the man's doing? Behaving improperly with his sister-in-law. Her husband has been missing since the war. I saw them together.'

With Kitty she did some showing off. 'Went for a spin with a friend in his motor, and told him to stop because there was a Punch and Judy on the prom. I loved them when I was small – remember they often had one down by the North Pier? A chap in the crowd turned round and it was my husband. He should have been in a train on his way to Scotland. I don't know which of us was more surprised. Of course, he twigged I was with a fellow.'

'So what happened?'

'I didn't think. I ran for the car. Our marriage is all ups and downs. The week before, he took me to the Adelphi Hotel in Liverpool and we had a suite with a bathroom. He can be generous when he feels like it.'

'Lucky you,' said Kitty, coating a dummy with raspberry jam and thrusting it in a baby's mouth. 'But then . . . why risk it? Is he kind to you?'

'From time to time.'

'Do you love him?'

'It's no use asking me questions. It's the kind of life we lead.' The story lost its edge; she was Mamie in a smoky back kitchen, frightened, not knowing what to do. 'I wish sometimes I'd never met him,' she said. 'You don't know the half.' Kitty was cutting bacon for her husband's tea. 'He was with a woman and a little boy. That's why he was at the Punch and Judy.'

'What was his explanation?'

'He lost a brother in the war and that was his wife.'

'So why did he say he was going to Scotland?'

'Oh, wanted to keep that side of his life separate. Grieves all the time for his brother and isn't able to talk about it with anyone. Yards of stuff. Can't stand the sister-in-law. Nasty little boy. My George is very convincing. He writes a good letter.'

'But you aren't convinced.'

'I could be if I wanted to.'

Her future could be anything she chose. Marriage was not her prison, as it was Kitty's; the riveter husband appeared in the yard as they were talking, and Mamie didn't stay. She walked through windy, treeless streets, past the town hall where they got married, thinking how she had taken a fancy to George because you had to marry somebody in the end, and the years were passing, and he aroused feelings of tenderness that she liked to find she had in herself. The tenderness had almost gone but the years were passing faster than ever.

In ten minutes she was to meet a chap at the Golden Lion. They had been going out for a week. He was an ex-warrant officer in the Engineers called Eddie, who was starting a rabbit farm at Whitburn. George was far away, so far she wondered if she would ever see him again.

She hadn't told Kitty how she went back next day to where the Punch and Judy had been, having thought about it all night. A quiet morning; light drizzle; no deckchairs. Perhaps woman, child and George were in a guesthouse sitting room, hoping the sky would clear. She began with the hotel opposite and found she was right first time.

'I am looking for my friends the Shottons,' she told a porter in a green apron. Ah, he said, a Mrs Shotton and her little boy had been and gone. Fumbling with her purse, she asked where they had gone to. He couldn't say, ma'am. They were whisked away yesterday by a man who said he was her brother-in-law, after some unpleasantness over a piece of fish which had only been out of the sea five minutes.

'I wonder,' said Mamie, handing over a coin, 'if these can be the right Shottons. Do you happen to know where the lady travelled from?'

'Was it Port Talbot?' said the porter. 'I tell a lie. It was Penarth.' Then the proprietor appeared, the porter vanished with his shilling, and it was made plain to Mamie that information about guests was confidential. Later on she looked up Penarth in a railway guide.

Eddie was a big bushy-haired man for whose benefit she removed her wedding ring and called herself Miss Stuart. They spent the night at his cottage, rented along with acres of sandy soil that he was busy fencing. Over breakfast he talked about the economics of rabbit farming and said shyly that a girl might do worse than take up with someone who was sitting on a little goldmine like the rabbit, which bred at a prodigious rate.

To stop herself giggling she said that rabbit on a plate made her feel ill, and changed the subject. She had been meaning to ask somebody for ages how one would set about discovering if a person of a particular name lived in a particular town. Eddie thought a bit and said, 'Electoral register.' That might do it, if the person had the vote. Now could they get back to rabbits?

Tyneside again, Mamie country; equinoctial weather, wind and rain sweeping the decks of steamers; a family gathering at Gateshead. Shotton senior had written to say that they intended to place a memorial to Everard in St Chad's, their local church; he was informing George as a courtesy. There was no deflecting them. His mother sobbed when George said he had no wish to see a brass plate in the Chapel of Remembrance. Any statement about 'b. 1886, d. 1918' was unverified. 'As you know,' he said, 'I went to Flanders, and I have my reasons for thinking he is still alive.'

'You need your head seeing to. Hasn't your mother suffered enough?'

It was no use: the thought of it made him shudder, Everard pinned under the weight of a brass plate inscribed in curly black-and-scarlet letters, alongside all the other plates, plaques, slabs of marble and the Book of the Fallen, one name per page, lit behind glass, a page turned every day until they reached the end and began again, for all eternity. He couldn't stop them; he wouldn't help them.

Chrissie came with him when he left. She had taken the morning off from the fever hospital, where she was now assistant matron, and George drove her there in a hired motor. Red knuckles in starched lap; polite questions about his wife and child.

'Arthur has started school. He has a dog that eats socks. May keeps in reasonable health. I have to remind myself that we have been married fourteen years. But I must have been away from home for the equivalent of ten of them. Under those circumstances, estrangement comes naturally.' The words slipped out. He drove fast across a bridge and a cyclist waved his fist. 'Marriage is a rum business.'

'Better not say that. I am getting married next spring.'

He stopped the car with a jerk and leaned over to kiss her. Women coming out of a factory gate waved to them. 'You're a dark horse, aren't you?' he said, his pleasure tinged with regret that the austere Christiana, single till her mid-thirties, had gone the way of all flesh. His name was Dick Vanderven; an electrical engineer, based in Gateshead, who travelled to power stations that used his company's turbines. 'He's older than me,' she said quickly. 'Thirteen years, to be exact.' She produced a photograph, and there he was, the bachelor with a weak chin, going thin on top, parents doubtless dead.

Would George come to the wedding at St Chad's? Of course he would. And bring May with him? Well, if it could be arranged.

The hospital appeared on the skyline, a red-brick tower with a clock; fields and grazing land around it, in case germs blew out of the isolation wards. 'So you and May are estranged,' she said.

'We manage.'

'I've never pryed. Was it because of your work?'

'I'm sure there are plenty of marine surveyors with happy marriages. Plenty of travelling husbands of one sort or another. I wouldn't worry about you and Dick. I myself go back to the bosom of my family from time to time. But I met a girl two years ago. That complicated things. You saw me with her on Newcastle station.'

'She was very attractive. Fond of you, I'd say.'

'Funny, I never tell anybody anything, except for Everard. I still write him letters, you know.' They pulled up on a forecourt behind an ambulance. 'She's called Mamie. Was a dancer. A single girl, very pretty, as you saw. Comes from these parts – when I was born, our parents were still in John Candlish Street, five minutes from her family. We've lived together all over the place. Now I find she's unfaithful.'

'Does she know about your wife?'

'I sincerely hope not. It's rather a mess. I have made my bed, et cetera. Actually, I've not seen her for some time. I'm waiting for her to come to her senses.'

'It wouldn't be wiser to forget all about her?'

'Very likely.' He helped Chrissie out of the car and gave her a kiss; already there was a trace of stoutness under the uniform. 'Easier said than done.' As she went up the steps he called after her, 'Write and say what you'd like for a wedding present,' but a coal lorry was going past, and she disappeared into the building without looking back.

Mamie reached the end of her tether. Farmer Eddie, bluntly handsome and not without merits in bed, fell deeper and deeper in love with rabbits. She owed money in all directions, had pawned the famous watch and the dressing-table set, and earned two pounds modelling corsets for Binns' autumn sale. Charlie, looking jaded, appeared with a Newcastle jeweller, the American having given her the slip, and there were parties in hotels and various unreliable men with motorcars. A pot-bellied dance-hall proprietor said, 'There's a fiver under the pillow in Room 11. It's yours for the taking.' Mamie almost said yes. A gust of his oniony breath saved her. After that she wrote to George to say she was missing him.

It took him a week to get there. Returning to Hawarden Crescent after a visit to the cinema, she saw her father in the street, on his way to join his tug. 'Good news!' he said. 'George has arrived in a motorcar.' A black vehicle with dirty headlamps was parked outside the house. 'He's in with your mother. He knows you're expected.'

With Ma boiling a kettle and rattling cups so as not to appear curious, Mamie put her arms around his neck and kissed him. They were reunited, sort of. His face was drawn and he had let the moustache grow again, giving him the Charlie Chaplin look that had made her smile when they first met. Perhaps there was more tenderness left than she thought.

'The tea's in the pot,' said Ma. 'I'm going out to the grocer's and the egg man's.'

'No need to go because of us,' said Mamie.

The door closed and George said, 'I'm glad you came to your senses. I shall find it hard to forgive you, but you meant a lot to me in the past.' He nodded towards the passage. 'Let us go in the bedroom.'

'Why?'

'Why do you think?'

Pushing her ahead of him, he unbuttoned his trousers and told her to lie on the bed.

'Please, Georgie,' she said. 'I can't do it now – not whoosh-bang, straight off the minute you get here.'

'You are being unreasonable. Knickers, please.'

What had she expected, butterfly kisses and a whispered 'Let's start again'? In some dim romantic corner of her brain, yes, she had. 'We'll do anything you want tonight. I'll write out some promises – you'd like that, wouldn't you?'

By this time he was climbing on top of her. She let it happen, thinking she might as well have said yes to the pot-belly and been five pounds better off.

'Enjoy that, did you?' she asked.

'We have a long way to go yet. I can't forget what happened in a hurry.'

'*You* can't forget? You do have a nerve, George. That little boy you were carrying had your mouth.'

'Hardly surprising, since he's my nephew.'

She made herself decent and dabbed some scent at random. 'You got them out of the hotel pretty fast.'

'I might have guessed you'd go back to spy on me. What a shabby way to treat your husband. If it's any of your business, the food was infected. Only your wicked imagination . . .' His voice trembled and he covered his eyes for a second. 'They are all I have left of Everard.'

She felt worn out by him already, George the spider, spinning webs of marvellous complexity. But not defeated; not any more. 'I'm fed up with our marriage,' she said. 'I want a decent place to live. I want some money of my own. I want to know where I stand.'

He had his arms folded, leaning against the wardrobe. 'How many times have you committed adultery?'

'Going for a spin in a motor isn't a crime.'

'How many times? How many men? I want to know who they were, every one.'

'I'm wicked and you're perfect, is that it?'

'I want to forgive you, but I want to know what I'm forgiving you for.'

There was something comic about his anxiety as he peered at her in the gloomy bedroom, hung with her clothes. 'What if I told you there'd been dozens?' she said.

'Have there?'

'Let's see.' She pretended to be adding up figures in her head. 'Thirty-seven in hotels, including the manager at the Grosvenor in Swansea and the hall porter at the Adelphi in Liverpool. We did it in the luggage room. And Mr Hearn in Trafalgar Terrace, when Flo was out shopping. Let's say forty in case I've missed one or two.'

'Don't try to be funny with me.'

'Motorcars, about twenty. Upstairs on a tram, once. Beaches and fields, let's say a round dozen. Are you counting, George?'

'I'd be very careful if I were you.'

'So can we stop all this?' she said. 'Let's go and spend the night at the Palatine. We could still be happy.'

'We're staying here and you'll answer my questions.'

'If you say so, but I want that cup of tea first.'

Instead of going to the kitchen she bolted through the front door and jumped into the car. George came after her, treading heavily like a stage policeman, and bent his head to speak through the window. 'Please leave the vehicle,' he said.

She gripped the wheel, pretending to drive. 'Off we go! Next stop the Palatine! One double room with all mod cons! Bread and cheese for supper!'

'You're making a spectacle of yourself.'

Children, playing in the gutter, shouted, 'Give us a ride! Take us to Roker, missus!' Motors were rare in Hawarden Crescent. She blew the horn and they cheered.

'For the last time, get out of the car.'

'Come on, Georgie. Be a sport. Let's be like we used to be.'

He pulled open the door and tried to get her hands off the steering wheel. Struggling, she let go suddenly and fell into the road, as Edith and Ma came hurrying along the pavement.

'She slipped. Didn't you, dear?'

'You dragged her out of the car,' said Edith. 'I saw you do it.'

Mamie's elbow hurt and a spot of blood came through the sleeve of her jacket. 'I don't want any fuss. Just go away, George.'

'You heard my sister,' said Edith, formidable with her thick legs and copious belly. 'I'm not having her bullied by you or anybody else.'

Faces were appearing at windows. 'Oh, damn the lot of you,' said George suddenly, and then, quietly, to Mamie, 'I always take the easy way out when I'm threatened.' He was paler than ever. 'I'm desperately sad about the state of our marriage. If I should have an accident, please forgive me and forget.'

The tyres squealed as he turned the corner, going at forty miles an hour to a dramatic death; or not, as the case might be. She would have liked to see them both as tragic figures, touched with nobility. But they were just George and Mamie.

Her sister, demanding explanations, was almost as difficult as her husband had been. Mamie told her as little as she could: they had rows, she wasn't happy.

'And he ill-treats you.'

'We ill-treat one another.'

Still, action of some sort was called for. She made sure where Penarth was, on the Glamorganshire coast, and spoke privately to Henry to say that if ever he moved furniture to or from South Wales, perhaps she could go with him. As it happened, he was taking a load to the Rhondda Valley in a week's time.

'Dear Everard, She is poisoning my life. When did her unfaithfulness start? I shall never know the answer. She held out an olive branch to me recently and I thought we might be reconciled, but I am expected to forget about her past, which I am unable to do. She doesn't have to forget about mine because she doesn't know what it is and please God won't. She will never know that a married man broke the law and lived a double life because of her. I honestly believe she has broken my heart. I ought to loathe the sight of her but she goes on being Mamie, same creamy skin, same feline eyes, etc., etc. Same body that I can't stop dreaming about. I have never been quite sane about sexual matters. Forgive my frankness. I am very much alone.'

Travelling took his mind off Mamie, but wherever he came to rest – an hotel room, Adelaide Chambers, his own house in Penarth – she was waiting for him, in the shadows, in the dark. He must learn to live without her. But in October there was a letter when he asked at Lloyd's in Leadenhall Street.

He opened it in the entrance hall, and a tiny gust of scent came off the pink writing paper inside. There was something odd about the contents; almost friendly. She still didn't have tuppence in the world but who cared? Agnes (remember Agnes?) and her Donald had been to stay at South Shields. Charlie came and went. There was a screamingly funny rabbit farmer whose rabbits kept escaping. Altogether she was managing very well as an abandoned wife.

It was hardly contrition. Was it defiance? He turned to the

last page, which hoped he was keeping out of mischief and was signed, 'Kind regards, Mamie Stuart.' There was a PS: 'Had a look round Penarth last week. Nearly bought a hat at Cash & Co.! Isn't the pier grand?'

Adhering to his schedule for the rest of the day helped steady his nerves. A flatiron collier tied up at Queenborough on the Medway was meticulously attended to. He met a Lloyd's agent in Leadenhall Street. It wasn't until he was on the night sleeper from King's Cross that he felt panic rising in his throat. If she knew about Penarth, what else did she know? He couldn't work out if they had been there at the same time. How long would it take to move May and Arthur somewhere else? Newport? Bristol? Glasgow? The Outer Hebrides?

But by the time he reached Sunderland and Hawarden Crescent, where he arrived while Mrs Stuart was still raking ashes out of the kitchen fire, George was calm, looking to the future. Immediately Mrs Stuart was banging the door – 'Mamie, dear, wake up, your husband's here.' The room crowded with clothes; Mamie yawning and stretching, hair under armpits visible in a crack of light through the curtains.

'I had to come the minute I got your letter,' he said. He sat on the bed and gave himself a crick in the back, embracing her. 'As if I'd ever abandon you. I've had enough of this. Everything is going to be different. I want us to start afresh. Only God understands how much you are to me.'

'Will it work, Georgie?' Her voice was thick, sleepy, petulant. 'It won't if you keep nagging me about my duties as a wife.'

'My precious girl needn't worry.' He kissed her breast through her nightdress and smelled the warmth of her body. The presence of other men seemed to cling to her. But he made himself go on. 'I intend to do the things you want. Find a house for us, in a nice part of Swansea. Hire a servant. Buy a motorcar and teach you to drive it, so you can come and go as you like. Let you have some money of your own. Think about moving to London in a year or two. How does that sound?'

'Splendiferous. Will you really? When can I come?'

'In a few weeks when I've found a house and all that.'

'Can we go to Binns today?'

'I don't see why not.'

Desperate to ask her about Penarth, he knew he mustn't sound too concerned; although it would be equally suspicious not to sound concerned at all, because she would be watching him. The right moment came when they were at the department store and she was trying on hats.

'Better choice here than Cash & Co.?' he smiled.

'Mm.' She caught his eye in the mirror. 'Nice little town, Penarth.'

In the restaurant afterwards he watched her eating a peach melba and said he supposed it was the George Hotel that had mentioned Penarth. Point one, it wasn't Penarth. It was *Peniarth*, a village in North Wales, not far from the charming resort of Aberdovey. Mamie's lips parted to let in a glazed cherry and a blob of ice cream. Everard had known people at Peniarth. Sister-in-law and child were staying there, and went on to South Wales in the hope of seeing George. Raspberry sauce ran down the side of the glass. Point two, whether it was Penarth or Peniarth, why bother to go there? Did she really think there was anything to find?

'I was curious.' The long spoon came up with a slice of peach, and she put on her dreamy voice to explain how Henry let her go with him to the Rhondda Valley, where he was taking a colliery manager's furniture.

'And then what?'

Then a train into Cardiff and a train to Penarth, not much over an hour all told, and there she was in the mysterious place where the mysterious Mrs Shotton came from.

'Except it isn't. She doesn't.'

The spoon rattled on the glass and gave up. She had walked about a bit – went to the Esplanade Gardens, found the pier. George tried to reconstruct her route from the station. Conceivably she had gone along Westbourne Road.

'They have a dock that ships coal. I have been there often.'

'I liked Penarth. Nice houses. Everything clean. I went to the town library.' Her eyes were fixed on him. 'A friend told me you could look people up in the electoral thingummy.'

'I believe you can.'

'What d'you think I found?'

'Nothing. There was nothing to find.'

Her serious-woman look broke down into giggles. Instead of being alphabetical the stupid list was street by street, so after a while she gave up. What a waste of time. That night she went back north with Henry.

It could have been a fatal curiosity; perhaps it still was. 'My darling girl is a silly-billy, is all I've got to say,' said George, but he had a sense of time running out. She might not have been bored so easily. Or a helpful librarian might have referred her to the current edition of *Kelly's South Wales Directory*, which listed better-off residents alphabetically. 'Shotton, G., 244 Westbourne Road' had been in it since before the war. There were ample traces of Shotton, G. for anyone who persevered.

Fortunately people were easily sidetracked. Visits to Binns did wonders for Mamie. The sight of George taking his wife to the pictures reassured Captain Stuart. Even Edith was softened by a bunch of lilies and his crisp admission of what a swine he'd been to her sister that day with the hired motor. 'Mind you look after her better next time,' she warned, and George's quiet 'I will, I will,' drew a line under the past. When he left Sunderland it was understood that Mamie would be sent for as soon as things were ready in the south. Nothing had changed, of course. He knew she meant to bleed him white. Adultery would be the order of the day. What mattered was his determination to survive.

18

Arriving at Swansea High Street at seven in the evening, Mamie was disappointed but not surprised to find no George in the station yard with the car he claimed to have bought. It was November the fifth; approaching the station, the train had passed waste ground where fires were burning, and she saw children's faces looking up as a rocket burst. If she had known the address she was going to, she could have taken a taxi, if she had had the money; if there had been a taxi.

The porter carried three suitcases and a hatbox back into the station and she sat in the ladies' waiting room, shivering despite her sealskin, remembering her lovely goodbye party over the weekend when Charlie brought sundry men and girls to the rabbit farm. Eddie thought she was going to a cabaret engagement in South America. When he wasn't looking, a man with gold cufflinks said he had to see her in London and gave her his card.

It was all George's fault. If he had taken more care of her, who could tell how faithful she might have been? A grain of her remaining affection blew away in the twenty minutes she spent wearing out her behind on the hard seat, before his knuckles rapped the window and he escorted her to a second-hand Morris four-seater, all apologies, blaming something called the magneto.

Still, the motorcar had come true. They went past the gas works and the prison and along Trafalgar Terrace, where she cried, 'Give Florence a toot!' and he sounded the horn obediently. The house had come true. The car pulled up outside a square old-fashioned villa with an overgrown garden, weakly lit by a streetlamp. 'Welcome to the House of Peace,' he said, pushing her into a tiled hallway. Gaslights pulsed on the wall. He called, 'Mrs Rees!' and a middle-aged woman appeared from the rear of the house, wiping her hands on her apron, looking nervously at her new mistress.

'Mrs Shotton is tired after her journey,' said George. 'She will discuss the household arrangements with you tomorrow. Please serve our supper now, and then you may go home.'

First impressions were discouraging – primitive bathroom with an iron tub like a cauldron on legs, lavatory with greenish copper fittings, brown blinds and a grate containing half a bird's nest in their bedroom. George told her not to worry, it was only a rented place. Their real house, which wasn't quite ready yet, was an eye-opener, modern, with a brand-new bathroom, electrical wiring overhauled, Kooksjoie stove in the kitchen, near cliffs and a beach. In her honour he was giving it a new name: Grey Home, to go with her eyes. They would go and see it soon. Was she excited?

'I've met men like you before,' she said, playing the sort of game she knew he liked. 'Tell a girl anything if it'll persuade her. I shall wear my little pink pettie from Peter in bed tonight and wrap it round my knees just in case.'

'There's a shed where you can keep your own motorcar, which I haven't bought yet. One day we shall have a telephone for you to talk to your friends. I shall be able to call you up from anywhere. "Hello, wifey, George speaking from Land's End." "Hello, George, pity you're not here. I've put rouge on my nipples."'

'Filthy beast,' she said, laughing.

In daylight the house was, if anything, worse. Several of the rooms were locked, although keys hung on a board of hooks in the kitchen. They were unfurnished, or contained only rolls of dusty carpet, a broken chair or two, some medical journals from earlier in the century. The words 'Waiting Room' showed faintly through the ochre paint on a downstairs door. Inside was a bare room with damp coming through the outside wall, and a child's slate, still bearing a chalk likeness of a face, thrown in a corner.

George had left early for Milford Haven. Mrs Rees, who preferred talking to working, told Mamie that a doctor had lived there twenty or more years before; she recalled a scandal and a sudden departure, that he was mad or ran off with a patient or committed suicide; some of his things were still down in the cellar. A woman in Carmarthen owned the place now.

'Mr Shotton says it's called House of Peace.'

'Ty Llonydd, in the Welsh. House of Peace and Quiet, you could say.'

There was a grocer and a butcher 'just round the corner', said Mrs Rees. Outside, Mamie realised where she was, near the top of the hill with a pub and a chapel where she and George had pushed their bicycles on her day out. The Mumbles Road itself was a mile away, so until her mythical motorcar arrived, she was landed with another of George's inconvenient addresses.

In bed he had hinted that a little two-seater might be ordered in time for her birthday, later in November. 'You do mean it this time, don't you?' she said, and let him have a line from the new Gladys Leslie picture, ''cause I'm not kidding, baby.' She had plans for the future.

George had ceased to be a problem. He appeared early one afternoon, drove the Morris to a terrace at the foot of the hill, and explained about the brake, the clutch and the difficult art of double-declutching. The steering wheel felt enormous. Grinding noises came from the gearbox when she tried to move off. They lurched forward, and for a few seconds she had a glorious feeling of power in her hands, until she trod on the brake pedal by mistake and the engine stalled. 'It takes time,' said George. 'You're doing very well.'

He came and went, giving her lessons when he could. What about Grey Home, she kept asking, when could they see it? Not ready, he said, be patient, I want it to be a grand surprise. Was it far? Not far. He would take her there soon. Workmen were busy. It was all in hand.

Ty Llonydd was a dismal place to be alone in. On Mrs Rees's evening off, Mamie built up the fires in sitting room and bedroom, ready for George's return from a trip to Bristol, and was annoyed to find that the lazy woman had left the coal scuttles half empty. Wind was blowing rain against the house. She looked into the road for any sign of the car, which George had left at the station. Nobody was about. Lights showed in neighbouring windows; nearer, a cat yowled in Ty Llonydd's undergrowth.

Taking a candle, she carried a scuttle down the cellar steps from the kitchen. Shadows leaped about on whitewashed surfaces streaked with dust and cobwebs. A wooden barrier kept the coal in a far corner, where bags were tipped down a chute at the side of the house. On the way back, Mamie stopped to rest her arm, and the candlelight glinted on something. A box of tools was open on a trestle table, alongside mildewed books and papers. Holding the candle close, she could see them slotted into compartments lined with what looked like rotting velvet – knives of varying sizes, a little fretsaw, a much heavier saw with powerful teeth. Rust had bitten into them all. An engraved plate screwed to the lid, which lay to one side, was legible. She read, 'Chas Burridge & Sons, Medical Instrument Makers'. They must have belonged to the mad doctor, or whatever he was.

A sudden banging terrified her. She dropped the candlestick and the flame went out. Shaking, she crept towards the gleam from the top of the steps. The noise came again, as if there was a lunatic upstairs. Until she emerged in the kitchen, she was bracing herself to run from the house. Then she realised it was someone banging the iron knocker on the front door.

A telegraph boy stood holding his bicycle, water streaming off his cape.

'Sorry, lady, Post Office says we must keep knocking if there's a light.'

A wire from George, handed in at Cardiff. 'DELAYED BY EMERGENCY RE VESSEL. ENSURE ALL DOORS BOLTED IN CASE OF VAGRANTS. BACK BY END OF WEEK. G.'

Twenty-four hours later Mamie had called on the under-employed Captain Andrews, they had been for an afternoon spin to a village inn twenty miles from Swansea, and he had half undressed her on the back seat. Wet foliage in the lane where they were parked brushed against the windows; the car steamed up, and it was early evening before he dropped her off in Newton, round the corner from the house.

The Morris was parked outside, and George was waiting. 'Been walking,' she said casually, and he nodded, acquiescing if not believing. It was thrilling to think she could do as she pleased. When she undressed for bed she left her underclothes in the bathroom, where a suspicious husband might conduct a furtive examination. Whether he did or not, it failed to stop him making love to her.

In the morning, it's true, he was remote, not quite himself. He was in the garden before breakfast, throwing stones at squirrels; later brooding over a book, which he left behind when he went out. It was a diary for 1919, every page blank except on the fifth of November, where he had written, 'Mamie has come back. For how long?' Was she meant to read it?

He had promised her another lesson in the afternoon, and

she was allowed to drive along the Mumbles Road and park outside the Pier Hotel; in reversing she hit a wall and gashed a mudguard; all George said was, 'Damn.' In the evening he was off again.

A curious letter came from her father, who never wrote anything unless he had to. Was it true that she was going back to London to be with her friends? Now that she and George were reunited, he and her mother would want nothing more to do with her if she abandoned him again.

She wondered if Albert could have written to her in Sunderland, and the letter been steamed open and read. Albert wasn't the sort to make mistakes like that. Otherwise, there was nothing to know; no journey had been planned, no ticket bought. Someone was reading her thoughts.

Captain Andrews was away. She was bored. The birthday motorcar would make her feel different; but even if it arrived on the day – and her common sense told her it might not arrive at all – she had another week and a half to go. Instead of waiting to visit Florence Hearn until she could show off the motor, she called at Trafalgar Terrace for a gossip.

The welcome was no more than polite; she was invited in and offered a cup of tea. 'I must say, I thought we'd seen the last of you,' said Flo.

'I had to rush off that day.'

'So you said. Not a word about why and not a word since. I thought of us as friends.'

'I *am* sorry, Flo. I didn't think.' The husband wheezed in the next room. 'Please forgive me. I'd seen Mr Shotton at the Mumbles with a woman and a small boy. That's why I left.'

'You don't mean Mr Shotton had a . . . had a . . .' The word escaped her, or was unsayable.

'It was all explained. She was a sister-in-law and the boy was his nephew, staying at the George. At least, that was his story.'

Now she and Mr Shotton were living together again; they were renting a house near the Mumbles, moving soon to a place of their own; they had tried to draw a veil over the past.

'Found true happiness at last,' sighed Flo.

'Mr Shotton and I aren't cut out for that, I've decided. Someone's been telling my folk in Sunderland that I intend leaving him again.'

'There's wicked! Who would do a thing like that?'

'Mr Shotton?' She felt better for putting the thought into words. 'If he wanted to blacken my character, he might.' But she had no evidence.

'He wouldn't do such a thing.'

'He wouldn't knock me about, according to some people. He did, though. Doesn't any more, I hasten to add.'

'What I remember saying to you was, least said, soonest mended.'

'I've come to the conclusion that Mr Shotton is a very odd man. If I ever disappear, you'd better come and look for me.'

He was the whoosh-bang man; now you see him, now you don't. Mamie had an overwhelming sense of his presence; knew, with illogical certainty, that he had returned to Swansea already. Or had not been away. His car was there again, outside Ty Llonydd, and he was waiting for her with a key in his hand. 'It's ready,' he said. 'I want to take you there.'

'Is that where you've been?'

'Pack some things. We'll come back for the rest in a day or two.'

Late afternoon; sea mists around the streetlamp. He drove through lanes to a church on a sharp bend. Beyond it the road descended past gorse and sheep, where they had cycled down to the beach. 'Caswell Bay,' he said. 'Remember?'

Past the black and white seascape at the base of the valley;

up the steep hill on the far side, winding among trees. She was on the Chester Road again, Mainsforth Terrace left behind, all around her the unknown fields.

'Nearly there,' said George.

There was enough daylight to catch the white frame of the house, built above the road and reached by six steps. A steep slope with trees rose behind it. The parking shed was further along the road. He locked up the car and said, 'Follow me.'

Smells of paint and plaster greeted her; George switched on electric lights, naked bulbs without shades, and said there were still things to be done. A coal stove was burning in the kitchen; a job lot of pots and pans lay on the table. Everything was second-hand. Mamie had been expecting new furniture, not chairs that didn't match and a dining-room table with a broken leg and a book to support the stump. 'Rome wasn't built in a day,' said George. A used gramophone and a pile of records were in what he called the morning room at the rear of the house.

What other delights? He was proud of the electric generator, humming in a wash house beyond the kitchen. 'Ugh!' she said. 'Horrid smell of oil.' She frowned at the dirt in the deep stone sink, the worn-out mangle, the patched copper for boiling clothes. 'Are we having Mrs Rees?'

'It's a long way for her to come.'

'Because I'm not going back to cleaning and cooking.'

'I shall think of something. Trust Georgie.'

At least the bath was adequate, and hot water came out when she opened the tap. But the windows had rags for curtains. So did most of the rooms. 'I admit, it needs a woman's touch,' he said.

'Why didn't you ask me what I wanted?'

'I am doing my best.'

'You said it was going to be so marvellous.'

'Be patient.'

'You keep saying that, but you're the one who wanted me back. You know where I want to live, in London, where my friends are.'

'One thing at a time.'

His meekness was uncanny, taking the edge off everything she said; making a fool of her, as he did that time he saved the lamb, and left her feeling like a child.

'Who told Ma and Pa that I mean to leave you?'

'Not me. I hope it isn't true.'

'It may be. It depends.'

'Let's not quarrel, not on our first night. There's a joint of meat in the oven. I have bought a bottle of sparkling wine.'

He helped her with supper and made her laugh when he burned the potatoes, but she found the new George unsettling. She couldn't provoke him. When she asked what he was thinking about, he said solemnly, 'The Kooksjoie. I may not be burning the right coal at present.'

The wine made her drowsy. She left him fiddling with the stove and lay in bed, in the dark, pretending to be asleep, having decided not to let him do what he was certain to want to do when he joined her. But he didn't appear. Noises came from downstairs, doors opening and shutting, what sounded like furniture being moved, water running and making the pipes shake. Real sleep came soon after.

When Mamie opened her eyes, she thought it was morning until she focused on the electric light. George, in his shirt sleeves, sat by the bed on a rickety chair, staring at her. For some reason her heart was pounding.

'What are you doing?'

'Looking at you.'

'What time is it?'

'Three a.m.'

She pulled the bedclothes over her head. 'Leave me alone. You're giving me the creeps.'

'Sleep tight,' he said, and the light went out.

He left the house before she was properly awake, saying he would be back by the evening. After the noise of the car faded, there was only wind dragging at the trees. Fortunately she had packed scented soap, bath salts, coconut oil, glycerine, emery boards, pumice stone, Scott's Fat Solvent for her calves and a bottle of La Rola never-failing skin protector. Lounging on the bed after her beauty treatment, she rather wished there was someone to be beautiful for, and wrote a few lines to Alberto, out of nostalgia more than anything.

In the afternoon, wearing a jumper and skirt, and an old mackintosh from the kitchen in case it rained, she went to have a walk and find a pillar box. Caswell in winter was deeply depressing. No one was about. The beach where she and George had walked was littered with storm debris thrown up almost to the road, coils of seaweed, splintered planks, a broken barrel.

Evidently the GPO didn't cater for letters in Caswell. She was walking up the road that led towards civilisation when rain began blowing in from the sea and drove her back. Everything went wrong. Needing to rub herself dry, the only big towel she could find was still damp on the bathroom floor. The house felt cold and she saw that his wonderful Kooksjoie thing had gone out. It took her an hour to relight it by stuffing wood and paraffin under the anthracite, after which she needed another bath, but couldn't have one until the water heated up again.

It was dusk when George came back. He listened patiently; said she would have her motorcar within days; got the Kooksjoie roaring; agreed to take her out to supper at the Pier Hotel. Nancy would have been proud of her. 'That's the way to treat 'em,' she would have said.

This time she was a mere half-hour in the bath. Dressing in the cold bedroom – biscuit costume, white silk blouse –

she heard the gramophone playing downstairs. George was in the breakfast room. 'You look very nice,' he said, and cranked the machine. 'Remember this?' It was 'Let's All Go Raving Mad'.

'I'm ready to go.'

'We used to play it in Elgin Crescent.' His face was discouragingly white and she wondered if there was trouble coming. 'You were all I wanted. I'd never been so happy.'

'Oddly enough, nor had I.'

'You were a hell of a dancer.'

'My dancing days are over.'

'But not your fucking days.'

Her legs were trembling but she wasn't afraid of him. 'I warn you –'

'That you'll leave me? You will anyway when it suits you. Go poking around in Penarth? Poke away. You've no idea what I sacrificed for you. You know nothing about me at all.'

'I didn't want any of this to happen, but it has, and that's that. If you like, give me a thousand pounds, and I shall go and live in London and you'll never hear from me again.'

The record finished and the needle scratched in the groove. 'Live with Albert, perhaps,' he said, and produced an envelope with her handwriting blurred by rain. 'You forgot to post this. "Coming your way again soon . . . make up for lost time . . ."'

'Serves you right for reading other people's letters.' She knocked the needle back into play and 'Let's All Go Raving Mad' croaked away for a second before he swept the gramophone to the floor, where it broke apart with a whirring noise and the horn fell off.

'"My old man seems to know quite a lot . . . what the eye doesn't see . . ."'

'What did you expect, the way you've treated me?'

'"Dying to feel your arms around me . . . sounds just like a novel! . . . bye-bye, fondest . . ."'

To her horror, she saw tears running down his face. His hands hung loose at his sides. 'You bitch,' he said.

'I'm not really. Shall we go to bed? It's you I love.'

'Too late,' he said.

19

As the war receded in one direction, the future came rushing from another; like England from a train, thought George, who was travelling home in a first-class compartment, seeing wintry moors above the line in Yorkshire swept away and replaced by a rash of blossom in a park far to the south, and a girl with a bicycle waiting bare-armed at a level crossing.

Spring 1920; one's son growing up; one's sister getting married. The engineer with the unreliable chin would have enjoyed her by now, twenty-four hours after the ceremony. George had been at St Chad's in Gateshead, as promised, and afterwards at the parents' house: persuaded by Chrissie, against his better judgement, to attend the wedding breakfast. Led into the parlour to see the gifts on show, he noted that his extremely expensive present – a silver fruit bowl the size of a hatbox, inscribed 'Christiana and Richard 15 March 1920' – seemed to be missing. Someone (his father?) had obscured it with a pair of bath towels and an alarm clock. He was gratified to see Chrissie restore it to its place of honour and rub off the fingermarks with her handkerchief.

An aunt whose name he couldn't remember told him what a consolation Everard's brass plate must be to them all. He gave her his invariable reply, 'I have seen no evidence of his death,' and saw her telling other relatives, who all took covert looks at this eccentric.

The husband was agreeable enough, although inclined to talk about electricity, and Chrissie seemed genuinely glad to have her brother there. When he was leaving, which he did as soon as it was decently possible, she made him promise to visit them when they were settled in their own place, and he said that indeed he might, and might even bring May.

'You didn't bring her today,' said Chrissie, who added a coquettish 'Naughty boy!' because she had been drinking sparkling wine. Through her lacy gloves came an unmistakable hint of chapped hands.

'No, but we are getting on better these days. We live in Swansea now. A change of scene can work wonders.'

'And the girl?' she whispered. 'The dancer?'

'She up and left, so that was that. Months ago. It was probably for the best.'

The future came to rest, for the moment, at Swansea High Street, where he had left his motorcar parked in a corner of the goods yard by arrangement with the stationmaster. At Adelaide Chambers he sat with his feet on the desk, looking at correspondence. An envelope with 'Private' stamped on it in purple ink contained a letter that led him to lower his feet to the floor and sit poring over its three and a half lines, typed with a worn-out ribbon, which asked respectfully if he would be kind enough to call on Sergeant Jenkins at the above address when convenient, in respect of a minor matter. The 'above address' was the central police station.

'What can I do for you, Sergeant?'

'Step this way, sir.' Jenkins was tall for a Welshman, bony, aged about fifty; catarrh enhanced his Swansea accent. 'The interview room's more comfortable.'

That was a relative term. The room reminded George of school – hard chairs, a table that was too small for the sergeant's legs, an inkwell and wooden pen, a railway map of Great Britain nailed to the wall. On a steel filing cabinet was a fish in a bowl, like an educational aid.

Sergeant Jenkins was in plain clothes, a brown suit, and

had brought some papers with him, inside a cardboard box tied with tape.

'Is this about my motorcar?' asked George. 'I bumped into the back of a fruit and vegetable lorry in Wind Street some weeks ago. I gave the driver a pound and assumed that that was the end of the matter.'

'It does get very crowded in that part of town.' Jenkins looked carefully at the three pieces of paper that the file contained. 'No, nothing here about that, Mr Shotton.'

'You mean that file is concerned with me?'

'Not necessarily.'

'Are you ever going to come to the point?'

'Yes I am, sir. Do you have a wife, Mr Shotton?'

'Has something happened to her?'

'Not that I'm aware of. Is Mrs Shotton in the town?'

'Of course she is. We've lived at Grey Home in Caswell since February. Now, I insist on knowing what you want.'

Jenkins blew his nose and sat back in the chair, which had the effect of levering his feet even further across the linoleum. 'You have seen your wife quite recently, I imagine.'

'A week ago, before I went away on business. I was on my way home when I found your letter at the office.'

'Would you have any objection if I asked a man from Mumbles police station to visit . . . Grey Home on his bicycle?'

'I have a better idea. See if Chief Inspector Haynes is in the building. He and I attend the same church with our families. We don't want your men toiling up and down hills unnecessarily.'

Jenkins departed with his file, looking uncomfortable, and was away for longer than George expected; he counted eight minutes on his watch before the sergeant came back by himself to say that Mr Haynes sent his compliments, but begged to be excused on account of a case of manslaughter that he was preparing to go before the magistrates in the morning.

'And your investigations?'

'At an end, sir. I regret not knowing that you and the chief inspector were acquainted, or I could have spared you the inconvenience. He and Mrs Haynes saw Mrs Shotton on Sunday, as it happens, at St Peter's. Your lad was there as well.'

'Which explains everything,' smiled George. 'Except what you were after.'

Jenkins had the door open, ready to show him to the street. 'I received an inquiry about the safety of a Mrs Shotton, whose husband is in the shipping business. So I asked on the docks. You are well known.'

'Why should anyone be worried about Mrs Shotton?'

'I'm not at liberty to say.'

'Malicious, would you think?'

'Whoever it was, sir, they will be told there are no grounds for concern. As far as I'm aware, the matter is closed.'

Mild bewilderment and a shrug of the shoulders were how an innocent man would respond. So George said that of course the police had their job to do, and it takes all sorts, doesn't it, Sergeant? He strolled to the car, brain spinning. Then he was at Grey Home, playing cricket with Arthur on the bit of steep grass behind the house that backed on to a wooded slope. He remembered nothing of the drive from town except that he nearly hit a tram.

When a sly delivery nicked Arthur's wicket, he made the boy surrender his bat and slammed the ball so hard, it went straight through the wash house window. Olwen, the servant, who had come with them from Penarth, was picking pieces of glass out of the long earthenware sink when father and son put their heads around the door. 'Daddy is very sorry,' said Arthur. The dog, chained up because otherwise he would have tried to eat the ball, barked happily. May called that they might as well come in now and have tea. Everything was reassuringly normal.

It was important to continue as if nothing had happened. Assume, as he must, that the inquiry came from Mamie's family. If they hadn't seen her for some time, they might have been sufficiently anxious to go to the police. When they heard that Mrs Shotton had been located, that should be the end of the matter. Danger would arise only if people got the idea that there were two Mrs Shottons. For a second he had to remind himself that there were.

Bigamy would be the end of him. But even if the worst happened, who was to say he had actually married Mamie? Who in his right mind would suppose that a man like him would marry a girl like her?

As for the marriage certificate, a document that certainly existed, the witnesses to the marriage were both officials at the register office. George congratulated himself on his foresight in not having friends present. Thousands must have got married at South Shields since March 1918, so who was going to remember a particular George and Mamie? The only evidence as such was his signature in the register, and his writing, which he at once began to change slightly, had nothing very distinctive; no flourishes, no funny Gs or Ss.

His travels went on as usual – east, then north-west, then south again, another web of journeys where he was lost for days on end. In Liverpool he avoided the Compton, where he was known, and stayed at a lodging house under the name of George Jones to prove to himself how easily one could change an identity. Not that he meant to run away, since where was there to run to?

The girl in the green hat was still plying her trade in Church Street. He said, 'Now then, Mamie my pet, kneel up so I can do it from behind.'

'I wasn't ever a Mamie before. Who are you tonight?'

'George.' In the dark his fingers traced shoulders, breasts and belly. 'Still George, worse luck.'

Machinery from German U-boats, broken up at Swansea and due to be put on sale, took him back to the town. The shipbreakers had hired him to spend a day at the Prince of Wales Dock, so he could write a report and advise the auctioneers. Half a warehouse was filled with the stuff, which two fitters were cleaning and oiling. Electric motors from AEG and Siemens Schuckert, diesels from Fried Krupp, generating sets by Ameg Hilpert, oil pumps, circulating pumps, compressors. The submarine that fired the torpedo that sank the *Cathays Park* in 1917, and did for that Norwegian captain he persuaded to go to sea – Solway? Solberg – might have been powered by the very engines he was inspecting. If he hadn't gone to Sunderland that day, Solberg wouldn't have died. Nor would George have met the girl who changed his life.

There were no messages from policemen at Adelaide Chambers. The builders had been at Grey Home, ripping out an unsatisfactory fireplace in the breakfast room, and May's dust sheets and newspapers were everywhere. Hercules had eaten wallpaper left in a bucket and been sick.

'I have written "DO NOT EAT" in big red letters to stop him,' said Arthur, who had stayed awake to see his father.

'You will have to teach him to read in that case.'

'I am training him so's he'll know RED letters mean DANGER.'

May thought that the little church school at Newton was doing wonders for the boy. She said shyly that the woman who ran it, wife of the vicar at St Peter's, had asked if May would join them as an assistant.

'If that's what you wish,' he said. 'If you have time on your hands.'

'I do. I am settling down splendidly here but I should like to meet more people. The school is five mornings a week. I shall walk there with Arthur.'

She had other things to discuss. A memorial service for

her father was being arranged at Penarth, and Elizabeth had written to ask if a date towards the end of April was convenient.

'There will be a good turn-out,' said George. The old boy had gone in a cold spell in January, a time of year when other old boys were not keen to expose themselves to funerals. They would make up for it now it was spring.

'She is suggesting we scatter the . . . the ashes from a ship. We are all supposed to go. It will be awful.'

Cremation hadn't appealed to May. But it was in the will (so was a bequest to her of eight thousand pounds). 'Let her have her ceremony,' said George. 'I will be there, of course, supporting you.'

Later that evening the bell rang when George was with the generator in the wash house, attending to a faulty ammeter. It was Olwen's evening off – she was walking out with the postman – and May had gone to bed early, so he answered it himself. A police constable was at the door. He was sorry to be a nuisance, but a break-in had been reported at a house in Newton, Ty Llonydd, and it was understood that Mr Shotton was the keyholder. An officer was on the premises, waiting for him.

George's six-month lease, taken the previous October – that other life! – expired in a few days, at the end of March. It was the last place he wanted to visit. But he preferred not to stand arguing on the doorstep, with May reading in bed in the room above. Having told her he was needed urgently on marine business – any lie would do – he took the car out; his headlights caught the constable, bent over the handlebars as he pushed his bike up the hill; he reached the house in a few minutes.

The front door swung in a breeze. Lights burned in the hall and beyond. 'Hello?' he called. Silence. Smell of gas and damp plaster. In the kitchen, he saw that the door to the cellar was open. Boots clumped on the wooden steps and Sergeant Jenkins appeared, carrying an electric lantern, and made a clumsy attempt to be friendly. He was still in the brown suit.

'Well, well, Mr Shotton. You will be getting tired of seeing me.'

'You obviously have a key. What do you want me for? I have had nothing to do with this house for months. My lease expires very shortly.' But he knew it was bad news.

'You occupied the house, sir. You might know what was in it.'

'I lived here for a few weeks last autumn. I returned once or twice to remove possessions. There is nothing I can tell you.'

'That depends. You took the place at Michaelmas. Long time to have a house and not live in it. Beg pardon for all these questions. Shall we sit around the table?'

George tried to fathom him: the hangdog look, the inflamed nostrils that he dabbed with his handkerchief; the small eyes that didn't blink much. He said, 'I suppose you're a detective.'

'For my sins.'

'So what are you after, Detective Jenkins?'

'A helping hand? I had an old guv'nor when I was a probationer – must have been in the eighties – used to say, "Jenkins, there is an answer for everything, but don't expect that even if you twig it, you'll always understand it." If I was to state some alleged facts, you could make comments as you saw fit.'

'Does Mr Haynes know that I've been brought here?'

'The chief inspector has gone down with pleurisy, worse luck.'

'I am helping you voluntarily.'

'Which I much appreciate.' Jenkins popped a pastille in his

mouth, and a whiff of menthol came across the table. 'Funny old business, missing persons.'

'Mrs Shotton isn't missing. We went through all this a week ago.'

'Put it like this. Somebody is. When you were living here at Ty Llonydd, you were keeping company with a girl.'

Damp and cold from the cellar were rising up George's legs. At the same time he was sweating badly. He said, 'Is that a question?'

'No, no, a statement of alleged facts. Which I wasn't aware of at our first interview. Her name was Mamie or Amy and she purported to be Mrs Shotton. Her family in the north-east – I can mention them now – say she *was* Mrs Shotton.'

'A ridiculous falsehood.'

'Well, we all know that not everyone who claims to be married, is. Even in religious districts of Wales '– he drew it out into 'Way-ulls' – 'it is not unknown. Her family wrote her letters to this house addressed to Mrs Shotton, and the postgirl remembers delivering them. It's her that the parents, a Mr and Mrs Stuart, are worried about. I suppose '– Detective Jenkins wiped a watering eye – 'you don't know where she's got to?'

'I have said nothing about knowing her at all.'

'I do have a photograph,' said Jenkins, and he took it from his pocket. There they were, caught by the bloody camera at Liverpool. 'The lady is the one they say is Mrs Shotton. The gentleman appears to be you.'

'Let me be frank. I'm not anxious to be reminded of that person. She left me some time ago. Before the end of last year, in fact. I am being completely straight with you. But you realise how harmful it would be if any whisper of this ever reached my wife.'

'This is between the two of us.'

'Has the girl's family not heard from her?'

'Not since last November, apparently. Except a telegram on Christmas Eve to say that she was going with you to London.'

'Which was certainly a lie. I was with my wife and child on Christmas Eve, in Penarth, where we were living at the time. The whole story is lies. The girl leads everyone a dance, including her family. I fail to understand why they are suddenly making a fuss.'

'In that respect,' said Jenkins, 'we do have some reliable facts. Bear with me. Fact number one. On a date unknown, a suitcase was left by a man who spent the night at the Grosvenor in Temple Street, in Swansea. I believe you know it.'

A pressure in his guts was distressing George. Would 'No' do more harm than 'Yes'? He said, 'It has a poor reputation. Edwards the manager is a drunkard.'

'That brings me to fact number two. Edwards was sacked for insobriety on March the first, St David's Day. Not the usual way we Welsh celebrate our patron saint, but as you remarked to me at the police station, it takes all sorts. A week later his successor, a smart young Irishman, found the suitcase in a locker and opened it up. As a result he informed the police, who took possession. Various items were in it. One of them contained addresses of persons in Sunderland.'

'You could have told me all this a week ago.'

'I wasn't sure it concerned you.'

'And now you think it does.'

'Look at it from my point of view, sir. We informed the Sunderland police about the suitcase and they informed the family. A routine matter. Mr and Mrs Stuart were anxious, not unnaturally, having heard nothing from their daughter for months. We were asked to make inquiries. After I'd spoken to you, a telegram was sent to Sunderland to say that Mrs Shotton and child were in good health. A constable cycled round to tell them. But all they said was, "What child?"'

'I have to use the WC.'

'Borrow my lantern,' Jenkins said, and George climbed the stairs to the bathroom containing the iron tub and the greenish lavatory, where he sat groaning, his insides turned to water. Edwards had been given a pound; the suitcase should have been safe. But George had blank spaces in his memory of the time after Mamie left.

'Everything all right, sir?' called Jenkins from the hall.

There was no paper in the holder. George had to flush away his handkerchief.

'I would like to clarify my relationship with Miss Stuart,' he said.

The detective had boiled a kettle and made tea. 'Right you are, sir. Fancy a cup? I made free of your gas.' There was no milk or sugar. Jenkins drank it from the saucer, eyes waiting above the rim.

'I sometimes referred to her as "Mrs Shotton" in order to avoid gossip. You might as well know the truth. She was a girl I picked up in the street. Nevertheless I was fond of her. I was upset when she left me. Couldn't bear to be in the house. It's ancient history now. I have put my indiscretion behind me.'

'And the suitcase?'

'They were things of Miss Stuart's that I found here after she'd gone. I couldn't bring myself to throw them out. She might even have returned. One is sentimental.'

'Bit like the Welsh.' Jenkins passed him a list compiled on the typewriter with the ragged ribbon. *Contents of brown leather suitcase recovered from Grosvenor Hotel. Two dress cases cut in pieces. Four pairs of lady's shoes all cut up*. Barely remembered now; kneeling on the floor in what had been their bedroom, slashing at things with a cut-throat razor. *Small brown leather bag with lady's silver wristlet watch*

No. 474051 inscribed 'From George Nov 24 1917 with love'. Should have smashed it with a hammer; couldn't do it; kept seeing her bare arm. *Lady's silver handbag engraved 'MS'. Silver vanity case with 'MS' scratched on it*. Acquisitive little monkey. *Bible with 'To Amy on her confirmation, November 1907' at front,* which he knew about, and *'J. S. Stuart, Hawarden Crescent, Sunderland. Edith Silver, 7 Queens Crescent, Sunderland,' at back,* which he didn't. A stupid mistake, but surely one's whole life couldn't turn on an oversight? Finally *Sovereign case containing one farthing*. My lost darling.

'I think we have both had enough for one night,' said Jenkins.

'You tricked me into coming here. You wanted an excuse to poke around the house. You are trying to frighten me. Well, you've picked the wrong man. My conscience is absolutely clear.'

The detective nodded sympathetically. 'But we all have our jobs to do,' he said, and added that further inquiries would have to be made.

Alone, George sat wondering how long Jenkins had been in the cellar. Then he turned off the gaslights, one by one, and drove back to Grey Home, whistling. At least he knew where he stood.

In the morning, due to leave early for the London docks, he went to Adelaide Chambers before eight o'clock and removed his letters to Everard from the safe, together with the revolver. When they were in his bag he slammed the door of the safe and spun the combination, just as footsteps came down the corridor. The bag went under the desk. A shape stopped outside the frosted glass and a fist rapped on the door. George flung it open. A woman with a mop and duster said, 'Never get to clean your room, do we? Saw you come in.'

'Another time,' he said.

Burning the letters might have been prudent, but he couldn't bring himself to do that. He broke his journey at Cardiff, opened an account with a trifling sum at a bank, away from the city centre where he wasn't known, and rented a safe-deposit box. The revolver went with him to London. He dropped it in one of the Surrey Commercial Docks when no one was looking.

20

As time passed, George told himself that he would hear no more, that the police thought it a matter not worth pursuing, even that Chief Inspector Haynes, who worshipped at the same church, had decided to turn a blind eye to a fellow communicant's private life. The policeman's illness kept him at home, but George saw Mrs Haynes one Sunday when he went to morning service with May, and they chatted afterwards in the porch.

'Please send Mr Haynes my warm wishes for a speedy recovery,' said George. 'I am in Swansea for the next day or two. Should I look in for two minutes?'

'How very kind.' But she looked uneasy. 'There have been complications. The doctor insists on absolute rest.'

The conversation came back to George when a telegram arrived at Adelaide Chambers first thing next day, to say that Detective Inspector Barry wished to call on him at 4 p.m. Barry, a sour-looking man, and Jenkins, whose cold seemed no better, were standing in the corridor when he arrived from Briton Ferry, across Swansea Bay, a few minutes late. A third chair had to be organised so they could all sit down.

'I see you know my movements, Mr Barry.'

'Do we, Jenkins?'

'Guessed lucky, sir, I believe.'

'Be that as it may,' said Barry. 'I have a particular question to put to you, Mr Shotton. You are under no obligation to answer it. You have not been cautioned. This is an informal conversation.'

'Like the one I had with Jenkins.'

'I believe that the sergeant was investigating an alleged break-in and that certain matters arose in passing.'

'Is that what he told you?'

Barry drew in his upper lip so that the inky moustache on it almost disappeared. 'I am now going to ask you the question. Did you undertake a form of marriage with Mamie Stuart of Notting Hill, London, at the South Shields register office on the twenty-fifth of March 1918?'

'I shall take proceedings for slander against anyone who says I did. I married my wife in 1905. The Mamie Stuart story is a wicked fabrication.'

Barry fingered a notebook. 'I have seen a certified copy of the entry, reference number TE814907. It refers to a George Shotton, aged thirty-seven, which I believe was your age then, and describes him as a marine superintendent, which I believe to be your profession.'

'Then all I can say is that someone has been impersonating me. Have you spoken to Mamie Stuart about this?'

'We can't find her.'

'Well, when you do, she will be able to tell you that the man she married wasn't me, whoever he was.'

'Do you have any idea where she is?'

'None. She is a girl with a violent temper. She left me more than once in the past, usually to go to London. I warned her that if she ever did it again, I wouldn't have her back. Last November we had a quarrel. I was out all next day on business, and when I returned home she had gone, taking most of her clothes with her. I have heard nothing from her since.'

Inspector Barry looked even sourer when he left, Jenkins plodding at his heels. They must know their case was precarious unless they could produce Mamie. George tried to think of her dispassionately, as the police would, a pretty girl with an artificial rose in her hat. He needed to strip away her history, to see her as their Mamie, not his Mamie, not as the someone he used to call his little monkey a thousand years ago, before she betrayed him, before she went away for ever. But it wasn't easy.

'A Service to Commemorate the Life and Work of William Loader, Esq., Master Mariner and Steamship Proprietor, at St Augustine's Church, Penarth. Friday, 30 April 1920.' Rousing hymns; May, silent in black silk; Elizabeth, bursting with vigour in her widow's weeds; clean-shaven men praising Billy on behalf of the Chamber of Shipping, Ocean Collieries, Lloyd's of London. 'And in conclusion,' said the vicar, a man with awkward limbs like a scarecrow, 'a tribute from someone who was both son-in-law and colleague, Mr George Shotton.'

'I first met Billy many years ago, when I was walking out with his daughter. He told me he only had one question to ask. He walked me down to a dry dock in Cardiff where he had a ship just in – the *Gwalia*, I believe it was. She had been in a collision. "Have a look at her," he said, "and assess the damage. Then come and see me in Channel Buildings and give me a verbal report. Down to the last rivet."'

Heads nodded; someone chuckled at the back.

'That was the genuine Billy Loader: practical and forthright. He wanted to know if I was any good at my job. If I was, and his daughter was agreeable, then as far as he was concerned we were old enough to know our own minds. It expressed the essence of the man. Blunt, honourable, and a good friend that I and hundreds of others were privileged to know.'

May thanked him afterwards. 'I am so proud of you,' she whispered. 'Did he really say that?'

'I may have exaggerated a trifle.' The story of the *Gwalia* sounded like the truth even to George, who had made the whole thing up. Lying came from the heart; it was only a complicated way of being honest. 'I was fond of him. You know that.'

Behind the black veil Elizabeth was bubbling with life. 'Thank heavens,' she was telling people as they waited outside the church for the charabanc that would take an invited party to Penarth dock, 'I was able to make William happy in the time we had together.' There was keen anticipation for a novel event. Considerably more than the intended thirty scrambled aboard the bus. George, putting his wife to sit with Bella James, saw the widow patting the seat for him to join her as they rattled downhill.

'I haven't seen either of you since you moved to Swansea,' she said. 'Does May like it there?'

'You must ask her yourself.'

'Oh, I don't think I will. When I knew her first I was someone to confide in, which she badly needed in those days. A fresh start will do her good.'

'We have moved from one town to another, that's all. You must come and see us one day. The beaches are very beautiful in summer.'

'I suspect that May blames me for taking William to America.'

'Yes, she does.'

Elizabeth lifted the veil to look at him. Shining teeth, heavily powdered cheeks. 'You made her life a misery,' she said, pitching her voice below the background of noise. 'Did you know that I know that?'

'I am making allowances for your grief.'

'Arthur treats Hercules better than you treated her. I'm glad you pulled your socks up in the end.' The throaty laugh. Then, 'There you are, George, you won't need to talk to me ever again.'

The charabanc stopped by the jetty beyond the locks where

the pilot cutter was waiting, her grimy red-and-white flag at half-mast, smoke leaking from the funnel. Passengers were helped aboard. An undertaker's man with a plain wooden box under his arm was last off the jetty, the shorelines came away, the telegraph on the bridge could be heard ringing for slow ahead, and George put his arm around May's shoulder as the cutter edged out into the Bristol Channel.

The sea sparkled in the sun, but a long swell coming at them diagonally started the cutter pitching. May went to join the rest of the ladies amidships, where, they were told, the effects would be less severe; perhaps they thought it their duty to look delicate and use smelling salts. George drifted among men he knew. He was keeping up his membership of the Yacht Club; retained the house in Westbourne Road, for that matter.

'Here he is, the emigrant himself,' said Oscar. 'The flesh-pots of Swansea have claimed him.' Some banter followed about the ancient rivalry between Swansea and Cardiff. The secretary to the Chamber of Shipping, laughing one minute, turned pale and was sick over the side, the ladies turning their backs politely.

George became aware of nods and signals from Oscar, and let himself be led into the stern, deserted because of the seesaw effect. The screw thudded under their feet. Gulls hovered, wings trembling in the slipstream of hot air from the stack.

'We're safe here,' said Oscar.

'From what?'

'There has been a visitor at the office, asking questions about you. I wasn't there. He spoke to Miss Boulton.'

George was encouraged. They were getting desperate.

'Who was he?'

A long pause. Oscar was braced against the after-cabin for the downward plunge. George held a stay above his head, like a man strap-hanging on a train. They rose again, the horizon widening to include Flat Holm, a tramp ship, the

English coast. The cutter was turning, ready to lie to for the ceremony.

'He said he was a policeman. Miss Boulton was so flummoxed, she didn't get his name. He showed her his warrant card.'

'So what did this policeman want?'

'Particulars of your movements, going back for months. She showed him the office log, and he made some notes.' Hands stuck in the pockets of his tight-belted mackintosh, Oscar looked as worried as if he was the one who might have done something wrong. 'Weren't you present when a solicitor with a writ came on board a ship in the Mersey? A Greek, last winter some time? My guess is we shall find it pertains to that. Perhaps you're needed as a witness.'

'Very likely.'

'In any case, I have instructed Miss Boulton not to tell a soul. To be on the safe side I gave her a box of marzipan delights and said there were more where that came from.'

'A friend could do no more,' said George.

They went amidships, where the undertaker had taken a small urn from the box and was holding it with both hands while he and the widow consulted the senior pilot about which side of the ship to use. The cutter was at dead-slow, broadside to the swell and beginning to roll. A coal broker was being quietly sick in the bows. None of the half-dozen ladies seemed affected, although May was gazing at the urn with a look of dismay.

'Stop engines, Skip,' the pilot shouted up to the wheelhouse, and in the silence, with the sea slapping the hull, the undertaker could be heard saying, 'When he gets to "We therefore commit his ashes", remove bung, hold at arm's length, tip and shake.'

The vicar strode from the midships cabin and began the service without a pause, presumably trying to get it over before anyone else was sick. A scene floated in George's memory. Behind the gawky figure with cassock flapping about his legs, in a hurry with the words, he saw the prison chaplain holding the crucifix and Bible, keeping himself between the yellow-faced prisoner with the pinioned arms and the scaffold where the executioner waited. Tussaud's waxworks, December 1917; with Mamie at the Chamber of Horrors.

'*Man that is born of a woman hath but a short time to live, and is full of misery. He cometh up, and is cut down, like a flower; he fleeth as it were a shadow, and never continueth in one stay.*' The vicar took a deep breath and nodded at Elizabeth. '*Forasmuch as it hath pleased Almighty God of his great mercy to take unto himself the soul of our dear brother here departed; we therefore commit his ashes to the deep . . .*'

Elizabeth, leaning over the side, was having difficulty with the bung. 'Allow me,' said the undertaker. He wrestled with it, red in the face. '*We therefore commit his ashes to the deep*,' the vicar repeated with a trace of annoyance.

Defeated, the undertaker asked if someone had a penknife. May had her eyes shut. Before there was any response, Elizabeth snatched the urn and threw it into the sea; a woman's half-hearted throw. The object disappeared, only to bob up beside the hull. The company peered over the rail, and George heard his wife say, 'Now my father's remains will be washed up on a beach.'

'Boathook!' he snapped to the nearest deckhand. With the pole in both hands he leaned over. 'Hold my legs,' he ordered, and with the seaman and Oscar securing him, he was able to touch the urn. But there was nothing for the hook to catch in. As the object began to drift away, he stabbed it as if he was using a spear. The urn shattered; a shadow ran through the water.

'*We therefore commit his ashes to the deep* –' the vicar's

teeth were clenched – '*looking for the resurrection of the body, (when the Sea shall give up her dead,) and the life of the world to come, through our Lord Jesus Christ. Amen.*'

'I am much obliged, George,' said Elizabeth, and there was a general murmur of congratulation as the telegraph rang for engines and the hull vibrated again.

'I was never so disgusted,' said May, when they were back at Westbourne Road, where George had agreed they spend the night. 'The urn might have been an old shoe for all the respect she showed. If it hadn't been for you, I don't know what would have happened.'

'There are times one has to act.'

He went from room to room, looking for damp or insects. The woman who kept an eye on it for them had been in to air their bed and turn on the water supply. Some of the furniture was in Caswell, and what he thought of as the bachelor's room no longer had a bed. George looked gloomily at the dents that the legs had left in the linoleum, wondering if he would be spared sexual intercourse.

They ate supper at the Esplanade Hotel and walked home via the steps from the promenade and the ornamental gardens. A light was on downstairs, shining through the glass panel above the door. George told her to stay on the pavement in case it was a burglar and turned the key, his heart nearly throttling him. But the house was silent, undisturbed; one of them must have switched on the hall light, though neither could remember doing it.

After May had gone to bed he sat alone with a whisky, planning his journeys over the week ahead. This was an exercise he usually enjoyed, constructing the timetable in his head, using Bradshaw only for a branch line to some obscure port, or to keep himself up to date with revisions. The thick lines of the railway map, the narrow columns of print, the typesetter's asterisks and pointing fingers, reflected the orderliness of a system that he admired; that he would have liked in his own affairs.

A connection at Lancaster eluded him, and he had to look it up. Then a night train to Scotland. It was absurd to be consulting Bradshaw for trains to the north. He needed a holiday; he needed peace to think. Yet the house was as peaceful as the grave. George thought nostalgically of the zigzag itineraries that he devised when he first knew Mamie. Rushing madly from one end of the country to the other, he would wait on blacked-out platforms, stand in corridors, on one occasion bribing a guard to let him travel in the van, all in order to spend an hour in her bed. It felt like memories of his youth, not 1917.

The need to write to Everard had been growing for weeks. He wondered if he dared. There was no point in writing if he had to hold things back. Having found notepad and pencil, he continued to hesitate. A tug hooted in the bay. For all he knew, Sergeant Jenkins was outside, watching the house.

'Dear Everard,' he wrote, 'there comes a time when calculation fails and one is cast adrift on a stream of events over which one has no control. My little monkey is no more – I have heard nothing of her for many months. The police are after me. They have traced my marriage to her, my "golden solution", as it seemed at the time, and they are hoping to charge me with bigamy. The whole world is my enemy. I expect May would try to understand, but I doubt whether she has the necessary imagination. Only you have that. I remember your words: "In matters of the heart, George, nothing is simple. It doesn't do for onlookers to make harsh judgements."

'All I did was follow my heart. I was under a spell. I was dreaming. *I don't know* is the answer. It is inconceivable to me now that I allowed the present situation to develop. But as I told you once, I have this capacity for not thinking about things. For all I know it is part of my neurasthenia.

However, I may fool them yet. If they can't find Mamie, I stand an excellent chance. In the process of course I have to say certain things about her. I have to deny her thrice, as it were. I have already told the grey-faced policemen that she was a whore. It is essential that I make her seem an unlikely person to have married. A friend of mine, Oscar James, once told me a vulgar riddle. *Q*. What is a mistress? *A*. Something between a mister and a mattress. When it seems appropriate I shall pass that on to the policemen. It will appeal to them, help to put them on my side. If you were here, I would hardly need to spell all this out. A few words and you would understand everything. My dearest boy, how I long to see you.'

He folded the pages small and zipped them into the back of his wallet, where he kept an Eggins's special, for emergencies, that left a faint circular indentation in the leather. Mamie noticed it once. 'Just like a boy scout,' she said. 'Always prepared.'

Lying next to May, after he had crept into the bedroom so as not to wake her, he was dismayed to feel the marble arm come his way.

'George,' she said, 'there is something I have been meaning to say.'

Silence. Perhaps he could fall asleep before she said it.

'Our marriage is strong enough for me to tell you. Whoever there was in your life, I have long since forgiven you for it. Some woman in some town. It doesn't matter now. Thank you for giving her up.'

Pain seemed to link every bone in his body, from skull to feet. He was all frame and no flesh; a dry remnant of George Shotton. His shape ached between the sheets.

'Coming back here,' she said, 'reminds me of the nights I've lain in this bed, so unhappy I could have died. I know it's over now. Do you know when I knew?'

'When?' said the skeleton.

'The day you told me about the house in Swansea, and you said you were calling it "Grey Home" after the song.'

Was that what he'd said? It sounded all too possible, God help him. George realised she was going to recite the lyric. The whisper crept into his ear:

> 'But with love brooding there, why, no place can compare,
> With my little grey home in the west.'

She sighed and said that at last they were like they used to be in the old days. The moment to tell her the truth, or enough of the truth to be going on with, had passed. George did the only thing possible and gave the marble arm a squeeze.

On an afternoon in the third week of May, returning to Swansea by train from London and the east coast, he was met at the barrier by Sergeant Jenkins and a uniformed constable.

'George Shotton,' said the detective, 'I have a warrant for your arrest on a charge of bigamy.'

George said, 'That's preposterous. You are making a grave mistake. I have a complete answer.'

A motorcar took them two hundred yards to the central police station, where he repeated that he was innocent; was told he would be kept in a cell until he came before a court in the morning; supplied the telephone number of a solicitor he wanted to instruct, and had his possessions removed and listed. 'One wallet,' said the desk sergeant, 'containing driving licence, four pound notes, one ten-shilling note . . . and zipped compartment containing –' the policeman zipped it up again quickly – 'one instrument for male use. Sign there.' George did his slightly altered signature.

The room they used for the interview was the one with

the railway map and the fish. This time it was two of them, Barry and Jenkins. George could hear the traffic outside in Alexandra Road. May would just be taking Arthur home from school.

21

'It is a curious case,' said Edward Harris, the solicitor, a short, bald man with an air of authority. 'In the ordinary way of things, if they accuse a fellow of bigamy, the second wife is their best witness. She's the one feeling vindictive.'

'What will happen if they can't find her?'

'They will make do.' Harris glanced at the statement that George had signed earlier. 'There is prima-facie evidence of a marriage.'

'Someone impersonated me. It's as simple as that.'

In the dim electric light, the cell looked as if it had been hacked from a single block of blackish stone. A chair had been brought in for the solicitor. George sat on a bed-frame with two blankets. He said, 'I don't like the tone of their questions.'

'One hardly ever does. Your robust denial will have made them sit up. You would be surprised how many people – people who *are* guilty – succumb to suggestions that they make a clean breast of things.'

'They are implying I have done away with her.' The solicitor opened his mouth and shut it again. 'It seems that inquiries have been made in London. As if that means anything with a girl like Mamie Stuart. The previous time she left me, she wrote saying she was going to be a dancer in South America.'

'Did you keep the letter?'

'Certainly not. But I can assure you that South America was

an obsession with her. Her real name is Amy. She called herself "Mamie" after an artiste known as Mamie Stuart, who went to sing in a casino at Buenos Aires.'

'I don't altogether see where this is leading,' said Harris.

'She – the other Mamie – refused to sing a vulgar song.' He could hear his own voice, deadened by the cell. 'It was all in the papers, before the war.' The solicitor shuffled documents on his knee, doing his best to look interested, but George had lost the thread. Where could he start the story of Mamie? How far back would he need to go?

The solicitor said, 'Let us assume that Miss Stuart turns up. She will be asked who it was that she married at South Shields. Will she name the man?'

'I very much hope so.'

'You have to admit that your account takes some believing. It is my duty as your solicitor to speak frankly. We shall need every scrap of evidence. Can you show that you were somewhere else when the marriage took place?'

'Very likely.'

'Yes or no?'

'I'll do my best to find someone.'

'You say that Miss Stuart married a man who pretended he was you. Did she spend the wedding night with this pretend Shotton?'

George thought about this. 'I assume she did.'

'It wasn't you?'

'I don't think so.'

'Was it or wasn't it? If it was spent at an hotel, as wedding nights usually are, the police are going to find a chambermaid. Be caught lying about that and you're in Queer Street.'

'I need time to think about all this.'

'I don't want to alarm you, but the courts take a harsh view of bigamy. The war is blamed for a loosening of morals, and the powers that be are anxious to tighten them up again.

Judges are anxious to stamp on anything that smacks of hanky-panky.'

'Quite right,' said George. 'As it happens, I attend the same church as Chief Inspector Haynes. My wife was a prominent member of the Moral Vigilance movement during the war. I addressed one of their meetings in Cardiff.'

Harris shook his head. 'I am afraid that that would be relevant, if at all, only in respect of a plea of mitigation. Which I sincerely hope it won't come to. First things first. You will appear in court in the morning. They mean to ask for an adjournment while they complete their inquiries. Formal hearing, no evidence from you required. I shall see you get bail, and you'll be free to go home.' He looked at his watch. 'So it isn't all bad news.' At the door he said, 'May I ask a personal question? Have you taken Mrs Shotton into your confidence?'

'I wouldn't like to worry her unless I have to.'

'Where does she think you are now?'

'I sent a telegram to say I had to be in Cardiff. She's used to that sort of thing.'

'A reporter will be in court tomorrow.'

'My wife rarely sees a newspaper.'

'This won't do, you know,' said Harris. 'She is inevitably going to find out. The police may not be Sherlock Holmeses but they aren't playing a game either. They may decide to question her. Or her family. Or your neighbours. The newspapers are going to take an indecent interest. If I know the police, they will circulate a description of Miss Stuart. That is invariably the prelude to speculation. Do you understand what I'm saying?'

'Yes, I do,' said George.

He told her when they were alone in the motor, after morning service next day, Arthur having been left at home with

Olwen. It was Whit Sunday and they had just been treated to a stirring sermon about the cloven tongues of fire that visited the Apostles at Pentecost and made them multilingual, the lesson being that in today's war-weary world, faith in Jesus could bring the nations together.

The vehicle seemed full of May's hat. George stopped at the foot of the gully, facing the sands at Caswell. Some bathers could be seen. Smoke rose from a family picnic under the cliff where a kettle was being boiled on a tripod. The surroundings, whatever occasion he chose, would be at odds with the story. In bed, after dark, the presence of night and silence would magnify the words. Over supper on Olwen's night off? 'That was excellent toasted cheese. By the way, I have a confession to make.' The interior of the car was merely a space in a piece of metal where their bodies were close together in the way that passengers on a crowded tram were close. It seemed to George as near as he could get to being nowhere at all.

She didn't cry or look angry, simply stared straight ahead at a lemonade stall. Stage One, tell her about the girl whose existence she had guessed at, and bring her to life as 'Mamie Stuart'. Stage Two, speak of this girl's mysterious life and her wicked pretence that she had married George; at this point he held May's gloved fingers. Stage Three, explain that the police, confused by these evil tales, had come to him for an explanation. Stage Four (take a deep breath, open bag, release unspeakable cat), he had been charged with bigamously marrying this Mamie. Never fear, he had instructed the best solicitor in Swansea. Truth would prevail.

The bathers came out of the sea. Sunlight flashed on a knife or a glass at the picnic.

'Shall we be all right?' said May.

He expected the fear in the question; what touched him was the loyalty. Her fingers were shaking and his weren't very steady. In an odd way they were closer than they had been for years; since before the war. That evening she told him shyly that she had kept all his telegrams over the years. They were in a brown envelope in her wardrobe and contained evidence of his whereabouts from time to time that might help disprove the false allegations. Would he like to see them?

Whoever they helped, it was not going to be George. Brooding on their date-stamps and town of origin, he found the telegram he sent from South Shields the day he married Mamie, 12.40 p.m., 25 March 1918. 'TYNE AND WEAR AT PRESENT. UNCERTAIN THEREAFTER.' He burned it in the Kooksjoie as soon as May was in bed. Unsure what else might be used against him, he crept downstairs in the middle of the night and burned the lot. The brown envelope he took with him into Swansea after the holiday, fattened by a folded-up newspaper, telling May that Edward Harris had better have it.

May's faith might be grounded in desperation; not to have it would be worse. Still, it existed, was visible, both pleased and frightened him, pricked his conscience; in his better moments even strengthened his conviction that without Mamie the case would collapse. For two nights running the marble hand came towards him, and to be fair, wasn't marble at all. But a warm, wriggly May merely engaged his pity.

Sleep, these days, was a long black silence without dreams, or without dreams he could recall. He woke in the night and heard an animal screaming. Or the scream had been in his sleep and he was left hearing the echo as he pushed a handful of sheet into his mouth, gnawing the cool linen until it was sodden against his tongue. In daylight he hoped to find evidence of some animal encounter. Blood on the grass; a poisoned fox; a rabbit in a snare in the woodland above the garden. There was nothing. Olwen had unlocked the wash-house door for Hercules, and the dog rushed about, barking, leaving a wake through the dewy grass. The morning had a healthy smell of salt air and vegetation.

George remembered when he was a boy, walking with his father by a creek of the River Wear above Sunderland. It was low tide, the water motionless, a pool in the mud. 'Now, watch,' said Father. 'Watch!' Nothing moved. A mollusc bubbled. Then the pool trembled and began to expand, very slowly, absorbing the bubbles, covering a tiny stone. 'It was slack water,' said Father, 'and now the tide is coming in.'

A paragraph appeared in the Swansea *Post*. The police were looking for a dancer named Mamie Stuart. George made sure the newspaper didn't come into the house. But by the time he went to see Harris next day, the solicitor had a bundle of press clippings. Mamie's height, hair, eyes, even her gold-and-ivory teeth, were already in the London papers. A photograph of her wearing a beret smiled at readers.

'They are unable to make up their minds if she's an actress, a singer or a chorus girl,' said Harris.

'They know nothing about her. They ought to be stopped.'

'Not at all. Unless she's gone into a nunnery, this will flush her out. Isn't that what we want?'

A clerk brought in a late-morning edition of the Swansea *Post*. 'You won't like this much,' said Harris. He read, '"The girl, who is associated with a bigamy charge now pending, stayed in 1919 with a man who gave the name of George Shotton at 28 Trafalgar Terrace, where they were regarded by Mrs Hearn, the occupier, as Mr and Mrs Shotton. She said he seemed quite a gentleman."'

'Are they allowed to print that?'

'I'm afraid they are. Mrs Hearn has evidently been talking to the police, who have tipped the wink to a reporter. Listen to this. "Her disappearance has reminded me of a very strange remark that Mamie made to me on one occasion. She said, 'If I ever disappear, you'd better come and look for me.'"'

'What are they trying to do?'

'Frighten you,' said Harris.

But all they had charged him with was bigamy. The magistrates would decide if there was a case to answer. If they rejected the evidence, said Harris, it would all be over. Otherwise they would send the case for trial, in which event he had his eye on a local KC, Sir Marlay Samson. Expensive but silver-tongued.

George was never sure how much of the story reached May. She continued to take Arthur to school and act as teacher's assistant. She called at the same shops in the Mumbles; the same delivery boys came down the hill on their bicycles. But she stopped speaking about the case. She continued to sleep in the same bed. But the hand no longer came his way.

As George was fumbling with the garage door – his fingers were unsteady, and he dropped the key – a stout man in a mackintosh stepped from behind a gorse bush and said he was special correspondent of the London *Chronicle*, hoping for a brief statement before Mr Shotton went into court. 'My position delicate,' said George, dragging the doors open. 'Things, however, not what they seem. Complete defence up my sleeve.' The car backed out in a cloud of smoke. The reporter scribbled in his notebook, trying to keep rain off the page. 'Writs for libel will follow acquittal as night follows day,' smiled George, and wound up the window.

The courtroom, lit by small squares of daylight and electric lamps high in the ceiling, was fuller and more purposeful than the last time he was in it. Solicitors' clerks in black coats, reporters lounging on a bench, police officers, three full rows of onlookers, not all of them men. George was allowed to sit in the body of court, behind Edward Harris. Mutterings, coughs, rustlings of paper. The clerk said angrily, 'Ink. Ordinary black ink,' and a lad with a stone bottle appeared and filled up wells in the magistrates' dais. He was still doing it when a faded red curtain behind their seats trembled and the three JPs came from behind it. Everyone stood up and sat down again. George folded his arms. The reporters were watching him.

The case seemed to crumble away as soon as it started. A lugubrious solicitor conceded that the prosecution couldn't produce the lady who got married at South Shields. Nor could anyone identify the man. He called Alan Coats, the first witness on the marriage certificate. Coats said he was the clerk in the register office. They performed nine hundred marriages a year and he didn't remember Shotton. 'I know the face,' he said, when George was asked to stand up, 'but I can't say where I've seen it before.'

George leaned forward and whispered, 'Is that the end of it?' He saw himself walking out into the town, a free man. Then he heard the clerk say, 'Kindly call Mrs Silver,' and a moment later the usher's voice was booming down the corridor, 'Mrs Edith Silver.'

'Hold tight!' said Harris through the corner of his mouth.

She stood in the witness box like a great frog, wrapped in greys and olive greens, bursting to harm him. Her voice was raw and hesitant at first, then hard, cold, hostile, the north-eastern twang overlaid with a furious gentility. Yes, her sister had showed her something. That something was the marriage lines. Yes, her sister and George Shotton often stayed in Sunderland, and he always addressed her as "wifey".' The clerk said, 'Whom do you mean by George Shotton?' The frog looked at George for the first and only time. 'The defendant,' she said.

Like an auctioneer, the lugubrious solicitor flourished a bundle of correspondence tied up with pink tape. She must have kept his letters and left them with Edith. The clerk read extracts to the magistrates. 'Darling little wifey' and 'Love and kisses from hubby George' made the court go quiet. The reporters crouched over their notebooks. '"July the fourth, 1919. Darling mine, let us start afresh,"' droned the clerk. '"It is two years yesterday since we met. Two years to the day. . . . *Come at once, wifey.*"'

Harris made a fluent speech about the failure to identify Shotton as the man at South Shields. George could see it was a waste of time. They sent him for trial at the assizes the following month and gave him bail. The police let him out through a side door – he had nothing to say to Harris – and he walked down High Street and along the Strand, dawdling at the North Dock and thinking of the rush and blackness of water. But it was amazing how badly one wanted to stay alive. He carried on to Adelaide Chambers instead and sat there planning another of his journeys.

A telegram warned Chrissie that he was coming, but only her husband was at home when George arrived. The house was in a respectable Gateshead terrace a quarter of a mile from the river. Boys in the street made rat-tat-tat noises and shot one another with sticks, but they wore decent boots and their legs didn't have the rickety look of the old-fashioned poor. 'Grand evening,' said Dick Vanderven, and led him through the house to the back. The smell inside was a blend of soap and linen and new wallpaper. George guessed they would never have children. Outside the back door was a patch of yellow grass and cucumbers in glass frames.

'Yes, grand.'

Tyneside dust or chemicals had tinted the clouds violet; below, the horizon was browned with smoke, like the ceiling of a pub. Dick, stuffing tobacco into his pipe with nervous gestures, asked after George's business and made an irrelevant remark about dry docks. He didn't ask after George's wife. He knew, of course. England was full of people who knew.

'Business doing well,' said George. 'Wife and son doing well too. And how about the dynamo and generating-set business? No complaints there?'

Dick wouldn't catch his eye. Power stations, he said, were springing up like mushrooms. He had been in Spain a week earlier.

'I tell you this,' confided George, 'if I had my time again, I'd think of a career abroad. Come to that, I have been thinking of it all summer. It's never too late to make a fresh start. Would you agree with that?'

'I don't know, I'm sure.' If anything, the chin had got weaker. He stooped over a frame and knocked an intruder from his vegetables, already enveloped by the shadow of the house. 'Poor soil around here,' he mumbled.

'Ours is nice and black and we have the Gulf Stream to keep the temperatures up. Not that I personally grow things.' He saw his sister appear in the doorway. 'I was just telling Dick about our new house at Caswell Bay. You must both come and stay with us.'

She took him into the front parlour. Dick, who wasn't allowed to smoke inside, was left to potter with his cucumbers. Marriage had changed her. She was harder, not softer; a Christiana, not a Chrissie.

'So you've been reading the papers,' he said.

'It would have been difficult not to, with that girl being a Geordie. What possessed you?'

'Error of judgement?'

'It's true, then?'

'If they can't find Mamie, they may still have difficulty proving it. My solicitor is going to get a KC. The jury will be more sympathetic than those damn magistrates.'

'But it's true. You married the girl, or she thought she was marrying you. You actually did that.'

'You seem to have made your mind up. I don't blame you. I wouldn't blame you if you said you never wanted to see me again. Nothing like this ever happened to a Shotton. That'll have been said a few times at home.'

'They've taken it very badly. I'd hoped they wouldn't see it, but of course someone had to rush round and say, "Oh, this can't be your George, can it?" You can imagine what Ma was like. Migraines. Curtains drawn.'

'And Pa saying he always expected something like this to happen. Don't tell me.'

'How is your wife taking it?'

'She believes in me, oddly enough.'

Chrissie swatted a fly and got rid of it in the grate, behind the fern in a brass pot. He patted the arm of his chair; after hesitating she sat on it. Her corset creaked and he caught the medicinal smell of her uniform.

'Dear Chrissie!'

'You want something. I can tell.'

'Would you give evidence at my trial?'

'About what?'

He put his arm around her waist. 'It could save me from prison. You and I have always been close. We may not have said much, but deep down we both know it.'

'Never mind all that.'

'They say I married the girl on a Monday morning. I shall say I wasn't there, so I can't have done. I was in South Wales that morning.' He recited the timetable: leave Cardiff 9.40, in London Paddington 1.15, go to King's Cross for the 1.45, arrive Newcastle Central 7.40 p.m. 'I was by myself, having a cup of tea in the refreshment room, and you came in and saw me. We talked about the German breakthrough. People were saying the war was lost. It was March the twenty-fifth. You said, "Where are you off to?" and I said, "South Shields. I'm staying at the Golden Lion." That's all.'

'The only time we met at the station, you had her with you, and you told me a pack of lies afterwards.'

'I am a fearful fellow. You might as well say it.'

'I wish I understood you.'

'I can go one better than that. Wish I understood myself.' He let her go and leaned forward, head in hands. 'I had no right to ask.'

'I read in the paper that the police thought the girl might have killed herself or had an accident in some lonely place.' Chrissie was standing at the window with her back to him. In the street the boys were still at war. 'It said they were combing the countryside.'

'Oh, they still think she'll turn up.' He gabbled off some of the sightings; perhaps overdoing it, he thought afterwards. She was working as a chambermaid in Bloomsbury (her sister Edith even went there to look). A sea captain in Liverpool swore she'd gone to Canada in a sailing ship. The police had reports of her in Hastings, in Kensington, in Dublin. 'Nothing would surprise me,' said George. 'Mamie Stuart is the rolling stone *par excellence*.'

Disapproval radiated from his sister. There was no question of his staying the night. He left in time to catch a sleeper to London. On the doorstep Chrissie kissed him and said, 'All right. I will.'

The police knew his movements, or at least they knew where he was every morning, when he had to report to a police station. It even occurred to him that he might be watched at other times. Every journey he made by train, he half expected to see detectives at the ticket barrier. When he travelled to Cardiff, having decided it was too dangerous to leave the Everard letters at the bank, he used the motorcar instead, and drove off with them on the back seat, tied up in a bundle.

They had to be burned. The Vale of Glamorgan was green and sunny. He revved the car up a track off the main road near Cowbridge, found a deserted strip of grazing, tore off the string; desperate to get it over. Letters slithered all over his lap, in ink, in pencil, on cream stationery, on lined pages ripped from notebooks; one on the back of a Lloyd's Open Form, another on Compton Hotel paper. Matches and a medicine bottle of petrol were ready in the boot, but he kept sifting the pages, reluctant to make a start. Phrases jumped out at him, 'this is the 60th day of the 5th year of the war' and 'I surprised her *in flagrante delicto*, damn near.' They weren't even his letters to destroy; they were waiting for Everard and the future. He tied them up again, returned to the road and drove on savagely towards Swansea.

As he approached the town, level with the dockside cranes and coal staithes on his left, a policeman stepped into the road and held up his hand. A slight adjustment of reality, this pedal instead of that one, and the man was dead, uniformed arms and legs sailing over the bonnet; last gesture of defiance. George braked sharply and the bundle bounced on the floor. He should have got rid of it when he had the chance.

The helmet was at the window. 'Swing bridge is stuck. If you want to get into town, turn right and carry on through Llansamlet.'

The road wound along the base of a hill. Reprieved, George turned up grey streets that petered out in scrubland. It was the hill where he came with Mamie on Peace Night. Rubbish was scattered around. A man burning paper attracted no attention. The petrol ignited with a pop and the pages began to curl inwards. George crouched in the sunlight, watching his brother die.

'I wanted to have a chat about Mamie Stuart before the assizes next week,' said Detective Jenkins in the interview room. He put a pinch of fish food in the bowl. 'Fifteen sightings in Great Britain to date. If they were all her, on the dates reported, she would need an aeroplane.' He surveyed the railway map, which had fifteen scraps of red paper pinned to it. 'I wish you could help us.'

'I'm as much in the dark as you.'

'We shall find her in the end, alive or dead. I shall be retiring next year. I would like to close the file before I do. Health not too good, you know. Terrible damp climate it is down here. The wife has got a uncle with a smallholding in Hereford that he wants help with. Go for weeks without rain there.'

'Was there something you wanted to ask me?'

'We had a postcard yesterday *re* Mamie to say the writer had seen her the day before near Redhill, in Yorkshire, with a theatrical company. Anonymous. Postmarked Paddington, London. Did you send it?'

'Of course I didn't.'

'It's awkward crabby writing. Could be disguised. You went through Paddington that day, I believe, en route to the London docks. Could have been you.'

'I'm surprised at you, Jenkins,' smiled George. 'You've been trying to put the wind up me ever since that night at Ty Llonydd. It doesn't work. I don't have a guilty conscience. By the way, who inspires the *Daily Chronicle* reporter to write stuff like this?' He fished out a newspaper cutting and read it aloud. '"If the girl took her life or met with an accident or foul play, there are a hundred spots where her body might remain concealed. Caves and deep clefts in the rocks abound. Rising above the foreshore are hills covered with bracken and boulders."'

'You know what these London journalists are like. When did you last see her alive?'

'In November or December, in Oxford Street in Swansea. She said she had found somebody who would look after her better than I could.'

'Was it you sent the telegram to Mr and Mrs Stuart on Christmas Eve, that purported to come from Mamie?'

'No.'

'Did you own a revolver at one time and go round threatening people with it?'

'I did once, as a joke. It wasn't loaded. You are wasting your time.'

The sergeant paused between each answer to write on sheets of lined paper, dipping a steel pen in the ink. 'A detective inspector is coming down from Scotland Yard,' he said, 'so I have to be able to put him in the picture. Mr Draper, a very experienced man. He is bringing a special instrument that shows if soil has been disturbed.'

'Or he could try the cellar,' said George. 'You see, I have nothing to fear.'

The day they began digging up the garden at Ty Llonydd, George went on the Caswell sands with Arthur and tried to teach him to swim without using his water wings. He took off shoes and socks and rolled up his trouser-legs so that he could supervise the boy's flounderings in two feet of sea. Sky and water were shades of blue; the bay was almost waveless; but every time George let go, Arthur kicked, struggled, gulped salt water and sank. He felt his temper rise at the white little face that was so implacably opposed to being manly. Then gathered him in his arms and carried him up the sand to where Hercules, similarly averse to water, was trying to eat a piece of rope, and rubbed him dry with a towel as if the child was a baby and the father was a different man, living in a different past.

22

'You have to be brave,' said George, driving away from Grey Home with his wife when the day came. 'Remember what Sir Marlay said: "The jury will want to hear that your marriage is like everyone else's." You are a normal wife. I am a normal husband.'

'Are there things you haven't told me?' she said.

'Nothing of any consequence. I confessed my adultery to you weeks ago. You have stood by me. You are a woman in a thousand.'

But he couldn't read her thoughts. The police had been to Grey Home, poking around in the garden. She must have heard about the digging at Ty Llonydd. These days she slept in the same bed as Arthur. It was what labourers' wives used to do in Sunderland, keep children with them in the bedroom on Saturday nights.

'I didn't do what the papers are hinting at, you know,' he said, as they came out on the Mumbles Road, to see the bay sprinkled with tugs and steamers, catching the tide. 'The idea is grotesque. The girl is leading them a dance. Can you seriously think that I could, that I would ever, that I would be *capable* of – no, you know me too well.'

'I don't know you at all,' she said.

'Very encouraging, I'm sure. Can't you see that once a thing like this starts, the police and the newspapers between them work everyone up into a fever? I am told that people often go missing. But we now have spiritualists saying they know she's dead. Is that responsible? Is that justice?'

He had woken in the night with a voice ringing in his head, as if he had been shouting a moment earlier. There was moonlight on the window. He sat up in bed, confused, thinking he was in Penarth, alone in his bedroom. Mamie was lying dead in a pit. There was enough blood to fill a bucket. Was this one of the dreams that you knew was a dream while you were having it? He put the light on; held his cold watch to his ear to hear it ticking – the time was shortly after four – and concluded it wasn't. The pit, he knew, referred to a gutter-press article of the day before, but he had another look at the newspaper to make sure. A Mrs Ida Barnes, spiritualist and occultist of Brixton Road, London, had written to the Swansea police, 'I myself have seen Mamie dead in her clothes in a pit one yard and two feet deep. She is lying on her right side. This is not beneath any brick floor but under grass. The sides of the pit are red and brown mixed mould and moist. There is above her an open space. It is not a house. I have not yet gone beyond this point.' The police, said the article, attached little importance to the letter.

George read it carefully, several times. At dawn he was still awake, watching trees across the road become individual shadows, below the cliff where the windmill stood. He didn't sleep again. Shaving, he cut himself badly, and appeared at breakfast with a piece of bloody lint stuck to the gash on his chin. But it was barely visible now. He glanced at himself in the driving mirror, as they crossed the foot of Wind Street and approached the Guildhall. Calm, impassive features; an ordinary man.

'Members of the jury. I have never presided over a case of such gravity where the so-called evidence consists of nothing but tittle-tattle. George Shotton is a man of impeccable character whose only failing as far as I can see – and I am a judge with considerable experience – is a fondness for the fair sex. But this is not a court of public morals. The charge against him is simply that he did bigamously marry, et cetera, et cetera. Where is the evidence? A signature in the register *might* be his. Do you ruin a man's life because of a "might be"? He freely admits the truth of the chambermaid's statement, that he and Mamie Stuart spent the night together at the Golden Lion, following the marriage of which we have heard so much. However, according to Mr Shotton, Miss Stuart must have married someone else and not told him. He was impersonated by this someone, for reasons we don't know, Miss Stuart not being available to tell us. Who are we to say that strange things never happen between men and women? I for one am prepared to believe Mr Shotton, who is a marine surveyor of no small repute. I hope you feel likewise, members of the jury. I look forward to your resounding verdict of Not Guilty, and trust you will join me afterwards for a glass of Madeira and a slice of seed cake.'

The Madeira and cake were taking things too far, but the happy endings that drifted through George's thoughts as the long day at Swansea Assizes before Mr Justice Avory dragged on were as real as if they had already happened. Wigs, gowns, green leather, coats of arms; a juryman with medal ribbons and a sleeve hanging empty; counsel bobbing up and down, Tweedledum and Tweedledee; the sound of his heart beating.

Familiar faces appeared in the witness box at the command of Tweedledum for the prosecution, a KC called Griffiths – Mrs Hearn, Edith the frog, Detective Jenkins, the chambermaid at South Shields, even Mamie's friend Nancy, all testifying in one way or another to the innocence of Mamie and the wickedness of George. Edith claimed to have seen him physically ill-treating her, a line of evidence that his expensive

Tweedledee jumped up to denounce. Sir Marlay attacked them all. Mamie Stuart, he said, led a double life. He read extracts from a letter she had written to 'a person called Albert' and said that such a woman might easily perpetrate a marriage fraud of the kind alleged.

Much later, it was George's turn. 'I was fond of her,' he said, 'but I formed a poor opinion of her character.' Was that true? Not as such, but the truth was hidden inside it somewhere. How could one possibly explain what was felt at the time, how one moved from happiness to despair, how sweetness turned bitter, how jealousy nibbled the guts?

'In July 1917 I was surveying a Norwegian ship at Sunderland. I met Mamie Stuart, who was with a friend. Misconduct took place that evening. I concluded that she was immoral.'

Life with two wives had seemed as necessary as life with one, but that could hardly be admitted to in court. One was thus compelled to tell untruths because of the impossibility of telling the truth as it appeared in the past, at the time, on actual railway stations, under real roofs, in real beds. That had all vanished. The real George who experienced those things had gone, along with the real Mamie, who was neither better nor worse than the caricature in the courtroom, merely different, a substance, not a shadow. What became of us?

He admitted addressing her as 'wife' and calling himself 'husband'; they had arranged to do it for convenience. That was why he gave her a wedding ring. 'I admit that I was at the Golden Lion on March the twenty-fifth, but I only met her there by accident.' He caught the 9.40 a.m. train from Cardiff, reaching Newcastle about 7.40, where he met his sister. He went to the Golden Lion and found Mamie Stuart with two other girls. As for the alleged likeness between the writing in the South Shields marriage register and his own, it was purely coincidental.

Tweedledum popped up to ask again about ill-treatment and bruises. Afternoon sun glared through the tall windows. Ushers were struggling with blinds. 'I never raised a hand to her,' said George.

Why did it matter if he had or hadn't? Below the surface ran the other trial, like a disease that was yet to manifest itself. The revolver was mentioned. So was the house at Caswell Bay – a very lonely house, said Detective Jenkins. Tweedledum: 'And is it removed from any other house?' Detective Jenkins: 'The house next door is unoccupied.' Sir Marlay complained, and the judge agreed that questions about lonely houses seemed directed at another issue.

The prosecution even brought up the incident outside the George Hotel, which the police must have got from Mrs Hearn, who must have heard it from Mamie. The question came at George like a punch in the face: 'Were Mrs Shotton and Mamie within a few yards of each other on the Mumbles Road on the twenty-first of July?' He bit his lip. 'I have no knowledge of it.'

May's nervousness was apparent from the way she gripped the edge of the witness box. 'I had no suspicion of the way my husband conducted himself between 1917 and 1919,' she said. 'I thought he was away on business.'

Sir Marlay's aquiline profile looked distinguished, not to mention expensive, in the slanting light that came through cracks in the blinds. 'Please describe your marriage, Mrs Shotton. Take your time.'

'It was just a marriage,' she said.

He seemed about to press her further; thought better of it; nodded and sat down.

George's other witness did better, insisting that she had no doubt of time and place. Her face hardened when Tweedledum suggested otherwise. She had seen her brother disembark from the London train; it was when the Germans were breaking through, and the station was full of soldiers. George was proud of her and mouthed, 'Thank you' when she looked his way.

'That concludes the case for the defence,' said Sir Marlay, and began to speak to the jury, man to man. George saw it was evening already. 'It is the rarest thing on earth to convict a man of the crime of bigamy when no one has been called to say "Yes" or "No" to his presence at the ceremony. My learned friend has tried to strengthen a weak case by hinting at matters that the prosecution lacks the courage to bring into a court of law. A determined effort has been made to poison your minds by suggesting that this man has done away with Mamie Stuart. Ignore these innuendoes.'

The juryman with the medal ribbons seemed to nod in agreement. George had watched him from time to time and wondered about his history. His cheeks had some of the redness of Everard's.

'There may be the best of reasons for her absence. The girl was thoroughly immoral and worthless in regard to her relationship with men. I submit that what really happened was this. She procured a man at a price and got him to go through a form of marriage, supplying him with the details that were given on the certificate. On that note, I leave you to ponder the gravity of your verdict.'

Tweedledum had the last word. The best he could do was speak of 'strong documentary evidence' and deride the defence's story. George imagined he saw the ex-soldier frown. Then Mr Justice Avory was summing up. George didn't listen. He preferred to think about Everard, the Everard of the letters.

The jury retired and George was escorted to his cell, but he was no sooner there than they took him back again. A hammering in his head was making him shake. He couldn't think properly. But he realised that the war hero was the foreman of the jury because he was the one who said, 'Guilty.'

The waxwork face of the man on the scaffold had always been his, of course; surprising that Mamie had never noticed. The jury had made no recommendation for mercy. How would he be able to live through the weeks before they whisked him into the execution shed? Any second now the judge would place that piece of black silk on his wig.

'George Shotton,' said Justice Avory, 'you have aggravated your offence by your wicked perjury. You must have given the jury small credit for their intelligence if you supposed they would believe your story. The sentence of the court is that you be imprisoned and kept to hard labour for eighteen calendar months.'

George came to himself. It was bigamy, that was all. Newspapers reported that he collapsed into the warder's arms and had to be assisted to the cells. But it was relief that made his legs give way.

23

George's cell at Swansea Gaol looked inwards to the exercise yard and a matching wing of barred windows, with a high slated roof where seagulls sat motionless for hours on end, as if they had lost their freedom too. The prison was as bad as expected, although the 'hard labour' was no more than an echo of Victorian times, and meant only that for two weeks he had to sleep on planks, before he was given the standard straw mattress. There was no stone-breaking. He did simple mechanical repairs in the workshop or just sat in the cell, waiting.

News from outside filtered through. May had fled to the George Hotel with Arthur because detectives had been to Grey Home, digging in the garden, pulling out fireplaces. It was difficult to imagine May managing on her own. But when he wrote asking her to visit him, a letter came from a solicitor to say she wished to have no communication, and in due course would be seeking a divorce.

The digging made no progress. Draper of the Yard visited him and said, 'Game's up.' George knew that if that happened there would be an air of ceremony, a chief constable in uniform, detectives with polished shoes standing in a ring to see him charged. All Draper did was light a cigarette and ask what he was doing parked up a lane near Cowbridge. 'No use denying it,' said Draper. 'A farmer saw you acting suspiciously and took the number of your motor.'

'Call of nature.'

'Don't forget I have a scientific instrument for detecting soil that's been disturbed. We suspect you took bits of her around the country in your motor and buried her here and there. Take my advice, Georgie, give us a confession. Did she drive you to it? Was she taunting you with another fellow? Was she threatening to tell the other Mrs Shotton? Throw yourself on the mercy of English justice and who knows? Plead temporary insanity. Man got a reprieve for that last year.'

'You have a one-track mind, Mr Draper. I hear she's been seen with an army officer in Canada.'

'She's been seen with a troupe of dancing girls in Karachi, but I don't believe any of those stories and neither do you.'

'It only needs one of them to be true.'

Draper was a bird of passage. It was Detective Jenkins, the local man with local memories, who troubled George. Jenkins wanted a moment of glory to take with him into retirement. His sly Welsh perseverance might give him ideas.

Jenkins appeared one morning in September. They brought George out of the workshop to a stale room used for prison visits, to sit opposite the detective at a table partitioned with plywood underneath to prevent contraband being passed. 'I thought it only fair to tell you, Mr Shotton,' he said, 'that we have recovered certain remains from the Gower coast. Mrs Edith Silver is arriving shortly from Sunderland to view them.'

'Do you want me to go pale?'

'You have, a bit.'

'That's what prison does to you.' George was fairly sure that a racing pulse wasn't detectable by sight. 'Whoever it is, I can be sure of one thing. Nobody thinks it's Mamie. Your Mr Draper would have been here if they did.'

'He's gone back to London, leaving us country coppers to get on with it. So we have.' Autumnal storms had begun and the Jenkins nose was watering again. 'It's a female, probably aged between twenty-six and thirty. Height and physical measurements commensurate with the description we have. One other thing. The body has been mutilated.'

Blank features and untwisted hands were the best George could do, but a twitching in his leg caught him unawares and his shoe banged against the partition.

'So where did you find this unsavoury object?'

'Where do you think?'

'You're the policeman. On the rocks, I would guess. A suicide, accidental drowning? Someone floating in the Bristol Channel, got caught by the screws of a ship? It's happened before.'

'You may be in for a nasty shock. I'll let you know what Mrs Silver says.'

Alone in his cell, George tried to think calmly. Whoever they had found, it couldn't be Mamie. But his anxiety undermined his certainty. They were still looking, digging up corners of gardens, tap-tapping at walls, ripping out floorboards. Carpenters had been sent to examine the house at Penarth. Jenkins had told him that men were out in the Gower countryside, looking in woods for signs of disturbed earth. The police were torturing him. They wanted to drive him mad, give him a nervous breakdown, make him babble a confession. They thought he was vulnerable; a man without friends.

'Dear Everard,' he wrote, 'I have a photograph of Arthur in the room where I am sitting, and you will be interested to know that he is beginning to look like a Shotton – he has the eyes and the mouth. Where did we come from, we Shottons? As far as I know we were coal miners, shipwrights, railway engineers, etc. What will future generations make of us? I can imagine a Shotton a hundred years from now saying, "Oh, they were either heroes" – meaning you – "or black sheep" – meaning me. Not that I regard myself as a scoundrel. A weakness, admittedly, something in the blood, or something *not* in the blood. A critical absence.

'Which leads me to the purpose of this letter. You are a veteran of the greatest war in the history of the world, so I need not mince my words. At the present moment I am in Swansea Gaol where I have been sent for unlawfully marrying Mamie. (Arthur's picture is pinned to a crack in the wall!) There was a trial, best forgotten. Suffice it to say that the prosecution obtained letters I had written, which she left behind in Sunderland, in which I said "wifey" and "hubby" and swore eternal devotion once too often. Well, we all make mistakes. You know better than anyone what I felt for my little monkey. *But she threw it in my face.* The last night I saw her – I told you in the spring that she had gone – I found a letter to a man called Albert. My barrister used it to show the sort of girl she was. *What was I supposed to do?*

'The London newspapers featured the trial as if it was the crime of the century. Not that they had any inkling of her life or mine. "In matters of the heart, nothing is simple" – I forget which of us said it first, you or me. I even thought of shooting myself with a revolver. You have to understand, she was close to finding out about May and Arthur. The trouble was that the more I gave her, the more she wanted. I can imagine you saying, "You were well rid of her." How could I ever be "rid" of Mamie? I can't describe the way thoughts went through my head, as if they were about someone *like* me and someone *like* Mamie, not actually us.

'I even started thinking, why not kill her? Every husband and wife gets ideas like that sooner or later. One can't be blamed for having them. Despite what she'd done to me, I still loved her. I think I deserve some credit for that, don't you?

'Let me be honest about this. The police think I killed her. They don't have any evidence. What do they know about me or how I felt? "In matters of the heart", etc. As if I woke up on a Monday morning and thought, "What are my plans for the week? I know, I'll do away with Mamie." Which is a travesty, e.g., I assumed that something would happen to stop me – Mamie would go to South America and never be seen again, or May, who has never been strong, would die of natural causes, or I would leave them both and go abroad (which might have meant not seeing Arthur for years). Can you imagine how I went round in circles? I even tossed a coin. Heads, I kill her. Tails, I don't. *What option did I have?*

'This went on for weeks, by which time we were living in a house by the sea. If you say to me, "Yes, but was it premeditated?" my answer is, "I was letting myself think about killing her." That isn't the same, is it? *The real truth is always something else.*

'Isn't finding a letter your wife has written to her lover enough to provoke anyone? *Everard, I was like a rat in a trap.* For Christ's sake, yes, yes, yes, I wanted to get rid of her.

'Afterwards I didn't know what to do with her clothes, there were so many of them, she had a sealskin coat, I knew it wouldn't burn like the dresses did, I took it on the Paddington train wrapped up in brown paper and stuck it on a luggage rack, but when I left another coat a woman came running after me and said, "You've forgotten this," and after that I was frightened and put shoes and things in a suitcase. I left it with an hotel. That was where the police found it.

'You keep looking at me but I am being as honest as possible. I can still see the clock, ten past seven. There was music on the gramophone that she used to dance to. It was raining. When she saw I had the letter, she got frightened and made out she wanted us to make love, as if nothing had happened, as if she could say, "OK, baby," and everything would be like it was. I didn't want to do it in cold blood. The letter was like a signal, telling me the time had come.

'Taking her being rid of moving her was harder than I could

ever than I could tell you what I had to Christ what I did what I had to. I put her where nobody will ever find her please God. I would give anything for you to be here now I am nearly am mad nearly mad now. *Try to understand.* He fastens your arms and legs and puts a bag over your head. Pray for me, Everard, don't let him don't let him. I did love her. Christ save me.'

The cell door opened and Detective Jenkins stood there, handkerchief in fist. He was unaccompanied. 'Writing a letter?' he said, and picked up a lined sheet of prison paper from the bed. 'You haven't started.'

'I was wondering what to say. I shan't bother.'

'Mrs Silver was unable to help us. It wasn't Mamie, so you can breathe again. But you looked pretty green this morning. I mean to get some men out on the cliffs again. I thought I'd tell you.'

The light was fading. When Jenkins had left, George lay listening to sounds from outside the prison, waiting for his heart to stop hammering. He would never know peace of mind again. How would he live, if he lived? A distant steam whistle and thunder of iron heralded a train on the London and North-Western line. That would be the 7 p.m., Swansea Victoria to Crewe, arrive 11.35, depart Crewe 2.13 a.m., change at Manchester, departing 7.05 on the east coast line, arrive Newcastle 11.34, change for Sunderland, arrive 12.15 p.m. If the wind was in the right direction, a man in Fawcett Street could hear the riveters at work, just below Wearmouth Bridge.

24

Forty-odd years was a long time to wait to conclude a murder investigation. Detective Inspector Horton, picking his way through the past in November 1961, remained sceptical. His superiors in South Wales were more eager than he. Once upon a time there was a woman who disappeared and a man who might have had a hand in it. They were shadows now; data in old files, most of which took some finding. Because the man lived in Bristol in later years, Horton went there first, dividing his attention between a glorified missing-person inquiry (little success) and a private inquiry into an old flame (no success at all). Now a name in a file had sent him to the north of England, leaving young Jones, his assistant, to poke about on the Welsh border. 'I have to be away longer than I expected,' he told his wife on the telephone. Lisa, the old flame, got a postcard saying 'I'll be back.'

Horton had never been to Sunderland, whose coastal greyness reminded him fleetingly of Swansea. Roker Park was evidently a genteel district. He needed a pee and a snooze, but supposed he must press on.

For the first time, ringing the bell of a large red house in dishevelled grounds, he felt drawn to the case. There was no obvious reason. A middle-aged woman appeared and said that Mrs Silver was resting.

'I'm a police officer. Nothing to worry about, I assure you.'

'Did he say police?' A stout spectacled figure came down a broad staircase, pausing on each step. 'Who is he?'

'Inspector Horton, ma'am. South Wales CID.'

'Mother is under the doctor. You haven't taken your tablets, Mother, have you?'

'Be quiet.' Sharp eyes looked at him from a face with broken veins. 'What do you want, Mr Horton?'

'Perhaps we could sit down and have a chat? It's a distressing matter. Ancient history, I hasten to say.'

'Is it about my sister?'

He was expecting a longer preamble. 'I'm afraid so. The Mamie Stuart who went missing.'

'Amy Stuart. She was christened Amy. Come inside. Put the electric fires on in the library, Dolly.'

It was hard to gauge how frank relatives wanted you to be. They could go from 'Yes, I'm fine' to hysteria within seconds. The daughter fiddled with plugs, and as the filaments glowed, the dark-panelled room filled with the burnt-dust smell of radiators that were never switched on. No books were visible.

There had been a discovery, said Horton, and as a result an inquiry had been opened. The discovery was made in a cave on the coast near Swansea. Some amateur potholers found human remains. He was sorry to bring such news.

'Why do you think it is my sister?'

'Forensic reports, approximate age, approximate date. No other missing person in that period who matches. A wedding ring assayed in Birmingham in 1917 was found.'

'With a broad band?'

'I believe so.'

'Was there an engagement ring? A split ring with three diamonds?'

'Yes, there was.'

'The poor child,' said Mrs Silver. She leaned across to her daughter, who was sobbing, and patted her knee. 'We've known all along that Amy was dead. Now we can see justice done. Go and get the blue notebook, there's a good girl.'

'At this stage, nothing is certain.' But he wondered what came next.

'Was it at Caswell Bay?'

'Nearby. I know this is very distressing for you.'

'I've been distressed for forty years, Inspector. You say she was found in a cave.'

'I used the wrong word. There used to be lead mines along the coast. There's an air shaft comes out on the clifftop between Caswell and a bay called Brandy Cove. It's at an angle, like that,' and he held his hand at sixty degrees.

'You mean people knew about it?'

'Apparently.'

'So why didn't the police look there?'

'Impossible to tell. The files have gone. I suspect they were never entirely convinced she was dead. For all we know they did go down. At the bottom there's a small chamber in the rock. There'd have been nothing to see, except an animal carcass or two. Farmers used it . . .'

'To throw dead sheep into. I understand. So how did the potholers find her?'

'There's a tunnel leading off the chamber, blocked by stones and a slab of rock. They moved the slab and got in.'

'And that's where she was?'

'Yes.'

Horton had been down the shaft; had seen the photographs and the pathologist's report. He hoped for Mrs Silver's sake that she was satisfied now.

'Do you have any idea how Shotton knew about this place?'

'None. But he lived in the Mumbles area.'

'They used to do a lot of walking, he and my sister.' She was lost in thought. Then came to herself when Dolly returned with the notebook. 'The Inspector hasn't found him yet or he'd have said.'

'We are still looking. He'd be an old man, of course.'

'He is eighty-one and he's alive. I can give you his address. I have kept an eye on George Shotton.'

He had to wait while she thumbed through the tattered pages in faded blue boards. 'It's all here, the lies he told, the things we knew. He had a gun. We think he had chloroform in a bottle once. He cut her clothes up and left them in a suitcase. It's all here. He was in London after he came out of prison. It ruined him, of course. He never went back to his career. His sister had a nursing home in Balham and he was the odd-job man. I believe the sister died. Anyway, he was in Monmouthshire with his parents in the 1930s, working as a motor engineer. People in Tintern still remember him. Same treacherous little man charming everyone, especially the ladies. Whenever he had a bit of money he would have a young girl in tow.'

'How do you know all this, Mrs Silver?'

'I made it my business. I engaged a private detective more than once. My late husband used to take me. I'd say, "Let's get the Rolls out and we'll do a Shotton." We always called it "doing a Shotton".' Decades of implacable patience shone in her face. 'He was working for a bus company in Lydney and I went to the manager and said, "Do you realise who George Shotton is? He's the man who murdered his mistress."'

'Dangerous thing to say, Mrs Silver.'

'When he was tried for bigamy, they as good as said it.'

'He was never charged.'

'Well, he didn't stay in Lydney, I can tell you. Then I lost touch in the war, and after it he went into the Bristol Home for the Aged. Here it is, "Admitted October the tenth 1947."'

'Is that where he is now?'

'No. One of the inmates, a simple-minded man he was kind to, had a sister called Vera Phillips who used to visit him. She got to know Shotton and said he could lodge with her and her husband. "Discharged June the seventh 1949." He's at Mrs Phillips's. Here's the address.'

'You didn't tell this lady about him?'

She shook her head. 'I wanted him to stay put. He was an old man. I knew he wouldn't move unless he had to.'

'Can I ask the latest date you have news of?'

'Oh, a year or so ago. The spring of 1958.'

'That's over three years ago.'

'Mother would have heard if he was dead,' said Dolly.

'It's been my life,' said Mrs Silver. 'My husband ran a very successful business and I have two other daughters as well as Dolly, but . . . I could never get Mamie and that terrible man out of my head. I should have stopped her going to Swansea that last time.' Her face brightened. 'You will hang him, won't you?'

'Not a man of eighty, Ma. Not even Shotton.'

'How did he kill her?'

'There's no forensic evidence,' said Horton. 'We only have . . .'

'The bones. That's what you mean. How did he get her down there, underground?'

'People can do surprising things when they're desperate.'

Mrs Silver shut the notebook and replaced the rubber band that held it together. 'My poor girl,' she said. Dolly was weeping again but her mother was serene. 'So now all you have to do is arrest him.'

'He'll be taken back to Swansea and questioned under caution. I don't think you need worry.'

Tearing south in the Humber, he was almost at Pontefract on the A1 when he stopped for the night at a roadside café with beds. He was on his way again at five a.m. with the first lorries, but the fan belt went at Birmingham and it was midday before he reached Bristol.

The street was near Temple Meads station. One end of it had been bombed in the war, and the terrace of shabby houses ended abruptly in scrubland, where foundations for a new building were being dug by a yellow machine. In theory Horton should have informed his superintendent, and the Bristol police as well, before approaching Shotton. But he had no intention of telling anyone yet.

An elderly woman with an intelligent face answered the door and invited him in at once when he said he was a police officer. 'Go straight through to the kitchen,' she said. As he walked down the passage, towards the coal fire and linoleum he could see ahead of him, there was a movement. A man stood up. It was Jones, his detective constable.

'Morning, sir. I got hold of Mrs Phillips's name by a lucky shot at Tintern and thought I should come at once. I hope that was in order, sir.'

'I shall hang you out to dry, Jones.'

There was no sign of Shotton. Mrs Phillips said, 'So you two know each other. Mr Shotton would have been tickled pink.'

'The gentleman is deceased, sir,' said Jones.

'I told your friend, it must be the wrong Mr Shotton, whatever it is you wanted him for.'

The only photograph of him in Horton's possession showed a man with closed-in features, next to the pretty young woman who was now a skeleton in a cardboard box. 'Brown, Barnes and Bell, Photographers, 32 Bold Street, Liverpool' was stamped on the back.

'It could be him,' admitted the woman. 'I think it probably is. Was that his wife? He never spoke of a wife.'

'So what did he talk about?' asked Horton.

'He had been an engineer – something to do with ships, I believe it was. But I don't think he was a seagoing man. He was a very refined sort of person. Kept himself to himself. He used to go to church with me at All Hallows. He kept in touch with a lady in Tintern – she sent flowers here for him when he passed away.'

Horton ploughed on, although the only result would be a report to the coroner, and if he was lucky a pat on the back. '*I would also like to commend Detective Inspector Horton for his useful work in filling in the background to this unusual case.*'

He said, 'Mr Shotton was from the north-east, wasn't he?'

'He made a remark about Sunderland once. Said he came from a big family but he had lost touch with them.'

'And he came to you in 1949?'

'He was in the Aged place, what we used to call the workhouse, but he treated my brother very kindly and I had him here, for nine years eventually. It was April 1958 he died.'

'So there was nothing unusual about him?'

'I told you,' Mrs Phillips said tartly, 'he was a cut above the ordinary. He was very quiet about the house. Never raised his voice. He used to appear behind you suddenly and make you jump. "Everard," I used to say, "you glide about the place like a restless spirit."'

'I thought his name was George.' Was there still hope?

'He was George as well, but he said Everard was the name he liked. It meant something special, I don't know what. That's the name he was buried with, Everard Shotton. He's in my parents' grave plot at Arnos Vale.'

At least it explained why he hadn't been found by the Births and Deaths people. Horton stood up. 'We mustn't take any more of your time.'

'You haven't said why you wanted to talk to him.'

'Just routine inquiries,' said Horton.

He wanted to know how Jones had found the address. 'The lady from Tintern, sir, the one who sent flowers for his funeral. An old girlfriend, if you ask me. She said much the same as

Mrs Phillips, "always a gentleman". Ladies' man up to the end, I'd say.'

'With your powers of observation, Jones, you'll go far.'

'Sir.'

'Take the train back. Your wife will be missing you. I have a few things to tidy up here.'

He rang Lisa, who said she was sorry for what had happened when he looked in the other evening. 'You mustn't be angry with me. But an old . . . friend doesn't like to think she's being taken for granted.'

'I'm sorry too. Apologies all round.'

'Have you found your murderer yet?'

'It didn't come to anything. My natural pessimism was justified. As usual.'

George and Mamie seemed closer now, more disturbing; nearer home.

'You mean he didn't do it?'

'I found he'd died. He got away with it.' Meeting the victim's sister had given him a different focus. 'It goes back forty years. He was a ship surveyor, highly respectable. Married a girl bigamously, killed her later on. Strangled her? Shot her? Never proved because there wasn't a body. Her skeleton turned up in a sort of cave near Swansea last week. He cut her up.'

'Charming.'

'The bones had saw marks where he was trying to get the blade in. She was probably fully clothed when he did it – there were fragments of skirt in the cave, as well as bits of sacking. Can you imagine carrying her there on a dark night?'

'I'd rather not.'

But Horton felt a need to unburden himself. The story of George and Mamie, which no one now would ever have the chance to investigate, had got under his guard. 'The upper severance went clean through the spine. Then he took the legs off. The pathologist said a layman who was desperate enough might have done it within the hour. But what an hour! What a bloodbath! He'd have had to saw through her breasts.'

'For God's sake, Harry. Nobody wants to hear such things.'

'I am getting morbid in my old age. I shouldn't have rung.' His wife and the girls waited for him; that other life a hundred miles away. 'I shall be going back to Swansea later today.'

'Pity. I was thinking, if nobody's replaced that button, you could bring your jacket over and I'll fix it.'

Horton hesitated, as George Shotton might have done. The thought made him shiver for a second, but there was no comparison, was there? A bit of fun was all a man wanted. The dead were dead and gone. He said, 'I'll be there by six. Dare I say Norwich?'

Lisa giggled, a good sign. He heard a soft 'Korwich' as she put down the phone.

George Shotton, born Sunderland, 20 June 1880.
Died Bristol, 30 April 1958.

Amy Stuart, born Sunderland, 24 November 1893.
Died Caswell Bay, Swansea, probably November 1919.
An inquest at Gowerton, West Glamorgan, on
14 December 1961, when her dismembered skeleton
was displayed in the courtroom, decided that she
was unlawfully killed, and that the evidence
pointed to Shotton as the murderer.